PRAISE FOR
RESTITUTION

"*Restitution* is a very affecting story . . . illuminating, as it does, the havoc caused by the uprooting of families, the secrets that cry out to be told and the extreme collateral damage . . . as well as the immense difficulty of finding 'just' solutions to loss."

> —LYNN H. NICHOLAS, world's leading researcher on Art pilfered during WWII and author of *The Rape of Europa*

"(An) intimate blend of family saga and historical struggle. How art looting defines its victims for decades to come, and the resilience the Rosenbergs find on the road to recovery."

> —SIMON GOODMAN, author of *The Orpheus Clock*

"Berg's second stand-alone novel is a blend of love, humor, and history, which captures generations through one family's amazing true story."

> —CHRISTOPHER SANTORA, Trial Attorney, United Nations War Crimes Court for Sierra Leone

Restitution

by Janet Lee Berg

ISBN 978-1-64663-074-5

Published by

köehlerbooks™

3705 Shore Drive
Virginia Beach, VA 23455
800-435-4811
www.koehlerbooks.com

Restitution

a novel

JANET LEE BERG

VIRGINIA BEACH
CAPE CHARLES

"Hope is the thing with feathers,

That perches in the soul,

And sings the tune without the words,

And never stops at all."

—Emily Dickinson

This book evolved under the instruction of Jules Feiffer, Ursula Hegi, Emma Walton Hamilton, Kaylie Jones, Heather Macadam, Robert Reeves, Roger Rosenblatt, Lou Ann Walker, John Westermann, and the late, great Frank McCourt.

The Courtroom

Holland 1980

Sylvie Rosenberg's knees buckled as she ascended the grand staircase leading to her fate. It was an unusually hot, sunny morning in Holland. She wrenched her neck studying the ornate Corinthian columns with their rows of acanthus leaves. Sylvie always took pride in her appreciation of aesthetic beauty, pausing between the Greek pillars until hurried along by the gathering crowd.

Upon entering the building, she had to steady herself as she wobbled in her heels on the shiny black-and-white checkered marble floor. It was the start of the fifth consecutive day of exhaustive questioning regarding the Rosenberg family paintings, including artworks of Rembrandt, Rubens, Nicholas Maes, VerMeer, and Van Steen.

Gretta, Sylvie's older sister, had already been questioned on a previous day, and it was accepted that their other siblings, Wilhelm and Ruthie, would not participate. Sylvie's Dutch lawyer was presenting a counter-argument for each painting that was challenged by the Dutch government clinging to these national treasures.

It seemed a lifetime ago when Sylvie's New York attorney, Harvey Adelstein, first submitted a claim for restitution of the many masterpieces taken from her father by the Nazis. The case was finally to be heard at the Rechtbank's-Gravenhage, the Dutch district court situated in The Hague.

But, given short notice before that fateful day, Sylvie received the startling phone call from Adelstein that there would be a change in the proceedings.

Sylvie held the phone to her good ear.

"Are you sitting?" Adelstein asked.

"Change? What change?" Sylvie asked. "I don't like change."

"Remember I had originally told you that typically court proceedings only have one presiding judge, except for high-profile cases? Well, let's just say they stepped it up a notch."

"Meaning?" Sylvie asked.

"Meaning, because of all the media attention and public interest, our case will be heard before a panel of three judges. And we'll be moved to the largest courthouse available to accommodate the demand."

"Oy! As if I wasn't nervous enough," she whined.

Sylvie had never been inside a courtroom and studied the layout: the elevated judge's bench, the counsels' tables, witness stand, and the gallery. The pews would be filled with the curious people viewing the proceedings. She nervously bit her lip.

Sylvie sighed as she looked up at the high ceiling. *To think this all started with the stroke of a brush—Rembrandt's brush. If he only knew.*

Pieter DeGroot, representing the Dutch government, looked intimidating in his flowing black barrister's robe. He stood ramrod tall and fastidiously groomed. He projected a grim, professional expression, bordering on arrogant. His demeanor screamed that the claim was without merit and everyone in the courtroom should share in his disgust with Sylvie and her family for wasting everyone's time.

Sylvie's American lawyer and their Dutch lawyer, Emanuel Van der Berg, looked meek in comparison. Adelstein, who had spent his years in American courtrooms wearing a simple suit, had clearly not adjusted to wearing his Dutch litigator's robe, constantly fidgeting with his sleeves, sometimes to the point of annoying his Dutch partner. The two lawyers hunched close to one another, whispering and writing notes.

They knew the timeline of events by heart:

1938—Hitler targets their art collection.

1940 May 10—Germany invades Holland. Five days later Holland surrenders.

1940 June–August—Art dealer brothers are forced to sell large quantities of art (500 paintings alone on August 2) for a fraction of their value.

1940 September—Hermann Goering visits the family home with a gun in his pocket.

1941 December—Nazis begin deportation trains.

1941 February—Art firm goes into liquidation.

1942 February—Arrangements are made for travel to Switzerland to obtain masterpieces for the Führermuseum.

1942 June—One quarter of family assets go to looting bank.

1942 September—Arrangements are made for the big trade; exchange of desired Rembrandt for twenty-five Jewish lives.

1943 October until end of 1943—Negotiations with high-level SS officials regarding fate of rest of family members left behind in the Netherlands, and who were arrested, taken to Westerbork concentration camps.

1944–1945—Sixty-five family members die in the camps or in a cattle car that drifted between enemy lines, shortly before liberation.

Post-War—Two brothers commit suicide.

Sylvie was called to the stand. Dressed in her conservative navy suit, she made her way to the front of the room. She appeared calm but tired from another sleepless night. She glanced at her sister Gretta, who, with Roger, accompanied her to court every day. They both offered her an encouraging nod and smile.

De Groot: As you have done for the four preceding days, speak your answers into the microphone. If you don't understand the question, please let me know and I will try to clarify. For the record, will you state your name.

Sylvie: My name is Sylvie Rosenberg.

De Groot: Where are you from?

Sylvie: I am originally from the Netherlands, but moved to America, eventually, after escaping the Holocaust.

De Groot: And when did you escape?

Sylvie: Can you speak up, Barrister De Groot? I am a little hard of hearing.

De Groot: Sorry. When did you escape?

Sylvie: We escaped two and a half years after Germany occupied our country on May 10, 1940. Only five days later, our country surrendered. And our Queen Wilhelmina was like a captain abandoning ship; she and most of the Dutch government fled to England. Proportionately, more Jews perished in Holland than any other European nation. Seventy-five percent. We had antiquated weaponry, no mountains or forests to hide in, and—

De Groot: That's enough, thank you. How old were you when Germany occupied?

Sylvie: Umm, that was 1940. I was thirteen. (She rolled her eyes as if he couldn't do the math.) Fourteen in 1941. And in 1942 I was fifteen. We left the Dieren train station October 20, 1942. (She referred to her notepad and read.) We were escorted by Willy Lages, the SS *Sturmbannführer* and *Generalkommisar fur das Sicherheitswesen Hans Rauter*, the highest police chief and one of the main officials in Holland, who objected to the plan. One of the officers remarked,

"I much rather would have shot all of you." I remember the guns and the soldiers barking orders at us . . . and the dogs snarling.

Judge: That will be enough!

The judge held up his hand.

De Groot: Ms. Rosenberg, we have a few questions for you concerning your father's business dealings with the Nazis.

Adelstein: Objection, Your Honor. Even in this kind of proceeding, the characterization as *business dealings* is unfair and has not been established.

De Groot: My Lord, I would like to assure the court and my learned colleagues on the other side that I will refrain from using the term going forward to allay Mr. Adelstein's concerns, but would note that while Mr. Adelstein is unfamiliar with Dutch proceedings, his learned partner Mr. Van der Berg is highly qualified and regarded and will undoubtedly ensure that their clients are treated with the utmost fairness throughout these proceedings.

Judge: Mr. Adelstein, I will remind you again, we are in a Dutch courtroom, not an American one, and my colleagues and I are not a jury and perfectly capable of ignoring the characterization if necessary. Overruled!

De Groot: Were you aware that your father was paid for many of these transactions and they were not *stolen* outright as you stated in your claim?

Sylvie: I cannot say I am aware of the figures or the dates of these transactions. It could have been anytime between the summer of 1940 up until our escape. But I can say for sure that my father sold them for a fraction of their value.

De Groot: And why is it you are so sure of that?

Sylvie: I can hear exceptionally well in my one ear. And I've been told I have *selective hearing.*

Snickers were heard.

De Groot: Were you aware that your father left the country specifically to make acquisitions to further these transactions?

Sylvie: Yes, I was aware he went on many business trips.

De Groot: Does the name Alois Miedl mean anything to you?

Sylvie: Miedl means nothing to me! He used my father. He was a messenger who worked directly under the Reichsmarschall. He was a Nazi banker and an art dealer.

De Groot: Isn't it true that he and your father were on friendly terms?

Sylvie: Haven't you ever heard the expression, "Keep your enemies close?" Friendly, you ask? Miedl didn't threaten my father's life with a gun. But he warned him that he was obliged to sell to the Germans whatever they wanted and that if things, meaning *sales,* did not go well, that it would end badly for the Rosenbergs.

De Groot: Your father and Miedl then worked together on these sales? Fair to say that the business your father conducted with Miedl was voluntary.

Sylvie: Please do not speak to me about *voluntary* sales.

De Groot: These transactions were voluntary, were they not?

Sylvie: There was nothing *voluntary* about our existence! It wasn't just Miedl. We also had to put together a collection for Dr. Hans Posse, the art director of the Führermuseum in Linz. I remember we had to give a painting for Hitler's April birthday.

De Groot: The paintings in question—were any of them returned to you? To your family, after the war?

Sylvie: Only a couple were returned to us that I know of out of the nearly 150 paintings. How very generous of the Dutch, wouldn't you say? The Dutch government threw us a bone.

There was an outburst in the courtroom.

Sylvie: My father and his brother were very smart businessmen and were forced to sell 500 paintings in one sitting in the summer of 1940. They never would have done that under normal circumstances. They weren't idiots!

Adelstein, who knew Sylvie had no filter, shot a warning look at her.

De Groot: Did you ever witness your father threatened by physical harm?

Sylvie: Well, I—

De Groot: Yes or no?

Sylvie: Well, no.

De Groot: In fact, isn't it so that the Rosenberg family was actually *protected* by the Third Reich?

Sylvie: Our *protection* was only temporary. We never knew when the ball would drop, so to speak.

De Groot: As far as you know, was any member of your family threatened by physical harm?

Sylvie: Yes. My grandmother was dragged off the street and taken to Westerbork Camp where she eventually died of dysentery. My mother—(she paused to look at Gretta for permission) and my sister were forced to have sex with the Gestapo officers and even the Dutch police.

Gasps were heard in the courtroom.

De Groot: *Forced?*

Sylvie: I'm not the only one with hearing problems? That is what I said—*forced!*

The presiding judge placed his hand on the gavel when Sylvie raised her voice, but he did not use it.

De Groot: That will be all for now, Your Honor.

Van der Berg walked to the front of the room and gave Sylvie a reassuring look.

Van der Berg: You said you were *twaalf* or *dertien* years old when the transactions occurred. Can you describe to us to the best of your recollection what transpired in your home during those terrible years, specifically, do you remember a visit by Hermann Goering in the spring of 1941?

Sylvie glanced at Roger sitting next to Gretta, who gave her a nod of encouragement. She looked back at Van der Berg with a distant look before answering.

Sylvie: I was an inquisitive child and listened in on conversations in my home at that time because I wanted to know what was going on.

Van der Berg: And what did you discover?

Sylvie: One day we saw a Mercedes pull up. Men in military uniforms got out and escorted an officer into our home. My mother ushered us children into the kitchen and instructed us to be silent. I snuck into the butler's pantry and then stood outside the dining room door, listening and peeking whenever I could. There he was, fat Hermann Goering.

Again, snickers were heard in the courtroom.

Van der Berg: Go on.

Sylvie: He was standing there in our room, the room where we had shared so many wonderful memories—dinners, birthdays, holiday celebrations. He was talking to my father about the paintings. I could see the shape of the revolver inside the pocket of his pants. My father was shaking.

Sylvie demonstrated her father's tremors by shaking her own shoulders and arms.

Van der Berg: Could you hear what they were saying?

Sylvie: Some of what they said, yes. Goering said he would like to procure these paintings and we would be compensated according to German law. I knew my father didn't want to sell so many paintings, which were his life's work.

De Groot: Objection, Your Honor. There has been no foundation established to show that this witness had any knowledge of what her father wanted.

Van der Berg: Your Honor, to the contrary of my learned colleague's assertion, there is rock-solid foundation. Ms. Rosenberg was very aware of what her father wanted, as the evidence has already been submitted that her father told her in no uncertain terms as Sylvie took an interest in her father's work at a young age.

Judge: Objection overruled!

Sylvie: My father could not hesitate—not for himself, I knew, but for his family, especially his children. The monsters did not have to verbally threaten him with physical harm because there was no doubt it hung in the air every minute of our lives.

From behind a piece of furniture, I could see Goering's shiny boots as he turned to leave our home with his henchmen. My father, such a big man, not only in stature, but in the respect and position he once held in our community, seemed all of a sudden to become smaller and weaker. I could hardly look at him; it was so painful. Once again, at bedtime, our parents had to comfort us and assure us we would be safe, but in the middle of the night, I heard my father downstairs and knew he was sitting at his desk. I could picture him with his head in his hands. I knew his heart was broken—our father whose spirit was always so strong.

Sylvie saw Gretta wiping her eyes with a tissue and Roger comforting her.

Sylvie: We did eventually escape with our lives (she choked on her words), but so many of our friends and family were not as fortunate. And there was always the guilt that we were the lucky ones.

There was quiet recrimination in the air. The judge loosened his collar.

Judge: That's all. Court will convene same time Monday morning at ten.

On the way out of the courtroom, Gretta approached Sylvie and squeezed her elbow with affection. "I knew you and Father shared a special bond about his art world, and for that I am no longer jealous. I am grateful."

Chapter 1

T he stealing started unintentionally.

Sylvie simply had to have that darling champagne-colored *crepe de Chine* blouse she saw in Lord & Taylor's storefront window. Once inside the iconic shop, she spotted only one blouse left in their newest French line. She could sacrifice some of the luxuries she had as a child in Holland, not all of them. Since her sisters living in England had stopped sending her designer clothes, she felt she was going through *haute couture* withdrawal cold turkey. Sylvie promised she'd reimburse them, perhaps after her next stipend from her father's estate. But no new pieces from her sisters arrived.

Yes, it has my name all over it, she thought, feeling the fabric of the blouse. As she reached into her bag for her eyeglasses to read the size on the tag, another woman grabbed the blouse from right under her.

Sylvie gasped, mouth ajar until she noticed the woman had a rather *large* neck, which reminded her of a tree trunk. Sylvie fingered her diamond *S* necklace that hung around her own neck.

"That blouse runs small, you know," Sylvie lied.

"Excuse me?" The woman glared.

"The blouse. I have the same one in another color. And it runs small. Especially trying to get it on and off over, you know, over your neck." Sylvie moved her fingers over her own slim throat.

"Well, I'll just have to take it home and see, now, won't I?" The woman stormed off toward the register.

"*Aagh,* all the nerve!" Sylvie huffed in her guttural tone. Over thirty years living in America, she couldn't rid herself of her Dutch accent. Aroused by such indignity, she threw her empty hands up in the air and shouted at the woman now out of earshot. "I'm a Rosenberg, I'll have you know—an aristocrat back in my country."

Why is it others always take what belongs to me?

Sylvie had to do something to squelch her temper. She had no more chocolate truffles in her purse, a usual quick fix to fill emptiness. She was anxious and desperate as she flipped through the one-of-a-kind skirts, dresses and slacks hanging on the rack, now minus the blouse. *My blouse.*

"Hmm. This one's not from the French line, but it's not *too* bad," she tried to convince herself, holding it up to the light, looking for its sheen. She picked through the other blouses until she decided on a peach-colored one. Methodically, she rubbed the plastic string tag back and forth over the teeth of her car key until the tag fell to the floor. She made sure no one was around before she slipped the garment into her shopping bag and casually headed for the exit.

For a minute, she panicked about where she had left the car. Like a mischievous child, she ran through the parking lot with her exaggerated pigeon-toed gait. Those years of ballet lessons, all for naught. Then she remembered the giant rabbit's foot she had recently stuck on top of the antennae. She giggled at her ingenuity as she squeezed her thin figure between the rows of cars, making her way to the gold Caddy glowing in the sunlight with the same gleam as her thick gold hair. She turned the key in the ignition, the same key she used to commit her first larceny, and pulled out of the busy shopping center.

"So what, I took one lousy blouse. It's not even satin. Besides, they should be thanking me. I'm the only one who sets a trend for fashion around here," she said aloud.

Lost in thought, she still had desire for something sweet and made a sharp turn off the highway, without signaling, into the parking lot of Simon's Bakery. Rewarding herself for her first misdemeanor, she blurted, "Mocha. Yes, I'm in the mood for mocha." She felt in command.

Lately she had the urge to steal, the most exciting of all her compulsions. It wasn't that she needed the blouse. She had a dozen new blouses hanging in her closet, most with the tags still on them. It was the conquest.

Between visits to her son's beach house, Sylvie became covetous of Michael and Angela's bond. She wondered if when a child came along, they'd have any time left for her. She feared she would be pushed out of the picture. *Although, it would be fun to take the kid out for ice cream cones and buy him or her lots of toys and fancy new outfits . . .*

As she approached the pastry counter, she wrapped her arms around herself, as if she needed a hug.

"You're cutting the line. You have to take a ticket, like everyone else. Ma'am?"

"Oh, all right, already!" Sylvie waved her purse at them, always sensitive about her hearing issues. "I can *hear*, you know!"

"Mommy, why is that lady yelling?" a little girl asked her mother.

"I think she *really* needs a cookie!" the mother answered.

"I want a cookie, too!"

"Don't cry, honey." Sylvie patted the child's cheek. "I'm going to get you the biggest cookie in the bakery—as big as your head."

The girl continued her crying, digging her face into her mother's side.

Sylvie bent and whispered, "When I was your age, my mother told me that every time I wanted a bite of my cookie, I had to take a sip of my milk. I didn't like milk, and I made it bubble out of my nose."

"I like chocolate milk. But I still want a cookie."

Sylvie poked the customer currently being served on the shoulder. "If you don't mind, perhaps you can wait for your babka so the little darling over there can get her cookie."

The woman stopped eyeing the fresh breads. "I beg your pardon?"

"Oh, here we go again," the Polish clerk moaned, recognizing Sylvie from previous visits.

"This child." Sylvie pointed. "You see the one crying? It's because she wants a cookie. She wants it now. Would you mind, terribly, if she—"

"Of course. Go ahead of me."

The child's mother was speechless while Sylvie stepped up to the counter ahead of five other customers. "I would like a black and white for the little girl, please."

The clerk grabbed a cookie and Sylvie held up her hand. "Not that one. The one in front of it looks an ounce bigger, wouldn't you say?"

The girl nodded.

"Oh. And while you're at it . . ." She tapped her fingernails on the glass. "Give me a piece of that mocha cake and I'll be on my way."

Sylvie licked the mocha off each finger while walking out of the bakery and looked back at the little girl taking bites out of her cookie.

That's what I like to do—help people. I'm good at it. Sylvie got into her car, and pulled out into heavy traffic, a cacophony of car horns in her wake.

After only five minutes in her small apartment, Sylvie paced. She was always pacing. She didn't know where she belonged—she was always running from something. She certainly didn't belong out east in the countryside where her son lived and where locals dressed in denim and overalls and wouldn't know a Gucci from a horse's feed sack. Sylvie thought of her son, now labeled a war veteran. She cringed thinking of the scars on his back, the limping and his cane.

She grabbed her light Burberry raincoat and headed out the door for a walk in the early evening chill. Immediately, she saw two women approach.

"Damn!" She pulled her silk scarf down over her eyes. Too late. Mrs. Silverman and her daughter, Rachel, started waving. Sylvie had run into them only the week before in the exact same spot outside her apartment building. *From now on I'll use the other exit.*

"Mrs. Rosenberg?"

Mrs. Silverman was pushing the stroller with her daughter's dozing toddler and was obviously in the mood for small talk. Rachel was almost nine months pregnant.

She needs another one like a hole in the head.

"How are you today, Mrs. Rosenberg?" Rachel asked in a nasal voice. "Nice weather, isn't it?

Sylvie stared at the toddler, who wore a ring of chocolate milk pasted over his mouth. *Like Hitler's mustache.* Sylvie was grateful they no longer called her Mrs. Beckman. Even after all the years since the scoundrel walked out on her and six-year-old Michael. She couldn't stand the thought of it. She was a Rosenberg, through and through. Sylvie contemplated turning down another street, but it would have been too obvious. She knew the questions would be coming.

"*So-o-o,* how's that good-looking son of yours?" Rachel said. "And his wife? What's her name, Angelica?"

Sylvie glared at Rachel's bloated midsection. She was wearing a lovely cardigan. *Cashmere?* "So, did you decide on a name yet? For the new baby?"

"We're not sure yet," Rachel replied. "If it's a boy, maybe Arnold, and if it's a girl, Amanda. Who knows, I may change my mind again."

Sylvie swallowed hard and looked away. *The nameless face in the old photo.* It hurt every time she thought about it. Only she knew the name she had secretly given the child, before he was taken away.

"What about you, Mrs. Rosenberg? No grandchildren yet?"

"No, no babies yet." Sylvie glanced at her watch.

"Well, once they have a baby, they forget we even exist, I can tell you that much," Mrs. Silverman said.

"Oh, Mom, that's not true. We ask you to come over quite often," Rachel said.

"Yeah, when you want me to babysit. I'm teasing, honey, of course."

Sylvie wasn't sure which she'd hate more, being called Mrs. Beckman or Grandma. Surely people wouldn't think she was an old woman. She liked the idea of pampering a new little one. And Michael and Angela would be so happy. *I'm sure in no time they'll conceive my first grandchild.*

Sylvie walked on, tightening the belt on her Burberry, and readjusted her scarf as it started to drizzle. She headed for the main street where she preferred strangers who'd simply walk by, complimenting her on her wardrobe. Sometimes she felt like Queen Wilhelmina on the avenue— the early days of the queen, before even she fled the Netherlands when the Nazis invaded. *Abandon is more like it. How shocked and angry my parents were.* Sylvie, as a teenager, overheard the queen's speech on BBC while eavesdropping on her parents.

"I wish those left behind the very best," the queen had said, bidding her people farewell. Sylvie grunted derisively at the memory of the queen's comment.

Sylvie was less irritable later in the week once she arrived at Michael and Angela's beach house on the eastern end of Long Island—even if it was a little rundown and crowded with Angela's art supplies. Sylvie was single with no interest in dating, so she was often invited to spend the weekends with them. She cherished her visits with her son and even got used to his gentile wife. She was a decent enough girl, surprisingly accommodating, keeping her cabinets filled with the things Sylvie loved to nosh on, like those Dutch licorice drops. Sylvie didn't have much else to look forward to, aside from her junkets to Vegas or trying a lucky hand at the Claridge Hotel and

Casino in Atlantic City. But, after a streak of bad luck, she swore off gambling. Yet every time she thought of entering the casinos with the flashing lights and ringing bells, her blood quickened!

It was after Angela retrieved a package from the mailbox that things changed. Angela walked back into the house with the screen door slapping at her heels and removed an envelope from the package. She held it up and read the words printed in bold letters. Sylvie peered over her shoulder at the return address, a small village outside of Bien Hoa, Vietnam. *Air Mail* was posted in red across the front of the envelope.

A small black-and-white photograph of a little girl named Linh—captioned *gentle spirit*—was attached to a letter with a small paper clip. At first sight, the photograph caught Sylvie mid-breath. It made her think of the old tarnished photo she'd kept since the age of sixteen hidden under the loose floorboard at the internment camp where she'd given birth to her first child. But then she noticed this child in the photo that her daughter-in-law held had pin-straight hair, broad cheeks, and slanted black eyes.

Since Michael and Angela married, whenever Sylvie came for her visit, she thought they would spring the news that they were expecting a baby. But then two years passed, then four years, going on five, and still nothing. Sylvie rationalized about Michael and Angela not being able to afford the mortgage payments; there was no way they'd be able to handle more expenses. *And what if they turned to me for help?* Sylvie had her own problems—problems she didn't share with them. Heavy debt was one of them.

With each passing year, the eyes of the infant in Sylvie's old snapshot looking back at her seemed to fade a bit more. *Melting eyes*, she thought, remembering the day the photo slipped out of her old journal. Once in a while, she'd fetch the picture and allow herself to feel some tenderness. That photograph was both her ruination and her salvation. She refused to become attached, knowing the baby would be taken away. But for those few moments, she couldn't deny the warmth she felt when the baby was in her arms.

It had been difficult for Sylvie to keep from Michael that he had an older brother. *I want to tell him that lately I've been thinking about trying to find his brother. Imagine what that would do for Michael's morale?* She pictured them tossing a ball in the yard, or swimming together in the ocean waves. *I can't tell him. Not yet, not until I know it could happen.*

"Sylv—I mean, Mom? Isn't she beautiful?" Angela asked, turning toward her mother-in-law, holding up the new picture of the small Vietnamese child.

Sylvie nodded, disregarding her question, and drifted off into her own world. She could still hear the squeaking of that one loose board in the floor. The ones the guards walked back and forth over for three long years, passing by her cot, scuffing up the wood planking. "Lights out," they barked.

She scoffed at the hypocrisy of the internment camp. They called it a *safety* camp. The image of the crucifix hanging from the guard's neck, the way it scraped across her smooth, young cheeks as his body jerked over hers, remained fresh in her mind.

Sylvie never stopped running from the Holocaust.

Soon after giving birth, Sylvie almost threw the old photo with its scalloped edges into the trash, but later told herself it would make a good bookmark in her writing journal. As a teenager, she would write boys' names in her journal, never settling on one, knowing she'd be giving the child away. *Who cares,* she had written. *He's only half Jewish. And the other half—monster.* She had torn the page of names from the journal and ripped it into little pieces so no one would ever know she even considered such a thing. She determined no one would ever know the name she had finally settled on in her mind.

Sylvie grimaced thinking of that British guard, how she revered him as a father figure, and how he turned on her, taking advantage of her innocence. During the three years she was held in the camp for Jewish refugees, she wrote about the many fears she had in her journal.

Sylvie pushed her chair back from the table and walked to the sink to wash her tea cup, even though Angela said she'd do the dishes later. As she stood at the sink, her back to Angela and Michael, Sylvie could see the young couple's reflection in the window, their fingers threaded together with love. She allowed the hot water to fill the sink, full force. After she turned off the spigot, a slight drip continued to splash into the basin.

The pink flowers painted on the delicate cup receded into the sudsy water, and Sylvie noticed one of the saucers didn't match the rest of the set. It was the set Sylvie had given the kids for their first Chanukah–Christmas gift as husband and wife.

Did she break it? Too delicate for that girl. Earthenware is more her style. Now the set is ruined—a mismatch. Like these two lovebirds, the gentile and the Jew.

Angela's heart-shaped face was pretty in a plain way, like the bone-colored saucer they tried to pass off as a proper mate for the teacup. But Sylvie had to keep reminding herself that Angela became Michael's savior when he had lost his will to live after his horrendous injuries in Vietnam. The only one who could bring him back was the girl with *angel* in her name, even if she wasn't one of Sylvie's kind.

The image of the silver-and-blue wrapping paper came to her—how odd the gift box looked under the Christmas tree. Angela had insisted on getting a tree.

What a ridiculous holiday! Taking a dead tree, planting it in the middle of your living room for one lousy week, so you can stare at all the stupid ornaments that make you remember the past. Who needs to remember the past?

Sylvie bought them a giant menorah the following day.

Years ago, Sylvie's mother had owned a Royal Albert set of dishes and instructed the servants to set the table with the dinnerware every Friday evening, though they were not traditionally observant Jews. The turquoise color and pattern was still rich in Sylvie's mind, as was everything in the Rosenberg house: the over-buffed silverware, the heavy tapestries of fruit bowls, the thick oil paintings of landscapes, and the value of the antiques that seeped through the crackling wood—all the elaborate things kept on each of the three floors of their mansion in Dieren.

"Mom?" Michael called, bringing her back from her thoughts. "If you scrub that tea cup any longer, the roses are going to come off. And didn't you hear Angela just ask you a quest—"

Angela pulled at Michael's shirt sleeve to be quiet. He rolled his eyes. She shrugged and rolled her eyes back at him. She whispered, "Maybe she changed her mind about wanting a grandchild . . . maybe—"

"I'm so sick of trying to figure out what my mother chooses to hear and what she chooses not to hear. I bet she's never missed anyone complimenting her newest Gucci."

"*Shhh*, Michael. You're getting all worked up," Angela whispered. "Maybe the idea of adoption is too painful a reminder for her."

"Maybe she never should have given up that baby—my brother."

"You said you wouldn't pass judgment on her for doing that. It's something she had to do at the time, that's all. Maybe she's not even thinking about him. Maybe she's upset that I almost didn't call her Mom."

"Sometimes, I don't even want to call her Mom," Michael grunted.

"That's a mean thing to say. Lately, you don't sound like yourself."

"Sorry." He looked at the photograph of the Asian child still in his wife's hand and kissed her on her cheek. "Linh. She really is beautiful."

Angela's eyes filled as she gently slipped the photograph into her sweater pocket. "We'll show your mother another time. Besides, we're not even sure if we're going to get her—there are other interested couples."

"Honey, don't assume."

Sylvie was preoccupied with dusk just outside the window—that in-between time of day where her eyes played tricks on her and she'd start to lose focus on the clarity of the day. There was a light mist drifting in over the ocean waves.

"It's supposed to storm, you know. Why don't you stay longer, until the weather passes, Mom?" Michael said, grudgingly.

"No, no. I'm on for the afternoon shift tomorrow."

After moving from the suburbs of Massapequa to Queens, Sylvie left her full-time position at the department store and worked ten hours a week at an upscale boutique called Erika's. She claimed she only wanted to work to show off her own wardrobe. "Otherwise my collection will never be seen, sitting in the closet."

"Maybe you should ask for more hours," her son hinted.

"Oh, you are a silly boy, Michael. Who wants more hours?"

"I thought you'd stay out of trouble if—"

"Well, you thought wrong."

The sky rumbled with those words. "Are you sure you want to drive in a storm?"

"No use trying to keep me here, Michael. I'm better off going back today."

Michael winked at Angela, and she softly elbowed him in the ribs.

"Besides, there's less traffic on Sundays. And the first thing I'm going to do is clean the sand out of my new shoes. I don't know how you people live on a beach every day. All this salty air isn't the best thing in the world for fine leather and—"

"Fine silk. We know, Mom," Michael said.

"How would you know?" She looked at Angela's torn jeans. "Anyway, I want to leave now before it gets dark. You know how I hate to drive in the dark." She regarded Michael's bad leg. "Angela, be a dear and carry my bags out to my car, will you?"

"Of course." Angela smiled at Michael.

The telephone rang as she went for the bags. "First, let me get the phone."

With Angela out of the room, Sylvie tried to slip a twenty-dollar bill to Michael to show her love, knowing he'd reject it. He wore the helpless expression of a misplaced soldier while leaning on his cane.

Angela sighed into the receiver. "No, not yet, Mom. In fact, we're bringing Sylvie's bags out to the car now. What are you doing? Meeting the ladies for your card game? Your life sure has changed since you moved to Florida. I bet you don't miss all your sewing jobs."

"*Angela,* where's my bags?" Sylvie's voice rang through the house like a fire alarm.

"Oops. Gotta go!" Angela hung up the phone.

The three of them stood awkwardly at the threshold, talking about the weather. Everything else had been avoided, as usual.

Michael had been working hard in rehab, gaining strength each year since he was released from the VA hospital. First he rid himself of the wheelchair, then the walker, and he promised that soon he'd break that damn cane in two, right over his knee. And when that happened, he'd go searching the island of Jamaica for his brother.

"Well, look at that. It even rains out here in God's country. I'm off," Sylvie held her hand out to the raindrops.

"Please, don't speed, Mom. They'll take away your license."

"Oh, Michael, my son, the novelist, so full of drama," Sylvie answered.

"Funny, one of my reviewers said something like that about my first book. How naïve I must have been thinking after I got one book published, the next one would be so easy."

"If anyone ever gives you a bad review, let me know." Sylvie wagged her finger. "I'll set them straight."

"You're still Michael's number one fan, Mom."

She called me Mom this time.

"That's what mothers are for, right?" Sylvie reminded.

Years after the kids' marriage, it was still strange having a *shiksa* call her Mom. Not that she minded. Sylvie's eyes filled every time she had to say goodbye to her, as she was becoming more like a daughter to her every day.

❧

On the drive back to Queens, Sylvie thought about the kids' wedding day. They had wanted a very simple wedding under a tent in their backyard of the beach house in Southampton, only inviting a few friends they had grown up with in Massapequa. A Unitarian minister pronounced them man and wife on top of dunes as the small crowd watched from below. Michael sat tall in his wheelchair, grinning wide, his eyes scanning the sky turning into the worst rainstorm of the year after they read their vows."

"It's good luck," someone said at the affair. Sylvie believed in luck most of the time, the bad and the good kind. The tent leaked, and the band played on. Angela's long white dress was splattered in dirt, and her dainty sandals were ruined, yet Sylvie noticed her son looking at his new wife adoringly, as if she were the most beautiful bride in the world.

Sylvie had shaken her head. *They look like two hippies, if you ask me.* Soon after they had wed, Sylvie made sure to give Angela some of her used designer clothes instead of selling them to the little secondhand shops in Manhasset. *Well, the girl won't look like a damn hippie in my yellow Chanel suit, that's for sure! Now that I think about it, I never do see her wearing any of my hand-me-downs . . . huh.*

Stuck in traffic on the Long Island Expressway, Sylvie had time to obsess, which was detrimental to her. When she was growing up in Holland with too much time on her hands alone in that big house, she was always in a heap of trouble. Unlike her siblings, who were conformists in every sense, Sylvie had a mind of her own, since the time she was propped up in her high chair tight-lipped to the pabulum, to the time she was a teenager stealing kisses with the curator's son behind her father's art gallery—from the fireworks of her first kiss to the first bombs of the war.

She thought of the family art. In their dining room alone there were thirteen Rembrandts, including early etchings, hanging over the table. *Someday, I will be repaid everything that was ever taken from me. Almost everything.*

Chapter 2

Another one of Michael's bad dreams woke Angela in the middle of the night. She reached for the light on her bedroom nightstand, knocking over the book she had been reading, and hovered over him. His jaw muscles flexed with tension. Small beads of perspiration specked his nose like perforations on a Band-Aid.

Michael stirred and blinked at her as if she were a stranger and then muttered, "Go back to sleep, babe." He rolled over on his side, not wanting to engage in the usual conversation they had when he emerged from one of his nightmares. Angela turned the light off, pulled Michael onto his back, and cuddled inside the crook of his arm. This was where she felt safe, she'd always told him. He tried hard to breathe gently, to reassure her that everything was fine, but she asked anyway. "Are you all right?"

He nodded, and let her fall back to sleep in his arms.

As he lay awake, Michael asked himself the same question. *Am I really fine?* Some days he was more all right than others. He inhaled the familiar scent of honeysuckle shampoo wafting from Angela's long, dark, wavy hair and closed his eyes.

Over toast and jam in the morning, Angela studied the open jar of raspberry Smuckers, avoiding his eyes.

"You know, you were dreaming again last night."

"I don't remember," he answered quickly.

"I guess that's good, because it wasn't a pleasant dream."

"Oh?"

"You were moaning. Do you need to talk about it, Michael?"

"Talk about what? There's nothing to talk about. I told you, I don't remember."

"Okay. Don't attack me. I'm only trying to help."

"Help how? You want me to rehash Nam? Again?"

Angela's eyes locked with his, his pupils larger than usual. "Watching my buddies get their heads blown apart, like—"

He held his head in the palms of his hands.

Angela started to cry.

"Sorry!" Michael stood and grabbed his cane hooked over the edge of the table.

"Maybe it's time to talk to someone again."

"Ange, we've been over this a hundred times—back off, okay?"

"But, Michael, you stopped going to the counselor over a year ago. I worry."

"You worry too much about everything! That's why you can't . . . why we can't get pregnant." He leaned his weight against the table. "Never mind."

"Huh. Face it, we weren't ready to have a baby at first, remember?"

"I know. I know. Because of my injury."

"You needed more healing time," Angela said. "We were both extremely anxious for a couple of years." Angela sniffled. "After you tested okay, they pointed the finger at me. All those days of taking my temperature and thyroid pills!"

Michael lowered his head. "Angela, I didn't mean to bring this up. This hasn't been easy on me either, you know."

Angela recoiled. "All those attempts at artificial insemination that didn't take, and—"

He put his hand on her shoulder. "I wish I hadn't said anything."

She pushed his hand away. "I was poked and prodded over and over again."

"Ange, really, stop! Goddamn it! I'm half-crippled, and you're complaining about being poked and prodded? Jesus!"

She looked up at him and then at his damaged leg.

"Oh my, God, Michael, after all you've been through, and I'm whining about—I'm so sorry, so sorry." She buried her head into his shoulder.

"It doesn't matter. Just know I love you." He brushed her hair from his chin and kissed her softly.

"It's that time of the month for me, I guess. And you know how screwed up I am with that. I wish sometimes I could know what the future will bring us." She looked at the clock over the kitchen sink. "I'm gonna be late for school." She smiled.

"What are you working on today?"

"Pollock—I'm in the mood to throw some paint around! What about you?"

"Me? I'm revising that god-awful chapter in the middle writers refer to as the muddle."

"I have a few errands to run after my last class. I'll pick up some Chinese or something for tonight, okay?"

"Sure. Tell them no fortune cookies."

"Hey, you're not off the hook yet, Mikey. We didn't finish our talk about you seeing someone again, you know."

Michael felt his blood pressure rise. "We'll see. Let's not dwell on that." *Why do people refer to seeing a shrink as seeing "someone"?*

They hugged goodbye.

Michael cleared the dishes and noticed that neither of them had eaten much of their toast. He was more tired than usual, more short-tempered. Recently, he thought maybe he should speak with *someone*, but he didn't want to admit it. He only wanted to work on his body; it was so much easier than dealing with the mind.

He grabbed his car keys and, with his left leg lurching to one side to catch up to his right leg, he headed for the door.

Physical therapy was grueling on Mondays. He especially looked forward to beating himself up today. He felt his manhood in regaining his muscle mass. As soon as his regimen was over, he'd return home to work on his book. Some days, he'd write for eight hours straight, then rip up what he'd written and throw it in the waste basket. It was exhausting.

"Who needs a shrink when I've got John?" he said aloud while driving to physical therapy. At rehab, the two had hit it off immediately. John was in his thirties, also a vet, who started working in the States as a rehab therapist soon after returning from Vietnam. The two of them spoke the same language, sharing their war stories.

Together, they plowed through the apparatus, the splints, the electrical treatments, massages, and the intense exercises, while John gave Michael pep talks and honed in on the source of his pain.

"So, you really wanna step it up a notch?" John asked, not waiting for an answer. "Let's do it!"

Michael closed his eyes, hoping to feel the burning pain that meant he was making progress. His mind went to the easy days, his surfing days, when his biggest worry was the size of the waves. By next summer he hoped both he and his board would be ding-free.

"You ever dream about Nam anymore?" Michael asked.

"Not for a while now. You?"

"Huh? Yeah. At least that's what my wife tells me."

"Put your hands here," John said, demonstrating. Michael placed his hands on either side of his hips. "About the boy again? About Tsan?"

Michael shook his head. "Yeah, mostly I dream about that kid, but I had a whole series of dreams last night."

"All for one price, heh?"

"I can't remember them all. They were pretty intense."

"How's it going lately with adopting that baby girl—Tsan's relative?"

"Not a done deal yet. I know it's a shot in the dark trying to get a specific kid, but I have this feeling in my gut about adopting Tsan's sister's kid. Like it's meant to be, like I'm doing it for Tsan to make up for not being there for him when he needed me. I think it would be good karma to give Linh a decent life, since I couldn't save Tsan's."

"Hey, you've got to stop beating yourself up over that."

"Angela and I argue over my obsession with this, especially because there's so many other Vietnamese babies that need to be adopted—since President Ford okayed Operation Baby Lift. But I think Tsan's still reaching out for me through his niece, to save her."

John patted Michael's knees when they were almost finished with their session. "Maybe Angela's thinking you should adopt an American child?"

"I thought of that," Michael said. "Maybe she's afraid a child from Vietnam will keep my head filled with too many bad memories." He stretched his legs. *I wish I could save all the children . . .*

"Hmm . . ."

"What? Do you agree with her?" Michael asked.

"I'm keeping out of this one," John answered. "Only you can answer that, Mike."

Michael studied the scars on John's legs as he stood on the floor mat and changed the subject. "Hey, remember when I first came to you, and we compared our scars?" He laughed.

"Ha. Yeah, I forget who won that match. Want to recount?" John asked. "Every scar is etched in us for life. Can't escape it, can we?"

"I was out in the bush for days with hardly any water," Michael said, staring at the wall. "I was beyond thirsty. After that, I was assigned gate duty for a while."

"Checking ID?"

"Yep. Gate watch from dawn to dusk, until I was reassigned to a different unit."

"Then what?" John asked.

"We had to sweep the villages. Which was pretty interesting, getting to see how the Vietnamese live. They became real people when we did that."

He thought of little Tsan again. How he had hoped to find him alive. How he had felt when he learned Tsan's family had been killed. Almost his entire family. His sister, Khanh, had barely survived, and she was moved to a different location. It was only by chance that Michael learned about the lone survivor who later died of a ruptured appendix two months after the birth of her daughter, Baby Linh.

"I know what you mean. Real people were only targets. That's all they were—targets." John squinted as if seeing them.

"Easy targets peeking out from those huts made of bamboo and corn stalks and twigs. After their six o'clock curfew, they went into the cellars like ratholes and went to sleep." Michael paused and wiped his brow with a towel.

John looked at Michael. "Hey, buddy, don't let it mess with you."

"Sometimes I don't even know what's bothering me. I get really down on myself, and I don't want to bring up stuff at home."

John nodded. "Yeah, I hear ya. You know you can talk to me, anytime."

"Thanks. There are times I need to talk to somebody who's been there, ya know? I still feel the red dirt under my feet, still taste the C-rations . . . Those days are never really gone, are they?"

John gave him a smack on the back. "You have nothing to be ashamed of, Michael. Sometimes I can't believe how lucky I am to have made it this far."

"Yeah, so you can torture guys like me." Michael winced and stood to stretch before doing his lunges.

"We're still breathing, talking, walking, which is amazing, considering over 60 percent of the guys killed over there were twenty-one or younger."

Michael thought of his friend Tom.

John pressed on Michael's wounded leg. "Hey, no cheating on this leg . . . go deeper on the lunge. You worked yourself hard today. Great job. I'll see you Thursday, then? Same time?"

"You know I'm a masochist. I'll be here."

Michael hung his keys on the hand-painted rack that Angela had created from seashells. Everywhere he turned there was Angela's art. He especially admired the oversized canvas above their fireplace in the living room. It was a turquoise beach scene of two children digging a giant sandcastle with an oncoming wave in the distance. Michael quickly settled at his desk to write the thoughts he'd collected on the car ride home, sitting in front of his new electric Smith Corona. He scanned his desk. "Oh, man! Ange! Where's all my typing paper? She must have reorganized the shelves again. Maybe she moved the . . . Damn it, Ange, leave my stuff alone! I know exactly where things are in my own mess."

He rooted through desk drawers, pulling them open one at a time. The bottom drawer was stuck. He jerked it so hard the drawer fell to the floor. Something had jammed it. He pulled out a wrinkled snapshot of him and Tom—*Texas Tom* from Amarillo, they called him in the platoon. He was a kid then, barely eighteen.

Michael choked up. He had been Tom's sole caretaker.

Suddenly, Michael realized what he had dreamt about the night before. In his dream, he met his half-brother for the first time. They looked nothing alike, but he knew it was his brother. He wore the same smile as Michael, that slightly turned upper lip. In the dream, his brother was coming toward him, arms extended, as if to embrace him.

"Hey, how are you, man?" He held his finger up to his lips. "Shhh . . . this is our secret, okay, Michael? Don't tell anyone we finally met, not anyone."

Michael had no voice in the dream. He was confused. Where were they? It wasn't home, that was certain. They were together in the jungle, in the middle of Nam. Both in uniform, covering their helmeted heads, as their Elvis smiles dissipated. Blasts of enemy fire were everywhere. They both went down hard. Michael crawled up to him, clawing at his legs, pulling him to safety, climbing up to see he had no face. And on his uniform, there was no name tag. He finally got to meet his nameless brother.

1969 was a doozy, he thought, the year he met Angela, the year of Woodstock; the same year he and Angela parted right before he went off to fight in a war he didn't believe in—the year he wanted to totally give up after nearly losing his life, until Angela found him again and gave him a reason to live. And the same year he found out about his mother's little secrets.

Michael blamed his mother for many things, including letting his father walk out on them. *My father's a stranger to me. I lost him the same day I lost my first tooth.* Michael could still see his six-year-old self in the mirror staring hard at the hole where the tooth had been, the toothbrush bristles against his sore gums. He remembered his tears running into his mouth, the salty taste mixed with blood. But he could hardly remember the back of his father's head when he had slammed the front door and walked out without looking back. Maybe by the time a new tooth replaced the empty spot his father would be back. But he didn't come back, not even long after Michael's adult tooth emerged.

Mom forgot to put a quarter under my pillow that night. What did I know, a dumb little Jewish kid? I never enjoyed the splendor of the Easter Bunny or Santa Claus . . . no way was I ever going to believe in the tooth fairy. Or in my father. I kept that pain to myself. I guess we all collect our own little secrets.

Michael wasn't just an only child. He was a *lonely* child. He didn't have much of a family and he wondered why, trying to put the puzzle together: his famous grandfather, the world-renowned art dealer; his grandmother, the socialite who had the servants dress the four children in their best clothes. Michael envisioned them running through the three-story house in Holland all those years ago.

Michael heard a few obscure anecdotes about the once-aristocratic family he'd never met; her siblings were still living in Europe. He could see the angst on his mother's face as she told him, particularly when she mentioned Gretta's name.

One thing his mother made perfectly clear was that people were not to be trusted, even family. "The ones you especially have to be leery about," she had said, "are the ones that profess their love for you."

He knew in the later years exactly who she was referring to. His mother wanted to be the only one in Michael's life because she would never abandon him—not like his father had done. *Never!* And she had done everything in her power to keep her only Jewish son apart from that gentile girl named Angela.

After a night out drinking with the guys, Michael had become irrational. With a hangover, he had enlisted in the Army the next morning. He immediately knew he had made a grave mistake. Soon after, he and Angela separated. The girl was right all along—Michael wasn't strong enough to stand up to his mother. Ironically, when Michael had lost his will to live, Sylvie reached out to his Christian girlfriend and told her where to find him. "Tell him the truth, Angela. Only you can. Tell him the secret his mother kept from him his entire life."

Michael finally confronted her.

"How could you not tell me that I have a brother, Mom? You could have told me ten, fifteen years ago. He could have been part of our family after Dad walked out."

"I'm sorry, Michael," she had repeated over and over through the tears. "I know it was a terrible secret to keep from you. Believe me, I lived with the guilt." She turned away. "I can't talk about this right now. Please, don't make me . . . I never could tell you because I wasn't sure you'd forgive me. I wasn't sure I had forgiven my own sin," she whimpered.

"Stop! I don't believe in sins. Being human means you're allowed to make mistakes. And mistakes can be forgiven."

Sylvie had covered her mouth in shame. "I was so young, Michael."

"I would have understood," he said.

Michael imagined his mother as a young girl who missed her father and who had only known about showy dresses and expensive jewelry back in her homeland. She had witnessed the suffering of others during the war and feared the same horror could befall her own family. Still, it was difficult for him to ignore her shallow lifestyle.

During college, Michael rebelled against Sylvie's materialism. He practiced meditation, read Indian philosophy, and smoked a lot of weed. It wasn't until the day he met Angela, when he shed his sandals on the beach and ran into the ocean waves to rescue the gentile girl, that he saved himself from going under.

Chapter 3

Angela studied the lifelike ceramic red apple on her desk, a gift from a former student. This was her second year teaching, although some days felt like an eternity. When she was fourteen, she was perpetually staring at the ceiling, pretending it was a map of the world, and each speck was a faraway place she'd visit someday—anywhere outside of that classroom would have sufficed.

She sighed. *At least I get to teach something I love.* She looked at the students' work decorating the walls and realized the weeks were melding into one another. Life was especially rough for her during the month of May. Her birthday, May 7, was the anniversary of when her seven-year-old sister drowned. Angela's birthdays always made her mother so sad that Angela tried to uplift her with a fake display of humor. She would run around the rooms trying to sit on each balloon until they popped, making her father laugh, and then, eventually, her mother. Her parents had moved to sunny Florida, and Angela missed them terribly.

Angela had a surrogate sister growing up. Katie had so towered over Angela's petite frame that when together they looked like a comedy team. Katie had sat behind Angela in their sixth-grade social studies class, and the two would laugh at the most inane things, like the way Tommy Dermont's cowlick stood straight up on the back of his coarse orange hair.

Back then, when Angela got home from school every day, her mom would be sitting at the sewing machine. A Norman Rockwell print of a World War II scene hung above her mother in the corner of the room. Angela could picture the neatly cluttered apothecary chest holding dozens of thin needles, bobbin cases, and multicolored buttons.

It was 1968. The smell of freshly cut grass had drifted in through the crack in the bottom window of the schoolroom, enticing Angela's adolescent thoughts to wander. The distant hum of a lawnmower made her feel drowsy. She blocked out the monotone voice of her teacher at the blackboard. She could still see his lips moving, going off into one of his dissertations about taxation without representation or something.

The smell of chalk replaced the sweet smell of grass, and the peaceful sound of the lawnmower was replaced by a clangorous bell. Angela dragged herself down the hall to her next class, which was English, and before she could even think, she was assigned to write a poem about love. The only love she ever knew was from her parents; she had gone out with a few boys, but none were right for her. None could join in her dream of seeing the world.

Angela loved her parents, but she couldn't wait for graduation when she'd become a stewardess, spread her wings, and fly away from her small town. Her classmates were like robots, unimaginative and uninspired, moving from class to class at the sound of a bell, but ultimately going nowhere. They were just outer shells, making her wonder what was on the inside.

Mrs. Lee tapped Angela's desk with her masterful fingers. "Angela, did you finish your poem?" Angela handed in her paper, thinking the rest of the class probably wrote poetry about boyfriends or girlfriends. Hers reminisced on her childhood. She titled the poem "A Terrycloth Towel":

Backyard picnics,
pretty little girls
whirling in circles
with auburn curls.
A lavender dress
of dotted-swiss
made with Mama's hands.
Black Maryjanes
shined with Vaseline
and cuffed lace anklets
that wouldn't stay clean.
Dolls thrown to the side
For a different toy,
Mama disenchanted with
Such a spunky tomboy.
Thrown in the tub,
Mama washed me clean
No dirt to be seen.
In a terrycloth towel
She held me tight.

She was a seamstress
by night
'til her fingers bled.
and Daddy kept two jobs
to keep us fed.
Years and years later . . .
and I think of those days
at Jones Beach
when Mama was in reach
after a swim in the water.
Such a lucky daughter,
swathed in a terrycloth towel,

who knew she was wrapped
in so much more.
That terrycloth towel
had said it all.
The summer ended,
the towel . . . frayed and gone,
but the warmth of its memory
will always live on.

Angela was guilt-ridden over her love of the beach where her sister's life was taken so abruptly. Her eyes welled up, thinking that her dead sister could no longer feel a mother's love. Or could she?

"Hi, Mrs. Beckman." A tall, slender girl's high-pitched voice startled Angela, taking her away from the memory of the poem. "Oh, my gosh, I'm sorry, Paula. I didn't even hear you come in." She brushed the corner of her eye with her fingertip.

Paula looked at the art teacher, as if amused she had caught her off guard. "I'm a few minutes early because I ran. I mean, I walked down the hall. Quickly. I walked, quickly."

Angela smiled at her.

"Do you want to know why I ran? Mr. Quinn let me leave first because I got an A+ on my science test," she rambled.

"Oh, so no lectures," Angela said. "Congratulations."

"Yeah, so what are we doin' today?" the girl asked, biting the inside of her cheek.

"You'll see. Get your paint supplies set up."

"Cool. I love painting!"

Soon, more students filed into the room.

Angela told the freshman class about her travels throughout Europe again, and how she was inspired by the masterpieces she saw when she was younger. She wanted to open their imaginations to the magnitude of such experiences. At that time, Angela had been so overcome that when her bus pulled into the city of Florence—the heart of art—and everyone else had exited, she had to stay on the bus for a while and breathe slowly into a paper bag to stop hyperventilating. She pictured herself now, staring out the bus's cloudy windows, unable to calm down. She thought of all the masters she'd read about. *Please, don't faint*, she had told herself.

Angela called on Jimmy Peterson, who asked loads of questions. "What else did you do in Europe, Mrs. B?" Jimmy had a way of making her feel uncomfortable, as if they were equals.

"Well, I started out with a sketchpad, sat on the bottom step of a narrow, ancient staircase in the middle of . . . Well, I don't know where I was. I was pretty lost. I drew what I saw, what I felt, moment by moment."

"Just with a blank piece of white paper?" someone else asked.

"You have to begin somewhere," she answered, knowing that the very idea still scared her silly. She used to wonder, *What if nothing happens? No motivation? No miracles? And the white piece of canvas remains just that—devoid of color and emotion.*

"Where else did you go?" Jimmy interjected.

"I went to Venice, Monaco, Provence. I tried to go to as many places as I could, every city and the small villages on the outskirts of the cities, every fruit stand, every train depot, every coastline . . ."

"Mrs. B?"

"Yesss, Jimmy?" The class laughed. She had told them about seeing *The David* in Florence, and of course they had tittered about that among themselves.

"What did ya see that really turned you on?"

"I know this will disappoint you, Jimmy, but I sketched images of little old Frenchmen wearing berets, carrying loaves of bread and tapping their walking sticks on the cobblestones. That's what turned me on."

"Oh. Bummer," he said. "I bet you drew nude models over there."

The class laughed again.

Angela thought about her early sketches while the kids painted with oil. Her favorite was a small dog jumping at an old man's side. She had stayed with a group of kids she met in a youth hostel. During her travels, she had frequently referred to her bible, a book called *Europe on $5 a Day*.

Angela squeezed between the desks as they painted. "No, Mary. Add a little blue to that area."

She remembered being in her glory, wandering aimlessly through the narrow alleyways of the Algerian section. This was her solo trip, with nothing but a backpack weighing her down. She was indeed *free*, no longer having to follow an airline work schedule. She had imagined what it would be like to be an artist and to teach it. Those feelings would solidify in Paris.

Angela was awestruck by the spectacular Palace of Versailles of Louis XIV. Each church more beautiful than the next. The Pantheon, the Eiffel Tower, and then a boat ride along the Seine. At night, from the Cathedral of Notre Dame, she could see the whole city in one heart-quickening glance. On another day it was the *Mona Lisa* at the Louvre. Mona's stare followed her around the museum, like she'd heard it would.

Later, she ate pizza with her newfound friends, and they laughed when the pizza came with a sunny-side-up egg on top; she had stopped questioning the unusual during her travels. To know everything would have ruined the magic.

Angela didn't share her hitchhiking experience with her students. After Paris she was off again. She stuck out her thumb on Highway 10 and got a ride with a trucker all the way to Madrid. With each city she stopped at, she felt a little less burdened.

"Mrs. Beckman? You're not going to make us write a paper on our sketches, are you?" Jimmy asked.

"If you keep calling out, I will," she said, taken away from her daydream.

"Jimmy, shut up," the class moaned.

"You made us write a paper last year," someone called out.

"That's because Jimmy had a big mouth last year, too," Susie, the class goody-goody, reminded everyone.

"Okay, that's enough." Angela looked up at the wall clock. "We're running out of time. The seniors will be here in less than ten minutes. So, get your work done, let it dry on the windowsills, and clean up this mess."

After the last student marched out of the room, the phone rang. Mrs. Noonan called to say the senior class wouldn't be coming to art today. "I have to leave early to attend a family funeral, so I'm forced to do makeup work with them."

"Of course. I'm so sorry, Mrs. Noonan, about your loss."

"Oh. It's my husband's crotchety old uncle Harry, whom I only met once. Poor fellow, never smiled." The phone clicked. Angela smiled nervously, thinking back to herself and Katie at the age of eleven or twelve, on the brink of teenybopper, when they were coaxed into attending the funeral of their neighbor, Mrs. Fitch. Angela had been playing stickball on the street corner when she saw her mother at their front door, waving her kitchen towel.

"Mom?" Angela was breathing hard. "Why'd you call me in? I was at third."

"Angela, I want to tell you something. Now sit down."

"What, Mom?"

"It's Mrs. Fitch. She passed."

Angela looked out the window.

"No, honey. She passed *on*. She died."

"Oh, that's too bad," Angela said, trying to see what was going on with her ballgame. Her friends were still in their same positions, as she had told them to wait for her. "Can I go back on base now?" Angela didn't like how serious her mother got when someone passed. She had been kept away from attending her grandparents' funerals.

"I think you're old enough now to give your condolences."

Why does she think that? "But, Mom—"

"No buts. She was our neighbor. Now, go wash up."

If you ask me, the neighborhood's too crowded, anyway.

When Angela walked up to Mrs. Fitch's coffin, she was horrified. *What the heck did they do to poor ol' Mrs. Fitch? Her lip—it's coming to a point!*

Mrs. Martino pulled Angela down by her elbow to a kneeling position.

"Say a prayer, Angela."

Dear God. What am I praying for? She's dead. Even though she was a mean old witch, I never would have wished for this.

"*Psssst.*"

Angela turned to see Katie and her mom standing in line behind them.

Katie shrugged.

Made sense—the neighborly thing to do.

Angela, dressed in black, smiled at her. She imagined they had both been getting the lowdown on what they had to wear at the same time from their mothers.

Angela rose and watched Katie as she approached the corpse. Obviously, it was Katie's first time, too. Their mothers walked to a table of Fitch family photos. The room suddenly got too quiet. There was an empty chair next to Angela. Katie grabbed a Bible and sat. She pointed to her own lip. "Did you get a load of Mrs. Fitch's—?"

"Don't start," Angela warned. But it was already too late. Angela buried her face in her hands. Katie's face was deep into the Bible. They both tried with all their might to hold back volcanic laughter. Angela's shoulders shook, violently.

A dark-haired woman with a streak of skunk white mid-forehead gave her a sorry look. "Maybe these girls are too young to be here," she said to another older woman.

"Here, dear." She handed Angela a tissue and patted her back.

This made Angela want to let the lava really flow; she knew she was in deep. She started to cry from laughing and pulled the tissue closer to her face to wipe the tears.

"I am going to kill you," she whispered to Katie, slapping her friend's knee.

Katie slapped her back. "Cut it out."

"No. You."

One at a time, the two girls stood and casually walked to the back of the room, then tore out the back door when no one was looking. They sighed as they slid down the back wall of the building, unladylike in their dresses, and landed hard on the sidewalk on their rear ends.

"Look what I got." Katie showed Angela half of a cigarette she had stolen from her mother's dirty ashtray. "Wanna try it?" She hit herself in the head and looked at Angela. "Got matches?"

"Yeah, sure. I always carry matches, knucklehead."

Katie threw the cigarette away in disgust.

"We laughed at a funeral. Laughed. Now, we're going straight to hell," Angela said.

"On an elevator," Katie responded.

"Express." Angela said.

Katie raised her hand flat in the air and dropped it to the sidewalk. "Splat."

Angela erased the blackboard, thinking about her youth when life seemed more promising. She lined the chalk up in color order, hit the light switch, and closed the door behind her. Maybe she'd cook a nice meal for Michael and try to avoid talking about all the things she really needed to talk about.

On the weekend, Angela saw Katie again, and she was excited. It had been months since Katie's twins had been born. They had so much fun catching up that the day came and went way too fast. It worked out well, since mother-in-law Sylvie agreed not to come for her usual weekend visit. Angela wished Katie could stay longer, like in the old days when they shared girl talk for hours on end.

"Remember when we talked 'til dawn?" Angela asked Katie, helping her tote baby bags back down the driveway of the beach house toward Katie's station wagon.

Katie nodded, sadly. "I miss those days."

"I hate to see you go," Angela confessed. "The last time I saw Kelly and Kevin, they were still in the hospital, fresh out of the oven." She sighed. "I hope they're not teenagers by the time I see them again."

"Bite your tongue. I dread the teen years. Remember the trouble we used to get into? I hear payback's a bitch."

"I think they've already started paying you back," Angela said, "making you schlep all this stuff."

"It's so worth it, visiting you. Too bad Michael isn't home. How is he doing with his—?"

"His short fuse?" Angela interjected. "He's still the sweetest man on the planet, although sometimes—sometimes, his short temper puts a strain on our marriage."

"Marriage is work, ain't it?" Katie rolled her eyes.

"Anyway, he would have loved seeing you guys. He won't believe how big the twins got in only four months."

"Yeah, too bad. He missed a great lunch, too."

"Yeah, right. BLTs are so gourmet."

"It's the love you put into them." Katie winked.

Angela leaned over the infants as she helped to strap them down, rubbing her cheek against theirs, inhaling their baby smell.

"Yes, that's right. I'm so happy to see you all. I'm just tickled pink," she said in baby talk. "And blue. Tickled pink and blue." She backed away from the car and gently closed the door.

"Wouldn't it be something if someday our kids turn out to be best friends, like we were?" Katie asked.

"Aren't you counting my chickens before they hatch?" Angela looked solemn.

"What do you mean? I saw the photograph, and Baby Linh appears pretty hatched to me."

Angela's eyes got watery. "I didn't want to tell you we've been going through a lot of red tape. I'm afraid we won't get her for a while—if we get her at all. We recently figured out the expenses of raising a child and, well, frankly, there are probably other interested couples that would be better financially suited."

"Oh my God," Katie yelped. "That's ridiculous! You and Michael would make the perfect parents."

"And also something to do with Michael's injuries and what happened while he was on his mission over in Nam, you know, and seeing a psychiatrist and everything." Angela dabbed her eyes with her sleeve.

Katie touched Angela's shoulder. "I'm sorry you have to deal with all this."

One of the twins began to cry. Katie made a face and opened the car door. "Ahh, kids. They can drive you crazy." She tried to joke. "Now, which one of you guys is making all the fuss? It's Kelly. No, it's Kevin. Uh-oh, it's both of them. Double trouble." Katie looked at Angela and choked mid-sentence. "Ange? Ange, are you okay? It's me, Katie. I know you better than anyone. Blood sisters, remember? You can call me anytime if you need to talk."

Angela laughed and cried, simultaneously, covering her mouth with a shaky hand. "I'm afraid we're running out of options."

The babies quieted. Katie gently closed the car door again and turned toward her friend.

"Angela, having little ones leaves you no time for anything else. It's not all fun. You absolutely have no freedom, and if I remember correctly, under your high school photo, you were coined with the nickname *Freebird*, right?"

"That was a long time ago," Angela said. She thought about her days flying for the airlines as a stewardess. It was her dream job. She never shared her fantasies of those days with anyone anymore, not even Katie. "Yeah, that was all great back then—"

"Ange," Katie interrupted. "I know you're done with the fertility treatments right now, but—"

"I'm done with a lot of things. You know how I hate being around doctors and needles and—ugh. I've never had it easy in that area. I've always been irregular with missed periods and whatnot. And to tell you the truth, I grew so tired of all the bullshit the doctors told me. What was the latest? Something to do with a possible obstruction in one of my fallopian tubes? Maybe they just don't know what they're talking about." She wiped the wetness from her cheeks.

Katie stroked Angela's arm. "I truly believe you and Michael will have children one day."

"Thank you. I know you want that for us. And that means a lot to me."

The two friends hugged goodbye, and Katie got into her car. Angela tapped lightly at the window of the back seat where the babies were already dozing off. She watched her friend's car drive down Dune Road until it was out of sight, still savoring the babies' breath, seeing the pinkness in their cheeks.

She went back inside and sat alone in the quiet. Then she took out her art supplies and prepared for Monday's lesson.

Michael came home late from his editorial meeting. He was managing editor for the local paper he'd been working at since college. The pay was still lousy, but at least he got to write. In between, he worked on his second book.

He looked for his wife and found her standing in the kitchen with a blank expression.

"Hi, babe. What's the matter? You look funny."

"Hi. No. It's nothing."

"Katie left?"

"Yeah. I already miss her. Mikey, can we get a dog?" she asked as he leaned in to give her a kiss and noticed a smudge of paint on the tip of her nose.

"A dog? What brought that on?" he asked, already knowing the answer. "Ange, we've been through this before. A dog ties you down. We're both out a lot, and besides, you have a yellow nose."

"Huh?" She held up the soup spoon and saw the yellow spot in her upside-down reflection. "Don't change the subject on me."

Michael inspected what she was working on. "Sunflowers. Really nice."

"Your dinner's still warm. Want me to heat it up? It's your favorite."

"Aha! I see. Lemon chicken at the same time you're asking for a dog. What strategy."

Angela laughed. "I'm serious. Well, half-serious."

Michael nuzzled up to her, kissing her on the neck behind her ear. "If you need to nurture, I'm here, babe."

She kissed him back. On his eyelids. She loved the flutter of his lashes when she did.

"Okay, maybe we'll have to wait on the dog . . . not too long, promise?" She held up two sample paintings. "Think my classes will like doing the sunflowers? They have a choice of either doing a field or a still life."

"If they turn out like yours, they'll love it," he said. "How the hell do you do this?"

"I don't know; it comes to me through the paint brush."

"Wish I could make the words come through my pen," Michael said.

She set Michael's plate down for him and went back to the sink to wash the greasy pan. She wondered how many times Katie checked on the babies during the night. She'd often heard her neighbors complain about how tiring that could be. She rested the palm of her hand across her flat belly, feeling empty. She imagined gaining thirty glorious pounds to her five-foot, two-inch frame.

Chapter 4

Sylvie felt the heat rise up her neck and into her cheeks. She wished she could slam the phone down on the lawyer who was making her regurgitate her past these past few months. She'd never met the man and had only hired him after her divorce years ago to legally change her name back to Rosenberg.

"Mr. Adelstein," she complained, "I've told you all of this already."

"Ms. Rosenberg, I know. Still, we need to review and fill in some gaps, that's all."

"About?"

"About how your family felt they were being persecuted more than being protected."

"By the way, please call me Sylvie. As I told you before, Mr. Adelstein, the only reason our family would remain unharmed was because of my father's connections to certain masterpieces which the Swiss consul had, and which Hitler desired. And the führer could only obtain them if we survived. We didn't really know what would happen once he got what he wanted; however, we played that scenario out in our minds many times."

She squeezed her eyes tight, her life story passing before her like flipping pages through the scary parts in a children's storybook. There were things that children never talked about, even years after.

"There were four of us—Gretta, the oldest, was our bossy sister; Wilhelm, the introverted brother; then me, in the middle—the obstinate one; and the last one—sweet Ruthie. But Ruthie was not the last one to be born. There was another girl, an infant who only survived a few days. Mother never told us about the baby who died in her sleep. It was later, when we discovered that Mother had suffered a *nervenzusammenbruch*—a nervous breakdown because of the way the child suffocated. It was during one of the raids—the day we hid behind the wine cellar. We heard the soldiers above us, their boots hard on our parquet floors. Mother held a pink blanket that day close to her chest while we hid and she seemed so brave and protective with the new infant that had joined our family only five days before. She was so new that she wasn't yet a part of us. Mother was afraid the baby would cry. She couldn't let that happen.

"Years later, we learned more about Baby Rose on Mother's medical records when she was at the Mental Health Institute of Amsterdam, stating the cause of death as 'suffocation.' Even then, we were in denial."

"That's tragic," Mr. Adelstein said softly.

Sylvie thought about the day when they finally had to leave their home; how surreal it was being escorted down the empty street by the SS men at such an early hour in the morning when all you could hear was the echo of your own shoes in the dark. She thought they'd all simply disappear at any moment. As they got farther away from their house, she turned around one last time to look back and swore she saw tears falling from its windows.

She often thought about her old house in the small town of Dieren while waiting out the war. If she inhaled deeply enough, she could still smell the different rooms on each of the three floors. The first floor where the servants cooked smelled spicy sweet; the second floor was the children's quarters, all powdery fresh; their mother and father's master suite on the third floor was a mix of hard-earned perspiration and lovelorn eau de cologne.

As they grew up, her siblings grew further apart from Sylvie. She was the different one. The others conformed to the rules of the house. Not Sylvie, however; she had a mind of her own. She was more like her father—willful and independent. Sylvie was also the only one in the litter curious about her father's art business. Over time, the secluded Sylvie discovered this was the only way to get her father's attention. Soon, her vested interest in the world of art became her passion, and this thrilled her father. She quickly became his pet.

Sylvie mumbled some of her thoughts into the phone with her lawyer.

"I'm having trouble hearing you, Sylvie," Mr. Adelstein said. "Let's go back," he nudged.

"Oh, and they tell me I'm the one with the bad hearing." She intuitively touched her left ear. He laughed obligingly.

"On October 20, 1942, we were escorted to the train depot . . . to the unknown. We waited on the cement platform for three and a half hours. It was windy and cold. My brother and sisters wore dead faces. My mother nearly passed out, and a stranger helped her to her feet. Then, there was that final moment of truth—the big trade."

Sylvie went off again into her own world. *A Rembrandt passing hands, unbeknownst to the late, great artist, himself—Rembrandt van Rijn—who saved innocent lives with the stroke of a brush.*

"Talk to me, Sylvie," the lawyer coaxed. "Tell me what happened before your escape."

She thought about the crude cargo boat at the port in Spain where they eventually met other relatives her father's negotiating had saved—twenty-five Jews in all—the biggest trade and his last one.

"Oh, so many times we were told we were the lucky Jews because we ended up at the British safety internment camp on the island of Jamaica in the West Indies. We were in the state of suspension there for three long years . . . where I was supposed to finish growing up."

"No, no. Go back. You're getting way ahead of me. Before the camp, before the occupation. What were some of your earliest fears?

When did you start to feel threatened?"

"I don't know. It's all so vague. Sometime in the late 1930s my father spoke about going to America, to New York, to look at art galleries and museums and eventually running a branch of his art business in the United States. I had no idea it was where he'd try to salvage whatever art would be left.

"At first, the idea of going to America was exciting, especially going on a big boat. Later on, when I started to enjoy the freedom of being a teen, I didn't want to leave my home, and I especially didn't want to leave Samuel."

"Samuel?"

"He was my first love. You know . . . there's nothing like your first love."

"Yes, let's not get off track again. We need to go even further back—when you first felt threatened?"

She still saw Samuel's eyes in her mind, full of promise. She'd been crying hard when she told him with tears running into her mouth that she'd be leaving the country soon with her family—they'd be on the run. That was when she received her first kiss, her first salty kiss.

Sylvie tried to focus and recalled when she was a little girl in the early 1930s.

"There was a man by the name of Maxwell from Germany who came on a regular basis to our hometown gallery on Spoorstraat 32, only a few kilometers from our home. I kept that number forever in my head—32, my lucky number."

"Go on. Tell me about Maxwell?"

"Then he stopped coming, Maxwell. Something to do with our being Jewish. We received reports from across the border that things were getting very bad for the Jewish population in Germany, only fifteen miles away from our home. And later, like the spread of a terminal disease, the Nazis expanded their power, country by country. The Germans implemented anti-Jewish policies immediately upon occupation in Holland, including the taking of Jewish property. You know that Holland lasted only five days before they surrendered. There was nowhere to hide—no mountains, no caves, no forests."

Sylvie tried to remember other names that Attorney Adelstein may find helpful.

"There was another man, Dr. Hans Posse, who came to our gallery. He's the one who wanted to send my father's art to the Linz Museum—for Hitler's private collection. It was right after Uncle Nathan and my father were forced to register their business."

She told Adelstein that according to documents in the trade register, non-Jewish business partners were appointed as directors who resigned after the war, and the Rosenberg brothers were to continue to do business with whatever was left.

"How did your father feel about losing his power?" Mr. Adelstein asked.

"Like a small dog giving up a big bone, that's how he felt. My parents wondered what to do with us kids regarding the fate of his business. If he lost the art, his children's futures would be jeopardized."

Sylvie was getting more upset and started to look through her jar of sweets for a soothing lozenge to clear her throat. "Tension increased daily at the dinner table, but without questions. It was a rule—at the dinner table, we only talked about pleasant things.

"The servants were let go, and we had to deal with setting the table, eating our mother's lousy cooking, clearing the table, and washing our own dishes. We passed the salt back and forth along the lavish length of our table under the pretense that all the unpleasantness would go away. As you know, things only got worse."

She told her lawyer that the Dutch police got word from the Germans to give the Rosenbergs special treatment. But the Germans were growing impatient with the family.

"So, you felt the clock ticking?"

"Louder by the day. As a warning of what could happen if we didn't cooperate with the art, my grandmother was taken away. To Westerbork."

"Yes, I have all the details of that on record. Terrible, for an old woman."

"My grandmother and I were very close. Oma was more a mother to me than my own mother. I never wanted to believe they laid a hand on her. She eventually succumbed to dysentery."

Sylvie shifted awkwardly in her seat.

"Anyway, my father knew certain people in high positions that could connect us to art that wasn't degenerate; art that Hitler wanted for his Führer Museum."

"Do you happen to know the names of the artwork?"

"No, I regret to say I don't. My father didn't share everything with us at such a frantic time. We were under great stress, constantly concerned that the plans would go wrong. It was such a relief to get so many family members out of Holland.

"I remember my father and his brother obtaining travel visas at the last moment by securing a number of artworks. The foreign police had to be cooperative, too. But everything was risky. Sometimes Mother left us children home alone. She seemed to disappear without a word.

"When things became more chaotic, we realized the entire family urgently needed to leave Holland. Soon, Uncle Nathan got permission to bring his family to Switzerland. He had to pay the Swiss large sums of money to keep his family safe. The pressure was too much for him coming from all sides. My father and the rest of us, on the other hand, wouldn't be able to make our exit for many months after Uncle Nathan."

"Yes, I have all my notes about that from our last conversation," Mr. Adelstein said. "And about the nights previous to your exit when you had to go into hiding . . . all of which will be helpful in proving persecution. To tell you the truth, I need more details. We must show that whenever paintings passed hands, it was not voluntary. And the more detail you can provide, the more credibility."

"I can assure you, as any other Jew living during those times, that we couldn't bat an eyelash, place our left foot before our right, or flush the goddamn toilet without thinking of consequences. Nothing was voluntary. *Nothing!*"

"Please, do me a favor; when you're sitting quietly at home, jot down anything that comes to your mind, like you are keeping a diary."

Sylvie thought of the journal she kept hidden under her coat that day at the train station. She'd kept two things in her travels—the journal and her gold star necklace. Wilhelm kept his "good luck" guilder, and Ruthie the smallest of her dolls that she could easily conceal. For the life of her, Sylvie couldn't remember what Gretta brought with her. Maybe nothing. Should she share these silly details with him? For what? She kept them to herself.

"I must be prepared to show the Dutch government that the only reason your father was negotiating art deals with the Germans was because he had to secure his family's safety. Do you think his dealing with the Germans was common knowledge in the community?"

"I'm not sure about that. I felt some resentment among others, never understanding why at the time . . . I was only fourteen. The Nazi agencies wished to keep the arrangements secret with their own administration office for emigration of the well-known Rosenbergs, before our family could flee Holland. The documents also required to list the assets through the regular agencies handling Jews."

"Hmm . . . your young age may work against you."

"I was very angry and upset with my father for leaving us at the train station that day. I felt he betrayed us. I blamed my mother because they had been arguing and were no longer on speaking terms. Somehow I felt it was her fault Papa had deserted us. I hated Mother for that. I had to wonder. What did she do to make him want to leave us?

"I wept like a willow tree for almost one month, the extent of our journey, which ended on the seventh day of December when we finally arrived. Although thankful for the vessel, it was a relief to finally get off the *Marque de Comillas,* the name painted on the side of the ship. It took days to wash its stench off our bodies. It took me years to wash off the resentment I held after our father abandoned us like that. How could he leave us on our own? How could he allow bad things to happen to us? Was his art business more important than his family?" Sylvie asked as if expecting an answer.

Her lawyer didn't reply. "It must have been very difficult to forgive your parents."

"I'm not sure about forgiveness. It's something I've had to deal with every day since the war ended. The Holocaust never really ends, you know."

Sylvie still had the picture in her mind of Camp Gibraltar, how the barracks looked—the cots lined up in rows like tombstones. She remembered the sleepless nights on her stiff, narrow army cot, and how she missed her queen-size bed at home in the elaborate décor of her bedroom. They weren't treated like prisoners, but there were bars on the windows.

To make the days go by at the camp, she marked her journal, writing about her fears and her guilt. Father had abandoned them, making her mother deeply depressed, yet Sylvie had to live with the guilt of her Jewish friends she'd left behind. The stories she'd heard about what may have happened to them were atrocious, including how girls were forced into sterilization rooms. Still, Sylvie, only a child herself, could not comprehend how she met a different fate because of a Rembrandt—a painting. She had a repetitious dream about their escape from Holland, how the train doors opened to the death camps, instead—

"As I said, I've always had to live with being a lucky Jew."

"Lucky?"

"Being the survivor is not easy." She sighed.

"Sounds like you suffer from survivor's guilt."

"You're a psychologist, too?"

She could hear him swallowing in the silence. "And so, that was the demise of your father's firm?"

"Within months of our departure from the Netherlands, the firm was Aryanized. A year later it was completely dissolved. The Nazis had permitted our family to leave only on the condition that we leave behind all paintings, jewelry and assets listed on the Rosenbergs' declaration."

"So, your family was left with nothing?"

"Not entirely. When we were forced to leave Holland, the settlement of the release of capital was still in progress. Some records were destroyed during the war, and an unaccounted sum of my father's bonds and securities were tied up in European banks. Under tight government restrictions, none of our father's assets were made available to us. It took over thirty years to finally get dribs and drabs from the banks . . . and only on an annual basis."

"I suppose it was a real readjustment to your previous lifestyle."

"I'm afraid I no longer have a chauffeur or a butler, if that's what you mean."

"Excuse me, Sylvie. I have to take another call. I will keep you posted on a weekly basis of my correspondence with the Dutch committee," he said, attempting to end the conversation. "Oh, wait a second . . . Sylvie, are you still there? Actually, my secretary's informing me it's the Dutch counsel on the other line right now. Can you hold on?"

While Sylvie waited, she thought of the strained relationship with her mother; they were always butting heads. A conversation came to mind, way before their troubles began:

"Sylvie, I have a lot going on today . . . We're having Father's clients as dinner guests, so you must wear that darling little Ricci jumper I bought you yesterday."

"Mother, please. I don't like showing off everything you buy me. I do have a mind of my own, and I prefer my black skirt with the white ruffled blouse."

"No arguing, young lady. I do think I know a little more about fashion than you do, my dear." She patted her daughter on the head and turned away.

Mother demanded all the attention, but Sylvie gave her a run for her money, always a competition between the two, especially when it came to getting Papa's mindfulness, until one day Sylvie found out how to get to her father's soft spot—through his art. For months upon end, Sylvie had sneaked a multitude of art books up to her room, like ammunition. That did not last, however, after her father became preoccupied with the Nazi invasion.

Not having found a throat lozenge, she instead poured herself a shot of Johnnie Walker. Mr. Adelstein interrupted her thoughts.

"Hello?"

"Yes, I'm still here." She swallowed the shot of whiskey and exhaled.

"Sorry for the wait. I have some news, and I don't know what to make of it."

"What? What is it?" Sylvie blurted.

"The Dutch—they've lost the Blue Book, the notebook identifying works that belonged to the stock of the gallery."

"What did you say?" she sighed. "Now I can imagine the obstacles my father had to put up with during the war if we're having this much trouble now."

"Inconceivable," he agreed.

She spoke slowly, still in shock. "*Oy vey!*"

"I know it's hard to believe."

"Hard to believe?" she snapped. "This is preposterous!"

"Calm down."

"Calm down? My memory can only help us so much. What about those documents I had sent you from Mr. Goodman, the old gentleman who discovered my father's papers in his storage closet after Papa . . . after my father passed on?"

"No, we're all right with those. I have copies."

Sylvie envisioned her father hanging for hours in his lonely New York City apartment, the chair kicked out beneath his dangling always-shiny business shoes. But he no longer had much of a business.

"At least we have something which ties in to questionable pieces being held at the moment in Dutch museums."

Sylvie rushed her words at the attorney. "Which museums?"

"Let me see. Looks like the Rijksmuseum in Amsterdam, the Frans Hals Museum in Haarlem, and Mauritshuis in The Hague. I didn't get all the names. They include works by seventeenth-century masters, among them Gerard Dou, Nicholas Maes, and Jan Steen. There's also some works by Flemish and Italian artists."

"That's a start, but they've lost the Blue Book?" Sylvie could not shake it. "If you ask me, it sounds a little too convenient for them. Without certain documentation, we have nothing. I certainly don't have anything . . . we were on the run, for God's sake!"

"In a way, their negligence may help us. The courts may decide that any remaining doubts about the origin of paintings be in favor of the claimants. By the way, there's two ways we can handle this— go into the Dutch court and make the claim for the property, or we can have the United States government make a diplomatic contact."

She bit the inside of her mouth, feeling more anxious. "I don't know how I feel about going back there, so I prefer the latter."

"Well, you may have no choice. I think it will be more likely they request the hearings in their own courts."

"Whatever it is, it is. I wish it was all over with."

She lowered the phone to her chest and counted to three before she went on to ask him about an entirely different subject. "I do have something else I would like you to do for me." She hesitated.

"Yes, go on."

"I told you I only have one child . . . but . . ."

"Go on."

"There is another. Believe it or not, I don't even know his name or exactly where he is . . . mostly likely he's still in Jamaica. I'd like to talk to you about it when we meet. Perhaps you can do some private investigating?"

"Yes, sure, give my secretary all the information after we're through here, and we'll discuss that, too, when we meet. For the moment, we have enough to deal with."

"Mr. Adelstein, my son, Michael, he knows nothing about this case right now. If the claim ever comes to fruition, then—"

"That's your prerogative," Mr. Adelstein answered. "I will keep you apprised of all correspondence with the Dutch committee. Listen, we're under the gun, but it's not high noon yet."

"What does that mean?"

"Oh, I forgot, you're Dutch. You didn't know much about the Wild West shows in the '40s."

"You certainly aren't giving me enough credit when it comes to wild, Mr. Adelstein."

Chapter 5

Angela was on the couch watching a rerun of *I Love Lucy* when Michael came into the family room. It was the episode where Lucy discovers she's pregnant, after trying for eleven years, and wants to tell Ricky the news, but Ricky's too preoccupied with work to listen. Lucy goes to the club and slips an anonymous note to the maître d' who gives it to Ricky. The note is about how someone in the audience wants to reveal the news of her pregnancy to her husband, and Ricky breaks into a song, "We're Having a Baby, My Baby and Me."

The band plays "Rock-a-bye Baby" as Ricky sings and goes from table to table to find the woman who wrote the note. When he gets to Lucy's table she nods and Ricky walks away without it registering, but then looks back at her again as if to say *"It's you? Really?"* They waltz around the room crying tears of joy.

Angela was crying. "What's up, babe?" Michael asked.

"Oh, nothing . . . Ricky," she answered.

"Ricky?" Michael looked at Angela and then at the television, as Lucy and Ricky were ending their promenade. He sat down beside her. "Yeah, this one gets to me, too." He smiled and put his hand on her shoulder.

"Michael, I was thinking."

"Uh-oh," he said. "What are you *tinking*?" he asked, mimicking Ricky's Cuban accent.

"What if—what if you sell your novel? What if it becomes a bestseller and you make a truckload of money?"

"Then we'll not only get Tsan's niece, we'll adopt a truckload of kids!" He grabbed her arm and pulled her closer, hugging her body up against his.

"That would be great, wouldn't it?"

"I'm glad we're on the same wavelength. Now, you should watch something much funnier. I like seeing you smile so much more." He traced her bottom lip with his thumb.

Michael didn't burden Angela about their mounting bills and financial problems. He wanted to keep her world full of sunflowers— and that included becoming a mother. He thought about Tsan again, how he had vowed, but failed, to protect the Vietnamese boy and his family. Tsan was dead, as was his sister. But her baby had survived, and that child would be Angela's sunflower.

"I know she's the one," Michael had said when first broaching the idea. "Raising her is the least I can do for Tsan."

At first Angela was opposed to an international adoption. Over time, she thought about the karma and came around.

"Michael, your dream is my dream," she had told him. From then on they moved forward on the adoption, while still hoping to conceive a child of their own.

The next morning, Angela found Michael in the guest room stirring a fresh bucket of paint. One pale pink swipe of the brush had been streaked over the dull green wall.

"What are you doing, Michael?" Angela asked, standing at the doorway.

"So, whaddaya think?"

"I don't know."

"Oh, come on, honey. It's positive thinking, that's all."

"I don't want to see you let down." She stared at the newspapers lining the floors. There was an ad with a fifty-cent coupon for diapers at their local supermarket.

"I'll tell you what—I'm so confident that if I'm wrong, you get to throw paint all over these walls in your Pollock-like tantrum."

"That's a deal," Angela said and left the room, but by the way her brow naturally furrowed, she wasn't fooling him.

Michael thought of Tsan with each sweep of the paintbrush. He remembered when they met that first day when Michael and his platoon entered Tsan's small village. Tsan stood out from the other boys and girls, who were all holding their hands out to the soldiers, hoping for a stick of gum. Instead of begging for sweets, Tsan was kneeling next to an old woman who was nearly blind and wearing shredded clothing; her pupils looked frozen and glazed. Michael admired how the boy generously shared his eyes with the hunched-over woman. There was something sacred about the two of them among the others who were hungry and scared amid the oxen and chickens scuttling about in the small village of their war-torn country. Michael knew he'd forever have the image in his mind.

"Mikeel? Mikeel?" Seven-year-old Tsan would call out whenever Michael visited his village. "Mikeel, we are friends, yes?"

"Yes," he'd answer, tousling the boy's feathery head of raven hair. One day Michael gave him a gift box. Tsan held it and stared at the colorful box and ribbon, admiring it, not knowing it was something to unwrap, until Michael coaxed him along. "Go ahead, open it. It's for you."

"For me?" Tsan anxiously pulled the red ribbon that Michael had started untying for him, and he tore at the bright wrapping paper with the blue and purple and yellow balloons, which Michael had purchased at the PX. Tsan's face lit up when he lifted the lid off the box and he took out the Yankee baseball T-shirt. The Yankee logo was on the front and number 7 was on the back under *Mantle.*

"Mickey Mantle," Michael said, with a gesture like swinging a baseball bat.

"Mikeel Man-tel?" Tsan tried to repeat after Michael. "Like you—same name like you."

"Well, not exactly, but Mickey and I both like the number seven." He turned the shirt over. "It's lucky. A lucky number."

"What is the luck?" Tsan turned his head like a puppy dog.

"It means whenever you wear this shirt, good things will come to you," Michael answered. Like his mother, he believed in luck. "Why don't you try it on? Go ahead."

Tsan tore off his soiled, tattered shirt. His ribs protruded like a carcass Michael had once seen while driving through the desert. Michael's voice cracked.

"Looks fantastic, Tsan. It's a natural fit."

He wished he had brought the kid extra food instead, realizing the hunger he must have suffered. He made a note to save up any leftovers from the guys in his platoon, and from that day on, Michael collected packages, whatever he could bring to Tsan, and with great joy watched him eat a variety of foods he hadn't before tasted.

Tsan wore that Mickey Mantle shirt all the time. Michael had wondered if the kid slept in it, too.

While painting the room, Michael choked, imagining poor Tsan wearing his lucky shirt during the last few breaths of his life. *Some damn lucky shirt,* he thought, dripping the paint onto his shoe. Michael tapped the lid back onto the paint can with a hammer and stood, his leg throbbing in pain as it did whenever he stayed in one position too long. He viewed the fresh pale pink enveloping him and felt it was ready for Linh. Their hearts were ready long before he decided to paint the room, and he wished she were here. He was determined that Tsan's niece would have a luckier life than her uncle.

"I promise you this time, Tsan," he said softly aloud as he carried the paintbrushes, wrapped in a rag, into the kitchen. He fell into a trance, watching the pink swirl down the drain as he washed the brushes. He jumped when Angela came up behind him.

"Ooh, sorry, did I startle you?" she asked. "The room is gorgeous." She gave Michael a squeeze. "It gives me such hope to stand within the four walls."

"It'll happen, hon. We gotta believe that."

"Michael, I wanted to tell you about something."

"What?" he asked, drying his hands on a towel.

"Please don't give me a hard time, but I found someone you can talk to—someone who talks to a lot of veterans."

"Funny, isn't that all I talk about? To you, to my mom, to my friends, to my physical therapist? I even write about it; how much more can I do?"

"You have to talk to the right person, one who will show you how to cope better."

"I'm not coping?" he asked.

"Well, lately, I don't think you hear yourself. You lose your temper, you snap at people. Michael, please go and see him. One time, that's all. Maybe it'll help."

"Help what? Turn back the clock? Make Tsan reappear?"

Angela backed away. "Of course it won't change the past. But it may change the future."

"I don't think—"

"Oh, forget it. Don't go. I don't know why I even bother."

"Angela?" Michael grabbed his cane and followed her as she walked away. "I'll go. I mean it. I'll give it a try. For you. And for Linh."

Angela put her arms around his neck and kissed his eyelids shut. "Tell me you're doing it for you, Michael. That's what I want to hear. Promise?"

"I promise," he said, flatly. "For me, too."

❧

Michael stood shirtless in his blue jeans, staring at his Army fatigues that hung in his closet, and purposely pulled his white polo shirt and his corduroy jacket with leather patches off the hanger. *This is how a real writer would dress.* He wanted the psychiatrist to believe he was an in-control professional rather than an out-of-control ex-soldier.

Michael read the nameplate on the doorframe—*Dr. S. Freid*—and laughed out loud. "For Christ's sake, she sent me to see Sigmund Freud." He knocked and walked in, standing taller and straighter, trying to hide his cane from view.

"Sit, sit, Michael," the psychiatrist said in a deep radio voice, pointing to a cushy burgundy leather chair. Michael inconspicuously placed his slender dark-brown cane on the floor next to him and looked directly at the doctor. Dr. Freid was probably in his mid-sixties, with a round red face and thick white eyebrows. He wore his eyeglasses so far on the tip of his nose that Michael concentrated on its balance.

"So, Michael Beckman, how are you? Your wife and I had a nice discussion. She's concerned about you."

"Oh boy," Michael said with a skeptical smile.

"Oh, not to worry. She sounds lovely. I'm pouring myself some coffee. Would you like a cup?" the doctor asked, as the muddy gray liquid filled a stained mug.

"Uh, no, no thank you, I think I'll pass."

"Let's get started then, shall we?"

Michael thought about how strange it was. *Get started? How do you get started when your life is already one-third over, and you're more confused than ever?* Should he talk about his father who had walked out on him? About his unfulfilled wife or his doting mother? About the brother he'd never met? About adopting a child? About feeling like less than a man because he couldn't get his wife pregnant? About Tsan? Or should he simply stick to the war, his nightmares?

"Um. Where would you like me to start, Doctor?"

"Wherever . . . it doesn't matter. It's up to you. Entirely up to you."

Michael squirmed, sinking deeper into the soft leather.

"I'll start with my brother. As far as I know, he has no name. My mother didn't give him one," he said scornfully. "So finding him won't be easy."

"Oh? Did she give him away when he was born? Is that it?"

"Yes. Yes, she did."

"I assume you intend to look for your brother, then?"

"That was my intention, yes sir—yes, Doctor."

"What happened to change your mind?"

"Nothing changed my mind. Life got in the way so far. I haven't been able to make the trip yet. I'm going through a recuperation period." Michael pointed to his leg. "I earned myself a nice medal, though."

Michael wished he could retract his words.

"I don't mean to sound so pitiful. I am . . . alive."

"No apology needed."

"Besides," Michael went on, "it hasn't been financially practical to go traipsing around the Caribbean, searching for my long-lost half brother. My wife and I have been saving every penny so we can start a family."

"Your wife didn't mention you are expecting."

"Expecting to *adopt*."

"I hope that goes well for you." The doctor smiled sincerely, and from that point on, Michael trusted him.

"I understand you have no other siblings?"

"That's right."

"Do you blame your mother for not letting you grow up with your brother?"

"Yeah, I guess deep down I do. I guess, deep down, I blame her for a lot of things. Then, I feel sorry for her at the same time. She didn't have it so easy herself. When she had him, she was only about sixteen, so she chooses not to talk about it whenever I bring it up. She only goes so far when we talk about him, then she usually ends the conversation abruptly."

"What was she doing in Jamaica?"

"She had escaped the Nazis with her family, and they were waiting out the war at a British internment camp."

"This life of hers must have been complicated."

"You have no idea."

"Well, why don't you start telling me the story."

"I only know tidbits of when my mother's family was victimized during the occupation in Holland. For her and her siblings, there was the bullying at school; then they were no longer allowed to attend their regular school and had to go to a Jewish school, until they weren't allowed to go to school at all. The restrictions came upon them gradually, leaving the Dutch Jews to believe it would all go away, that things would get better. Of course, things only got worse. The German soldiers took their bikes away, then their grandmother. Neighbors disappeared. My mother thought because her father was a prominent figure in their community, that they'd be safe. She'd felt privileged.

"There was a lot of negotiating going on, I heard. Because of my grandfather's art. He was a bigwig in the art industry in Europe. There were bombings in Rotterdam, getting closer to their small town of Dieren. By this point they knew about the death camps, and every day they lived in terror of being rounded up—that my grandfather's power couldn't save them. Some nights they had to go into hiding in the root cellar of their home or in abandoned buildings . . . and finally, there was their great escape. My mother didn't believe the Nazis would live up to their end of the deal and thought the train doors would open up to the death camps. They were fortunate enough to continue on to Spain where they boarded a boat for Jamaica—to their freedom."

Michael's voice trailed off, feeling compassion for a teenaged Sylvie Rosenberg and what she'd had to endure. He felt guilty for losing his patience with her and guilty for believing his life had been harder than hers.

"There's more, Michael?" Dr. Freid pressed.

"A lot more."

He told the doctor what he knew about what went on at the camp. By the time he finished, he felt fatigued. On the way out the door, he looked again at the doctor's shingle—*Dr. S. Freid*—but no longer found it funny. He wiped the sweat from his brow and headed for the stairwell.

Chapter 6

"What are ya reading, Mrs. B?"

"Oh, gee. Where does the time go?"

Angela looked at her attendance book and knew she would be marking a lot of absentees because of the stomach bug going around.

She closed the thick book and looked up at the large white clock with its bold black numbers and then around the room. Sunshine passed through the windows, crossing over the three long rows of paint-speckled desks. Angela rubbed the back of her stiff neck and took in the familiar smell of chalk dust and patchouli oil, bringing her back to where she was—teaching another art class to high school students from wealthy Southampton families.

Sarah peeked over Angela's shoulder at the title of the thick book. "*World's Greatest Pilfered Art*," the girl read aloud. "Hmm . . . there's an awful lot of information. Is it boring?"

"Actually, no, it's incredibly interesting to me."

"Why?"

"Well, I know someone who had this happen to her—her family's entire art collection was taken."

"Yeah? Who?" Sarah pressed.

Angela paused, debating whether to share the truth. "My husband's mother."

"Wow. And she won't get them back?"

"Doesn't seem fair, does it, if the Germans aren't forced to make restitution?"

"What's *restitution*?"

"It's the giving back of what's been taken away. I'm afraid they can't give back the six million lives, though."

"I wonder where all those paintings are now," Paula interrupted.

"I want to sound more optimistic, but I doubt she'll ever see them again," Angela said.

"What happened to them? Were they destroyed?" piped another student who had been eavesdropping.

"I'm sure some were destroyed during the war, but the German army wanted as much art as they could get for Hitler's museum. Many pieces are unaccounted for."

Seeing their growing interest, Angela opened the book again and went back to the art history, reading as other students crowded around her desk.

She picked her head up. "Gee, looks like the time got away from me again . . . sorry."

"No, keep reading," the students chanted.

"I didn't know art was such a big deal to Hitler."

Sarah proudly announced, "Yeah, listen to this: Mrs. B's mother—"

"Mother-in-law," Angela corrected.

"Okay, mother-in-law . . . lost all her paintings back then."

"Where are the paintings now?" a student asked.

"In the museums?" another student asked.

"Guys, you know, if you'd like, I can show you more next time. I have a lot of books I took out of the library that I'll bring in, okay?"

"Yeah, cool," a female student said. "My grandfather was in World War II, and he told me how they went in and took hundreds of paintings the Nazis had confiscated."

"Really? Maybe some belonged to Mrs. B.'s family," Sarah said.

The interest from her class made Angela's heart flutter. "Okay, guys, let's settle down and finish up with last week's project."

Angela decided that the students' interest in stolen art presented a great learning opportunity about the value and importance of art. So, she decided to break the subject into three segments during her next class. For the first twenty minutes, she read the facts on the quantity of masterpieces looted; next, she read personal accounts from Holocaust survivors; and last, she assigned the kids to draw a quick sketch of a famous work of art from that period and write a three-paragraph summary of what they thought became of the particular piece of art they chose.

Angela was anxious for them to share their assignments. Ron Miller was the fourth student to get up in front of the class. He wore a grim expression when he spoke.

"My grandfather was a fighter pilot during the war. He annihilated hundreds of those Krauts with—"

Mr. Horton, the principal, walked in the classroom and stared hard at the boy speaking. Everyone froze, and Ron took a seat immediately. Angela fretted over his timing. *Damn, if Mr. Horton had come in a minute before.*

"Mrs. Beckman, may I see you for a moment, please."

Angela followed him into the hallway, giving the kids the quiet signal.

"Are you unaware of the seriousness of the subject matter you're involving your students with?"

"Subject matter? I'm afraid I don't follow. Maybe Ronald shouldn't have used the word *Kraut*, which I will certainly reprimand him for—"

"Yesss, that too, but I'm referring more to the whole topic on the Holocaust. We've already had a complaint from a parent that the topic is too . . . disturbing."

"*Disturbing*?" Angela was incredulous. "With all due respect, Mr. Horton, these young people want to learn—must learn—about what you call disturbing."

"Mrs. Beckman, I appreciate the time you've put into this, but I suggest you drop it."

"I can't. I can't drop it, Mr. Horton. We can't pretend it didn't happen. It's not like they're kindergartners. They can handle it. Besides . . . it's too close to me."

"What do you mean?"

After Angela explained the family history, Mr. Horton hemmed and hawed, then finally agreed to her request to have a guest speaker come to the classroom. "To talk only about the art," he clarified.

"Yes, only about the art, Mr. Horton."

"Let me think about this, Miss Beckman."

It's Mrs. *Beckman,* and "Thank you, Mr. Horton."

Angela reentered her room and realized the period was over. "That'll be all today, class."

"What happened, Mrs. B.?" Timmy asked. "I was getting into this, and I haven't had my turn yet."

"There's been a change of plans and I'll let you know more about that. Meanwhile, for those of you who haven't gotten their turn, please hand in your work, and I'll read them. I'm sorry about this, guys. I promise you we're not done yet talking about the Holocaust. In fact, I may have a guest speaker visit our classroom."

Someone raised their hand in the back of the room, asking, "Is it someone who lived through the Holocaust?"

"Yes," Angela said. "The woman I'm inviting lived there when she was your age." She looked at her students, so wide-eyed and innocent, and tried to picture any one of them in Sylvie's shoes. It was impossible to imagine.

By the time Angela got home, she was furious. "How dare that man stifle me and suppress the information from my kids," she huffed.

Michael touched her shoulder as she sat at the kitchen table, but she was too angry to be coddled. "No, don't. I really have to cool down. I especially felt bad for my Jewish students. They lost grandparents who were slaughtered during the war," Angela choked, resting her head in the palm of her hands.

"Maybe you should give this a rest."

"Are you serious? Give what a rest? How can you say that? You're a Jew. Aren't you infuriated? These kids have to know about this stuff. They have to know about the horrors, they have to be aware."

"Hey, maybe Horton's hands are tied. Maybe he's got to answer to the parents."

"Well, it's time someone changes this!"

"Don't tell me—that someone is you?" Michael said.

"How about your mother getting on the bandwagon?"

"My *mother*? Are you kidding?"

"No, I'm not kidding," she said, trying to convince herself. "She'll be my guest speaker. It will be like a cleansing for her to talk about it. You know it's unhealthy how she sometimes clams up over her past."

"Angela, of all people. My mother? It wouldn't work out."

"Why not? She's perfect because of her knowledge about the art, not about actually suffering in a concentration camp."

"Because of my mother's unfiltered social skills. You know how blunt and condescending she can be."

"I'll rehearse it with her and tell her what she should and should not say beforehand."

"What if she goes on and on about the Nazis? She'll call them worse things than Krauts."

"Let me handle her. I'll be there to guide her every step of the way."

"Okay, don't make me say I told you so when this backfires on you. And what about Horton?"

"Mr. Horton objected to discussing the horrors of the Holocaust, but I think he'll be very pleased to have a woman who owned the real masterpieces share the actual history of the art."

"I hope you're not jeopardizing your job, Ange? You are a new teacher."

"I know, and already I want to climb the walls because you know how much I really want to teach art history on the college level."

"I believe you will someday," Michael said. "In fact, with your determination, I know you will. About my mother—hey, do what you gotta do."

Angela smiled. "Thanks." She picked up the phone.

"You sure don't waste any time," Michael said with a grimace.

She put her hand over the receiver and whispered, "Besides, she'll love the attention, don't you think? Hello? Hello, Sylv—Mom?"

Michael chuckled and walked away.

Sylvie showed up in grand style, wearing her gold lamé blouse and her dark-gray flare skirt and her black alligator heels. Angela smiled to herself, thinking how well she knew her mother-in-law.

"Kids, I'd like to introduce you to Ms. Rosenberg, a Holocaust survivor, actually an escapee whose family traded the old masters to the Germans in exchange for their lives."

"You can call me Sylvie," she corrected with a sparkle in her eye.

"Please, everyone, give *Ms. Rosenberg* your full attention and then you can start asking your questions." Angela took a seat by the windowsill.

"Thank you, Angela—I mean, Mrs. Beckman."

The students laughed.

"I know your teacher recently talked to you about all the famous works of art stolen from the Jews during World War II. Well, I am one of those Jews," she said, and began describing many of her father's masterpieces that hung in his galleries.

Angela came to the front of the room and whispered in Sylvie's ear. She looked pale.

"You're doing great. Just keep going. I'm suddenly feeling sick to my stomach. Must be that stupid stomach virus going around. I think it got to me now. Sorry, I have to run to the bath—" She covered her mouth with her hand and bolted toward the door.

"Is Mrs. B. okay?" one of the students asked Sylvie.

"Oh yes, she's fine. She'll be right back," she said, before diving into the horrors of World War II. "So, let's see . . . hands up for any questions you may have," Sylvie said as Angela was heaving over the toilet bowl.

Sylvie was having a staring contest with the rows of pubescent faces when Angela returned to her classroom. She could tell by the quiet in the room that something was very wrong. Was it something Sylvie had said? *God forbid . . . what did she say? What damage did she do in such a short amount of time?* Angela thought.

Odd, how her usually chatty and inquisitive class sat there, stunned and eyes wide-open, practically crouched down under their desks. "Well, I did my job here . . . gotta go." Sylvie actually took a bow.

Angela escorted her to the door and asked if anything had happened. "Why are the kids so quiet?"

Sylvie denied saying anything to make them the introverts that they now were.

By Friday afternoon, minutes after the dismissal bell, Angela received a note in her mailbox from the principal. "Mrs. Beckman, please see me—it's urgent!"

"Uh-oh," she mumbled.

It was a humiliating moment for her, being summoned to the principal's office like a delinquent student. She tapped lightly on Horton's door.

On Saturday, Sylvie came out to Southampton for her regular visit, wearing a guilty expression, yet she did not admit to anything.

Her acting like nothing was wrong made Angela furious. She stuck her face in Sylvie's and demanded some answers.

"I don't understand how you let this happen when I only left the room for such a short time. It was an emergency, Sylvie. My head was stuck in the toilet. I was only gone for seven minutes. Seven lousy minutes! . . . I mean really, Sylvie; firing squads, sterilizations, gassings—you didn't see any of that! You weren't even at those camps!"

Angela paused to cool off, trying not to get further agitated by Sylvie's nonchalance.

"Sylvie, are you listening to me? Don't you have anything to say?"

Sylvie gave a little shrug and sighed, flicking at an imaginary piece of lint on the shoulder of her taupe silk blouse. "I was filling in the gaps . . . what could have happened to my family if it wasn't for the art. I was showing them how important art is—for your sake, Angela. To give credence to your job."

"My job? Are you kidding? Don't do me any more favors, please."

"I'm sorry you feel that way."

"Saying you're sorry isn't enough, this time, Sylvie. We went over this—I explained to you how to choose your words carefully."

"I can't help it if they asked questions. I told them answers."

"Didn't you notice after a while they stopped asking questions because you were freaking them out?" Angela turned to see Michael hovering over her. "You were right. I'm such a fool," she said to her husband.

Michael clenched his jaw, giving his mother a *you did it again* look before turning to Angela. "I suppose Horton got bombarded with phone calls from the parents?"

Angela hiccupped three short times in a row—something she did when she got nervous. "Ooh yeah!"

"You should know my mother better by now."

"Right now, I wish I didn't know her at all," Angela said.

Sylvie turned pale but remained steadfast. "Okay, I'm sorry, Angela. I'm sorry. I'm sorry . . . all right?" Sylvie faked a tear.

Michael glared at his mother. "Don't let her do this to you, Ange. I know how she can play people, turn on the tears."

Sylvie tried to defend herself, in between sniffles. "I don't know what happened that day, honestly. It all poured out of me . . . What do they call that?"

"A catharsis? You had a catharsis," Angela answered.

"Catharsis, my ass!" Michael yelled. "You are the most selfish, narcissistic woman on earth, always have been, always will be, and I'm fed up with you!"

Angela stood and grabbed at Michael's shoulder. "Okay, it's okay, Michael. That's enough. Watch your temper."

Michael shrugged her away. "No. It's not enough. It's never enough for my mother. Never!" he screamed and left the room.

A week passed before the three of them were on speaking terms again. Sylvie called every day, apologizing. Right after they technically made up, she called Angela on the sly and asked if they could meet for lunch, halfway between Southampton and Queens.

"Let's go to Krisch's in Massapequa—where you and Michael grew up. You went there a lot in your teens, didn't you?"

Angela ran out of excuses for not reconciling, and going to Krisch's was tempting. "Okay, I'll meet you there."

"Michael will still be at his book convention, right?" Sylvie asked.

Angela hesitated. "Yeah. Why?"

"I have to tell you some exciting news, but we must keep it secret."

"Oh no, not again."

Sylvie ignored Angela's last comment.

"So, let's meet at Krisch's. Say one o'clock? They have the world's best burgers. And we can get their homemade ice cream, too."

Angela kept all four windows down in her Volkswagen Beetle, letting her hair blow wildly around her face as she turned the volume dial up on the radio when "Tangled up in Blue" came on.

She thought about Dylan's lyrics, about the meaning of freedom, how she too could only *keep on* like a bird that flew. Angela wished she could flap her wings in the opposite direction as she drove closer to the meeting with her mother-in-law. At the same time, she was curious, the bright-orange carrot dangling before her like a trap as she pulled into Krisch's parking lot.

She spotted Sylvie in the corner booth wearing a rhinestone-trimmed top reflecting off the wall like Tinker Bell in Peter Pan. She felt sorry for the woman. Sylvie was like a child in so many ways, always seeking attention. Angela knew what a façade it was when she searched the gray flecks of her eyes. These flecks represented pain, secrets, and lies.

Angela waved and walked to the table where Sylvie was already giving her order.

"I'd like my burger fat and juicy and very rare with extra pickles and onions and extra cheese and extra everything."

"You mean, the works?" the waitress smiled.

"Yeah, that's it, give me the *vorks*."

"How in the world do you stay so slim?" Angela asked, taking a seat.

Sylvie beamed. "And when I'm through with that, I'm going to get one of your gigantic ice cream sundaes with the *vorks*, too."

"Oh, now you're showing off." The waitress winked.

Angela ordered and took a deep breath when the waitress left. *Here goes*, she thought.

"Okay, Sylvie, I'm sitting down. What is it that you have to tell me?"

"Well, I got a phone call from my sister in England. You know, Gretta?"

"The one you call *Sourpuss?*" Angela asked.

Sylvie laughed. "That's the one. Well, she shocked me when she said that the three of them—Gretta, Wilhelm and Ruthie—will be coming to the United States for the first time."

"Wow," Angela said. "I can't believe it. When?"

"Next week."

"Next week?"

"I told her you and Michael would put them up at your place."

Angela gulped. "What? For how long?"

"They couldn't possibly be comfortable in my small apartment," Sylvie said.

Angela recognized that Sylvie's siblings lived a different lifestyle by not blowing all their money on gambling. "For how long?" Angela repeated.

"I figure my sisters can stay in your guest room and I'll sleep on the cot next to them, and my brother can stay on the pullout couch in the living room. I promise, after they leave I'll stay on with you to help get the house back in order."

"For *how* long?" Angela pressed.

"Only for eleven days." Sylvie said, while sipping her drink. Angela's soda backed up into her nose, and she choked.

"Are you okay, dear?" Sylvie asked her daughter-in-law, getting up to pat her on the back.

"I see you've been doing a lot of—" Angela made more choking noises. "Excuse me, a lot of . . figuring."

"I hope you don't mind. I promise to help in the kitchen."

"In the kitchen?" Angela couldn't believe her ears.

"You do have a wall phone in there, don't you?" Sylvie tried to be cute. "I'll pick it up and dial for takeout."

The tickle in Angela's throat persisted as she imagined more Rosenbergs filling every inch of her small house. "Well, I suppose Michael will be very excited to meet them."

"I know he's always complained about never meeting my family, and that's why I want it to be a surprise for him."

"Oh, he'll be surprised, all right."

"So, it's our little secret?' Sylvie asked, sweetly.

"Yeah, sure, it's our little secret." Angela winced, starting to feel queasy. *Michael better be overjoyed about his newfound family and not lose his cool again over another one of his mother's little surprises.*

On the night their little secret was to be played out, Sylvie pretended to have an upset stomach and she sent Michael to the pharmacy for Alka-Seltzer and ingredients for soup. Sylvie waved at Michael as he got into his car. "No rush, we'll be eating late tonight."

Angela's stomach hurt, regretting that she offered to cook an old family recipe her mother-in-law had long forgotten about—brisket with cranberry and onion gravy. *Michael's trip to the pharmacy for Alka-Seltzer won't be a waste after all,* she thought.

Sylvie nervously went back and forth from the kitchen to the dining room, assessing the table setting. Angela knew her mother-in-law was ashamed at her lack of elegance, not wanting her siblings to look down their noses at them.

Sylvie took a serving spoon and tasted Angela's gravy. "Hmm, not quite the *borststuk* I remember, but it'll have to do."

Sylvie then pointed out the tiny stain of red wine on the linen tablecloth from a previous meal. "I suppose we could put this saltshaker over the spot." She picked up the shaker and examined the chip on one side. "Maybe they won't notice the chip because they'll be too busy wondering what happened to the missing dishes from your service."

Sylvie looked out the front window and announced, "I think that's the airport shuttle pulling up right now."

"They're unloading a zillion suitcases," Angela said, joining her at the window. She knew who Gretta was immediately—the one who walked with authority, broad shouldered, with a bobbed haircut. Ruthie and Wilhelm were smaller and a step behind. Gretta wore old-fashioned European tweed, while Wilhelm and Ruthie wore hipper London clothing.

Angela felt uncomfortable and foolish in the yellow Chanel suit Sylvie talked her into wearing.

"Good timing," Sylvie bellowed with a glowing smile. "Michael will be so surprised when he gets back." Sylvie ran out the door to greet them.

"What am I getting into?" Angela asked herself.

"Please pass those *aardappelpuree* around, will you, Michael?" Sylvie said of the bowl of mashed potatoes. "I made sure to add a lot of butter," she said as if she made them, even though Angela did all the peeling, boiling, mashing, and seasoning.

Angela kept her mouth shut and smiled politely as to not ruin it for Michael. He looked so thrilled when he got home and faced the surprise of instant relatives.

"We grew up on lots of butter in Holland, didn't we?" Sylvie made eye contact with each of her three siblings, who nodded.

"The butter in England is very good. Not as pure as in Holland," Gretta said.

Angela wondered if butter was all they had to talk about after all these years.

Michael pinched Angela under the table, directing her attention to the half-Dutch, half-English conversation going on between his mother and her sister Gretta when Gretta asked if they'd be moving over to the *big house* after dinner. His mother mentioned something about a "heating problem," which might take a few days to fix, stringing them along. She said she had intended on them staying at the "small beach house" only for the weekend.

"What exactly are the sleeping arrangements?" Gretta asked.

Angela overheard them muttering in Dutch about expecting something more palatial, no doubt the result of years of Sylvie's bragging over the phone and never expecting them to actually come to America.

"We can stay at a hotel rather than cramping up together here," Gretta offered.

After that, the conversation went strictly to Dutch.

Gretta stared, seemingly unimpressed with Angela's artwork hanging in the dining room, making Angela's left eye twitch uncontrollably. Angela knew Gretta had grown up with masterpieces, while she had grown up with pedestrian Norman Rockwell prints.

"Michael, tell us what your novel is about," Gretta said, shifting her gaze across the table to her nephew.

"It's about my time in Vietnam and the real life of a boy named Tsan, whom I met there."

"You mean it's a war story?" Gretta asked.

"Yes, I guess you could say that," Michael said.

"Why would you want to write about such a thing? I do everything humanly possible to forget the war we lived through." She sniffed regally.

"Well, not everything that happens during the wartime is bad."

"It's an unpleasant subject no matter how you look at it. And a waste of your time, in my opinion," Gretta said dismissively.

"You're right, that's your damn opinion, not mine," Michael returned.

Angela gulped. "Michael," she hushed him.

Wilhelm cleared his throat. "Can you pass the peas?" Sylvie didn't utter a word, which was unusual for her. Ruthie reached across the table to pass the bowl. Angela thought how odd it was that everyone handled the tragedies of war differently. Sylvie had bottled up her feelings for years, until the day she exploded in Angela's classroom.

"Let's talk about your plans while you're here," Angela suggested, wanting to smooth everything over. "We can go into the city and see the Statue of Liberty."

Gretta delicately patted her mouth with her napkin. "We saw it when we flew into New York."

"How about the Empire State building?" Ruthie added. "Like in *King Kong*. I've seen it a dozen times."

"I don't mind playing tour guide," Michael said. "But what just happened here? Weren't we talking about my book? Why'd you all cut me off?"

"Uh, Michael." Angela grazed his arm with her hand. "Another time, okay?"

"Another time? Why? You're as bad as your principal, Horton," he whispered to her.

"You're right. You're right, but it's their first night here," Angela whispered back. "Let's put war talk on the back burner."

Sylvie saw the tension between Michael and Angela and changed the subject. "Gretta, I bet you'll love going into the city. Maybe see a show?"

"We see many plays in London. I'm curious if the American stage is comparable."

"It's one of the many reasons why New York is the best city in the world," Michael said with attitude.

"The city that never sleeps," Angela added.

"Don't you live close to the city, Sylvie?" Wilhelm asked.

"Err, yes. I was telling Gretta earlier that's why we had last-minute change of plans and cannot go there. The heat is turned off and the painters are redoing my apartment right now," Sylvie lied.

"Really, Mom?" Michael asked. "You didn't tell me—ouch!" Angela kicked him under the table.

"Honey, can you follow me into the kitchen and help me bring out the coffee and dessert?"

He followed her into the kitchen. "What's going on?"

"Can't you figure it out? Your mother's mortified to show them her dingy little place. Did you forget they were raised like royalty?"

"Yeah, and did you forget how she gambled her way into the poor house?"

"The last thing she needs at their reunion is for them to pass judgment on her."

"After what my mother pulled on you last week, I can't believe you're putting up with this."

"Your mother's apartment really is way too small, and besides, they'll enjoy our ocean view tomorrow in the daylight."

Michael helped her stack the dinner plates near the sink. She carried the dessert dishes and headed toward the dining area again.

Michael followed, aware of their staring at him, walking with the cane and balancing the pie. He tripped as he entered, falling against the hutch but managing to hold on to the pie. Gretta was the first one to jump to his aid.

"I'm so sorry, my purse was in the way. Please forgive me."

"It's okay, really."

She handed him his cane. "No, I mean, please forgive me for what I said about your book."

"You're forgiven, Aunt Gretta."

The six of them passed yawns around the table, as they compared similarities and differences in their countries and their adopted England. The evening ended on a favorable note and Angela suggested they all "hit the sack."

"Hit the sack?" Ruthie asked.

Michael laughed. "It's slang—it means go to sleep."

Double-cheek kisses were accompanied with "goodnights" and "sleep tights."

Angela and Michael talked in bed for a while before going to sleep.

"You had to say it, didn't you?" Angela asked.

"Say what?"

"Don't let the bed bugs bite?"

"Yeah, they take everything literally, don't they?" Michael teased. "There was some serious instantaneous scratching going on among siblings."

Angela smiled. "So, what do you think?"

"Think about what?"

"You know, about your family?"

"I think Gretta has a stick up her butt. I think Ruthie's a bit gullible, and I think Wilhelm is, well, withdrawn, to say the least."

"He's definitely hard to read," Angela said. "I bet he has a lot of stuff going on in his mind because of the war. I guess they're all carrying that around with them. Oh my God, Aunt Gretta should have been there in my classroom the day your mother detonated about the Holocaust."

"Ha, really!" They both laughed. Angela whispered to Michael, "Shhh. These walls are paper thin. They shouldn't hear us laughing."

"Are you kidding? It's our house. I think we're allowed to laugh."

Michael got on his knees and bounced over her in the bed, tickling her until she was ready to burst.

"Stop. Michael, stop. Please." She buried her head under the pillow laughing until she cried.

"I love you," he said.

"I love you, too."

Angela reached for the light switch, but with the moonglow coming in the window, she could still see Michael's hair—the color of sand.

Chapter 7

Sylvie poured sugar into her coffee cup and stirred vigorously. She felt drained from the previous night at the dinner table. Everything she'd repressed over the years came flooding back to her. *How will I ever get through* ten *more days with my family?*

She turned toward the shuffling sound of slippers along the linoleum to see Ruthie behind her in the sun-filled kitchen. She was relieved it wasn't Gretta.

Childlike, Ruthie rubbed her eyes. "*Goedemorgen,*" Sylvie said.

"*Goedemorgen.*"

"Did you sleep well?" Sylvie asked. "How do you like your coffee?"

"Black."

Sylvie felt awkward not knowing how her sister took her coffee. It made her realize she knew nothing about her after the age of seven. She wanted to believe she knew Ruthie very well, yet she was a stranger in many ways.

"Was the bed comfortable?"

"Yes, very comfortable," she answered. "I could not believe the lovely ocean view this morning out the back window."

"Yes, isn't it? Michael rented this house during his college years and purchased it right before he married Angela. He used to ride those waves on his surfboard. He still tries to get up on the board, but it's difficult for him . . . with his leg. Someday, you'll have to see him surf. And Angela surfs, too."

"You'll have to tell me more about Michael and Angela, how they met. Her name before, it was Martino, you say? So, I guess they didn't meet at the synagogue?"

They both laughed. Sylvie thought, *If Ruthie only knew how I tried keeping those two apart. She'd think I was so small-minded.*

"Religious, we weren't," Sylvie said, as if she were modern and liberal enough to accept the changes of the younger generation. "Is Gretta still sleeping?"

"I think she's going into the shower." Ruthie glanced at the living room couch. "And I see Wilhelm is sleeping like a dead man."

"Every few minutes he comes back to life and snores like a jet engine." They both laughed again.

Sylvie flashed back, remembering Ruthie climbing up onto her bed when she was a toddler and the two of them reading bedtime stories together. She brushed a strand of wild blonde hair from Ruthie's eyes.

"You haven't changed that much over the years. You still have that peachy complexion."

Ruthie blushed and softly squeezed Sylvie's hand. "It's been a long time, Sylvie. We're mature women now."

"The last time I saw you—"

"I know. I know," Ruthie cried. "We left on the plane to the United Kingdom, after staying at the Gibraltar camp . . . You stayed behind, Sylvie. Why?"

"Agh, it was a lifetime ago. Who knows why we do what we do when we're young. You were only a little girl."

"You were a teenager," Ruthie returned.

"So?" Sylvie shrugged. "Look at us now."

"Now what?" Ruthie shrugged.

"Want to talk about it?" Sylvie asked.

"About what?"

"You know . . . about being forced from our home, about the interminable train ride. About the past—our past."

"Gretta made it obvious last night that she doesn't want to talk about it."

"You're not Gretta. You should feel free to talk about anything you want to talk about."

"Sometimes, it's not worth talking about," Ruthie said. "My husband, James, tells me the same thing you're telling me, Sylvie. But I found out that it was either let Gretta have her way, or else."

"Or else what?" Sylvie scowled.

"Or else she'd keep her children away from my children. It's important to me that they don't ever feel lonely, that they have cousins in their life. I want them to grow up with cheerful family memories."

Sylvie sniffled. "Unlike us, you mean."

"Yes, unlike us." Ruthie said.

"I know my relationship with Gretta is not as profound as it could be. But there's less tension this way. We take turns; they come to our flat, and then we go to theirs on the next occasion. Holidays are less lonely."

"Wilhelm's included?" Sylvie asked.

"Without children of his own, he's a very special uncle. There's not that many of us left, aside from you and Michael, and now Angela. Once in a while Aunt Chelley comes by even though she's now old and sickly." Ruthie wiped a tear from her cheek.

"It's not easy for me either. So many times I start telling Michael about those years, but I don't get very far. Wouldn't it be wise if you and I could talk, now? Right now."

"About what, about the horror and the fear we faced as Jews?"

Sylvie said, "Maybe Gretta's right. Maybe we should forget. But how do you forget? How do you forget them ripping Oma out of our lives like that? You were only little; still you must remember how she held you on her lap for hours, singing nursery rhymes. How do you forget what happened to our relatives? To our friends? How do you forget how they forced us—"

"Stop! Please, Sylvie. Stop." Ruthie put her hands over her ears.

"Why should I stop? For Gretta?"

"I told you why. Maybe you didn't hear me."

At first Sylvie thought Ruthie was making fun of her hearing, like all the kids used to do when she was young. But not Ruthie; she didn't have a mean streak.

"For God's sake, Ruthie. The children are adults now, why hide—?"

"Maybe we should let the past be the past. I'm not so sure they want to know more than the facts. Why should our guilt be carried over to the next generation? We survived. It's a simple fact."

"Do you know, I've been searching for something ever since. I think I needed to go home again. It was the last place I left my heart."

"Oh, Sylvie." Ruthie dabbed her eyes with a napkin.

Sylvie shivered. Again, she envisioned them lined up at the train depot, standing on the platform, cold and frightened. "At least we should know everything . . . We should never forget."

"What do you mean?" Ruthie asked.

Sylvie stood and then paced the floor as she spoke.

"There's things you don't know. I remember the first time Michael asked me questions about the Holocaust. He was thirteen. He was supposed to be a man at that age. And because his father wasn't around, he was my little man. I told him bits and pieces—you know, about our upbringing and about our escape. I couldn't bring myself to tell him my personal story, you know, about what happened at the camp."

"You mean about the baby?" Ruthie whispered.

Sylvie turned, still disgraced.

Sylvie had looked for the guard every day, wanting his approval, his affection. She had missed her father so much. It was Gretta who took the baby from her arms that day—the ultimate punishment for all the attention Sylvie constantly craved. This was all part of her resentment toward her older sister, for what she had done.

"It took me years to tell Michael about the baby's existence. Michael calls him the brother he may never meet. To think he's a grown man now, too, yet I still think of him with his baby face."

Sylvie thought about the irony of new life, how precious, how it could turn tragic so quickly. She reflected on her five-day-old baby sister, Rose, who suffocated in her mother's arms the day they hid in the root cellar—another one of those things they didn't talk about. Like their mother's pregnancy, which they called "her condition."

"Our family kept many secrets," Ruthie said.

"And lies, too." Sylvie huffed. *Was it Papa's child? Was Rose a Nazi baby? No one will ever know.*

Sylvie lowered herself into the chair next to her sister again. "Do you think of your first baby often?" Ruthie asked.

"I blocked it out for years. When Michael was old enough, I told him about it, and ever since, Michael talks about how he will find his brother soon, but I try not to think—"

"Because you find it too painful?" Ruthie admonished. "Then you should understand why Gretta—" Ruthie put her hand over her mouth. "I'm sorry, I don't want to fight with you."

Sylvie rested her face in both hands and shook her head. "You were such a sweet child. That's why I'm afraid for you—that you're clay in Gretta's hands."

"I know you think Gretta controls me. And maybe she does to a certain extent. But she's there for me when I need her."

Sylvie was silent, wondering if her sisters held it against her that she had come to America while they relocated in England. Did they feel she abandoned them like their parents?

Sylvie had chosen to settle in New York where her father's intention was to rekindle his art business. She remembered her father talked about moving to America, and then took his own life shortly after arriving, no doubt from shame, guilt and financial ruin.

Mrs. Rosenberg became reclusive and lived alone in Amsterdam with her tortured mind.

A deep ache settled in Sylvie's chest.

Ruthie interrupted. "I admired you, Sylvie, the way you didn't let Gretta get to you. You're your own person. You don't let anyone order you around."

"That's usually why people don't like me," Sylvie said.

"Me? I'm—I'm frozen," Ruthie admitted. "When it's too much, I shut down."

"And Wilhelm? What are his feelings?" Sylvie asked.

"Wilhelm?" Ruthie glanced into the living room and her brother still snoring on the couch. "He's afraid of everything," she said faintly. "That's why he didn't have children. He still believes there's evil in the world—everywhere."

"Good morning, everyone," Michael said as he walked into the kitchen, immediately opening the refrigerator door. "What's all this talk about evil? Sounds like a pretty heavy conversation going on for this early hour, heh?"

"Evil? What about evil?" Angela asked, right behind him. "What kind of a good mornin' is that?" She smiled at Ruthie. "I'll make all of us some eggs for breakfast."

Ruthie patted Angela's hand between both of hers. "Your home on the beach is so lovely. The sea breeze came in my window to greet me this morning."

Michael poured orange juice into four small glasses, without asking, while noticing the family resemblance between his aunt and mother.

"So, what's this about evil?" he asked. "Talking about the war again?"

Wilhelm entered the kitchen. "Which war?"

Gretta followed close behind, her hair damp. "Aagh, the war— *Godverdomme!*" she cursed in Dutch.

Ruthie turned bright red. Sylvie could see her trepidation.

"Oh boy, here we go again," Angela said. "Do you want to know what all this commotion sounds like to me? It sounds like family."

"Family with a ton of history," Michael said.

"Coffee's still hot. Help yourselves," Angela said to Wilhelm and Gretta, as she whisked the egg mixture.

"Okay, so which part do you want to talk about?" Gretta spewed. "Which part? When the Germans first occupied our hometown? When Papa's skin turned ashen and he plowed on with his feeble attempts at keeping our family safe from harm? When we were restricted from everything our Christian friends could do because we were suddenly not the elite, but the scum of the earth?"

Ruthie stood closer to Gretta. "You, you don't have to—"

Gretta ignored her and continued.

"You don't want to hear about when we huddled together when the bombs were getting closer? When the letters from Westerbork stopped coming from Oma? When soldiers marched through our home and forced us to—"

Wilhelm stepped in and touched Greta's arm to console her. After a moment she continued.

"You don't want to hear about when the stench on the train made us puke into our own coat pockets? Shall I go on? Or shall I reiterate the incredible guilt we must endure because we are the ones who were spared—all because of Papa's art. It's always about the damn art!"

"Not only because of the art." Sylvie choked. "Mother had something to do with it, too. What do you know about that?"

"Really, Sylvie, is that necessary?" Wilhelm piped.

"You owe me that!" Sylvie said.

"I owe you nothing!" Gretta spat.

Sylvie backed down, thinking about how they had competed years ago for their parents' love. With downcast eyes and a shaky hand, Sylvie took the envelope from her pocket and unfolded it.

"I have the letter our mother sent to our father. Mr. Goodman, who had moved into Papa's apartment in New York, sent it along with other documents and things. May I read it?"

Sylvie exchanged glances with her siblings. "Gretta, I think it's only fair to let Wilhelm and Ruthie know that I made you aware of this letter years ago, after Papa's suicide. I kept my promise not to mention it. Now, I am asking, again, for your permission."

Gretta didn't answer at first, which seemed like forever to Sylvie. "Oh dear God. Go on."

Sylvie swallowed, nervously. "This is one of the letters Mother had sent to Papa while he was away on still another business trip trying to obtain the art the Germans wanted." Sylvie put on her reading glasses:

> *My Dear Josef, my love,*
>
> *You were so perturbed when you left, and I didn't get the chance to explain . . . I had to do what I had to do, my darling, there was no choice with those men. They knew when you were away on business because you required special permission to travel. They warned me not to mention their visits.*
>
> *One night it was one officer, the next night, another—each repulsive. But after what happened to my mother being sent to Westerbork, I was afraid to refuse. What would become of the children if I was sent away? I wasn't certain that the art, alone, would protect them. What if something went wrong?*
>
> *It can still go wrong at any time, even though you are in the midst of negotiating our exit visas. How can we trust them? Please understand me, my sweet husband. I am alone here to protect our children. It pains me that you must know of this ugliness. You must know there is no man on Earth who has my love and respect but you, Josef. I beg of you to find it in your heart to forgive me.*
>
> *Your loving wife, Helene*

Ruthie slammed the palm of her hand on the table and then tried to compose herself. "Poor Mama. She asked our father for forgiveness? For saving us?"

Gretta took a seat at the kitchen table. Her voice was calm.

"There's more. I'm afraid that our family life was not the fairy tale you want it to be. You want to know the whole story?"

Angela stood close to Michael and grabbed his hand. All eyes and ears were on Gretta, the oldest of the Rosenberg children.

Gretta took a tissue from the pocket of her robe, as if in preparation. "I've lived my entire life, pretending—" She broke down. She had never shed tears like these, even on the day the Nazis took Oma off the streets, even when Sylvie handed the baby over to her at the camp, even when they found out that Papa hanged himself. Gretta's voice trembled. "I lived with such shame my whole life," she started.

Wilhelm jiggled his foot, nervously, under the table. "Gretta, you don't have to do this."

"It's all right, Wilhelm," Gretta said. "Sylvie, do you remember the first time the Dutch military came to our home? Papa was away on business, and they apologized to Mama that they had the wrong house?"

"Yes, I couldn't forget how frightening that was."

"Do you remember how the officer touched Mother? The way he slid the palm of his hand down the back of her dress? The way only a husband has the right to touch a wife?"

"Yes, I knew that was strange at the time."

"I don't remember," Ruthie said. "I was too little." Wilhelm said nothing, his eyes darting around the room.

"And you remember the soldier in the foyer who looked up at us where we were gathered at the top of the stairs, spying on them, and the comment he made to you?"

"I do," Sylvie said. "Why is that important?"

"He said you were pretty, like Mother, remember? And that someday he'd return to listen to you play piano."

"The soldier said that?" Ruthie asked. "How revolting."

"Sylvie, you generally got the attention from everyone," Gretta added. "That was one time I was not jealous. I was afraid for you."

Sylvie tilted her head at her sister and let her go on.

"One day Mother called me into her bedroom for a serious talk. She had told me something that was very difficult for her to share. It was about being with those men—the Dutch military police, even the goddamn Nazis, whenever any of them felt the need."

Ruthie gasped. "Oh, poor Mama."

Gretta handed Ruthie a tissue. "I'm sorry you weren't told sooner about the letter. I've already talked about this with Sylvie, when she was sent the box of Father's belongings."

Ruthie dabbed her eyes, twisting the tissue for a dry spot.

"What you don't know, even you, Sylvie," Gretta sighed, "is that Mother also asked me to be with those men. Not exactly asked—she ordered me to make the sacrifice, or else we'd risk being killed."

Sylvie cried out. "How could she? How could Mother make you? You did that for us?"

"Yes, and I've been ashamed. So ashamed."

"You were only a teenager. Maybe Father could have stopped—" Ruthie paused.

"Father didn't know," Gretta said. "He was away, forever trying to arrange art trades for the Nazis. During the war, when he found out, Mother asked him in a letter to forgive her for being with the other men, but she refused to tell him the truth about me.

"I was so afraid you would be next, Sylvie," Gretta said. "You had Mother's good looks, and they—those swine—they had their eyes on you."

"Oh my God!" Ruthie cried out. "Oh my God!"

Wilhelm stopped jiggling his foot and stood up at the table. "Now that all the truth is coming out, I have to tell you that once I woke up in the middle of the night and walked down the hallway to use the bathroom. I heard whimpering coming from your room, Gretta, so I stood outside your door, which was partially open, and—and at first I thought you were having a bad dream. Then—" Wilhelm squeezed his eyes closed. "Then I saw the soldier's uniform in a heap on the floor next to your bed, and—"

Ruthie jumped up and hugged Gretta.

Wilhelm's shoulders shook as he spoke. "I wanted to save you from that bastard—I was a coward. When I went to tell Mother, she sent me back to my room, and I had to make believe it hadn't happened, like she was pretending. But, after I left her room, I knew by the sound of Mother's muffled crying that it was really happening."

"You did the right thing, Wilhelm," Gretta said. "If we refused to cooperate, who knows what may have happened. Maybe they would have shot all of us. None of us believed the canvases were enough to save us."

Sylvie squirmed in her chair. It occurred to her why it was Gretta who took away her illegitimate child that day at the camp. Watching that boy grow up would have been a painful memory of the men who violated them.

Sylvie came very close to telling them that she hired a lawyer to get the Germans to return their art. She was so tired of disappointing everyone, so she kept quiet, hoping that someday they'd get the paintings back, and then she could surprise them with the wonderful news.

Gretta looked at Michael. "I'm sorry I insulted your writing about war. I imagine you also witnessed horrible things. War does terrible things to people. Much of what happened to its victims goes to the grave with them. It's not that I want to deny you your ancestors, your family history."

"No, I'm the one who should be sorry," Michael whispered. "After your reaction, I should have realized it wasn't a topic you felt comfortable with. I shouldn't have pushed you like that." He hugged his stern aunt Gretta, whose face suddenly softened. "Thank you for being so brave."

The six family members huddled together. The sound of the ocean waves rumbled through an open window, and the gulls cried.

Michael and Angela stood at the end of their driveway watching the airport shuttle go down Dune Road, taking away the family he was finally getting to know. Angela embraced him, as if reading his mind. "I can't believe I'm saying this—those eleven days went by really quickly."

"You were great, babe. Thanks. I know it was a lot on you, with the extra cooking and laundry and cleaning up. Who knows when and if we'll ever see them again?"

Michael and Angela turned around to Sylvie, standing with a blank expression.

"Mom, are you okay?"

"Huh? Yeah, I'm all right. I was thinking the same thing. Who knows when we'll ever see them again?" She blew her nose into her hanky.

"Aww, Mom. Next time, maybe we can go to England to visit them."

She faced her son. "You mean well, but you know what it would cost for all of us to fly to Europe."

"Maybe Michael will sell his novel," Angela suggested.

"Yeah, and I'll dedicate it to your sisters and brother, Mom."

They walked back into the beach house. He knew his mother had changed her whole attitude about her older sister. Now, for the first time in her life, maybe his mother could understand and forgive Gretta's shortcomings.

Chapter 8

Sylvie had driven back to Queens, dropped her luggage by the laundry room door and immediately turned on the television to keep her company. As she hung her coat in the closet, lost in thought, the phone rang.

"Oh, Mr. Adelstein, how are you?"

"I've been trying to reach you, Sylvie. Where've you been?" her lawyer asked.

"What? I'm not allowed to get some R and R?"

"Sylvie, I'm afraid I don't have good news to share with you."

"About the art?"

"The news about the art is encouraging, but the investigation I did on your missing son—well, I'm sorry for what I'm about to tell you—"

Sylvie knew she'd have to call Michael the following day with the bad news. She still wouldn't tell him anything about the art— not yet. Besides, the lawyer only mentioned that the feedback was encouraging, not good. *One thing at a time.* She waited until Michael and Angela would be through with working and finished with their dinner before phoning.

"Hello, Angela, is Michael there?"

"Sure, hold on." Angela handed the phone to him.

Sylvie made sure to have a drink to bolster her courage. "Michael, I have to tell you something. It's about your brother."

"Oh no," he said. "I don't like the tone of your voice."

"I don't know how to tell you this, but—"

"Mom, what is it?"

"He's gone, Michael. He's dead." She let out a small cry.

"What?" He sat. "How do you know this?"

"I hired a detective to find your brother, and—"

"And what?"

"And the detective got back to me with this horrible news. I was hoping to learn where he was, so you could meet him."

"Oh no," Michael cried. "Damn it, Mom. How? How did it happen?" He heard the word "drugs" and threw the phone onto the floor, breaking a piece of plastic off it. Sylvie heard Angela calling after him and calling his name.

She picked up the telephone and asked Sylvie what happened. "Oh my God, no. When? How?"

"Michael never gave me a chance to say much," Sylvie said. "Apparently, he recently died when some drug deal went bad. The lawyer said something about drugs."

"What lawyer?" Angela asked.

"The lawyer I hired to help find Michael's brother. He said it was drug related. Something went terribly wrong. He died of stab wounds."

"Sylvie, I'm very sorry. Why don't you give me the lawyer's name and number when you feel up to it, and when Michael's calm, maybe he'll call him to get more details."

Sylvie hesitated. "Okay, I will give it to you later when we both calm down."

Angela hung up and ran out onto the beach to find Michael sitting by the dunes, digging a hole in the sand.

She put her arm around him without saying anything.

"I wish I could climb into this hole right now. I really wanted to meet him. For years now, that's what I imagined, dreamt about. Especially after seeing my mother reunited with her family—what it did for her. I wanted that for me and my brother."

"I know. I know, hon." She rubbed the back of his head. "Maybe you should call your mother back. She sounds upset."

"No, I don't feel like talking to her."

"Please, be reasonable—"

"Ange—stop. Don't tell me what to do about my mother. She's the reason he had a hard life on drugs."

"Michael, look at how many years she wasted judging her sister, and she was wrong. Do you want to assume the worst about your mother, too? She had to do what she had to do back then."

"Don't you see? It's not the giving him up part that angers me. It's the not getting him back part. She should have let me know as soon as I was old enough—back in those lonely days after my father walked out on us." He openly cried now in her arms.

This scared Angela, who had never seen him so distraught. At that moment he turned into that six-year-old little boy again while she held him. "I'm sorry. I'm so sorry, Michael."

Sylvie called the next day asking if it was okay to visit. Angela held her hand over the receiver and mouthed to Michael if it was okay if his mother came. "Just for one night?"

Michael shook his head, emphatically. "I'm afraid he needs more time," Angela said.

"Tell him there's a lot we can talk about."

"I know there's a lot to talk about, Mom," Angela repeated so Michael could hear.

Michael grabbed the phone out of Angela's hand and accidentally knocked her lip into her tooth with the receiver. Blood surfaced immediately.

"Now? Now, you have a lot to talk about? Why didn't you hire a private detective years ago before it was too late?" Michael paced back and forth not looking at his wife. "Why, Mom?"

"I'm sorry. I'm sorry about a lot of things, Michael. Please don't hate me."

"I can't get my brother back. I can't get my father back. You almost broke up Angela and me. All because of those years in the past, you've been destroying the future."

Again, he threw the phone, but this time, it hit the small glass window, cracking it. Angela did not go after him. Michael bolted out the door. She heard his tires screech on the pavement as he sped away.

She picked up the chipped phone and, too upset to speak, she hung up on Sylvie. She went to the freezer and took ice cubes out, wrapped them in a towel, and applied them to her swollen lip.

Their two dinner plates of macaroni and cheese sat on the kitchen table cold and uneaten. She did not want to fight with her husband or her mother-in-law. She was just plain tired—of everything.

"Has he come home yet?" Sylvie sounded concerned on the phone.

"No, he hasn't. I'm going crazy worrying." Angela nervously pressed down on her swollen lip. She didn't mention Michael's infantile rage.

"This isn't like him. Something's wrong. Call the police. Call now!" Sylvie yelled.

"Calm down. Let's not panic, okay? I'll call at midnight."

"Why wait until midnight? That makes no sense," Sylvie argued.

"Nothing makes any sense, does it?" Angela scolded.

"No, maybe not," Sylvie sighed.

"I'll let you know," Angela said, trying to control her breathing.

"Please, call me the minute he comes home, no matter if it's three in the morning."

"Okay, I promise." She looked at the hands on the cuckoo clock, thinking it would take forever for that damn bird to come out of the house and cuckoo twelve times.

"Southampton Village, Sgt. Noonan, here. Go ahead."

"I'm calling because my husband left the house very upset and hasn't returned, and it's after midnight."

"Name, please."

"My name is Angela Beckman."

"When did you say your husband left?"

"A little after five," she sniffled.

"And his name?"

"Michael. His name is Michael Beckman."

"You have to wait twenty-four hours before filing a missing persons report."

"What if something's happened to him?"

"There are no accident reports since that time. You'll have to wait. Call back tomorrow after five if he doesn't show up."

Angela thought about calling Sylvie and then changed her mind. *Maybe he's on his way home. Maybe—*

She heard the front door slam, and she jumped up. "Michael, is that you?"

He stood in the doorway, staring at his wife, and he let his coat fall onto the chair. Without uttering a word, Michael walked up to Angela and grabbed her face in both of his hands and kissed her, moaning between breaths.

"I love you, babe. I'm so sorry, so, so sorry that I lost my cool . . . What happened to your lip?"

"You knocked the phone into my mouth, remember?"

"No! I did that? Oh God, honey, I'm so sorry."

"It's okay. It was an accident."

"I'm sorry. I don't re—"

"Michael, I'm okay. Now, where were we?" She grabbed his face now and kissed him in the same way he had kissed her, with desire.

"Oh, yeah." He scooped her up in his arms and carried her down the hallway and into the bedroom, gently placing her onto the queen-size bed, where he slowly undressed her.

"You know what," he said.

"What?"

"Tonight's the night. I feel it, Angela. I can't explain it, but I feel it in my gut."

Angela concentrated on his eyes. "I believe you. We're going to make our baby tonight."

He got playful, which she always loved. "You're such a treasure," he said.

"Like a treasure chest?"

"Yeah, like a treasure chest I found at the bottom of the sea. And I'm ready to unveil your hidden beauty, one gem at a time." He tucked her long, silky hair behind her ears. "Even your ears are beautiful," he said in a soft voice. "They're little pink seashells."

"Go on," she coaxed him, turning her head sideways.

He pulled off her hoop earrings and placed them on the night table. He gently tugged at her bottom lip with his, avoiding hurting her. "Your lips are so full like—"

"Like a blow fish?" she teased.

"Sorry about that." He gently opened her mouth wider with his and pressed into her, kissing her neck and undoing the clasp on her necklace. "Your neck is as elegant as a—"

"A seahorse. I want to be a seahorse."

"Okay, a seahorse." He tickled her ribs and she giggled. "Yeah, and what else?" she asked, with her eyes half-closed.

He unbuttoned her blouse and pulled it off her body. Then he laid his head on her chest.

"I love the sound of your heart ticking as precisely as the gold pocket watch inside the treasure chest." He continued kissing each body part, praising and critiquing her like a museum curator would a piece of art. "You're perfect."

She moaned his name and opened one eye, watching as Michael sat up and quickly removed his shirt and jeans. She was no longer squeamish about the hideous scar that ran along his back. He slid next to her again and put her hand on his chest.

"Feel my heartbeat?" he asked her. "It's in perfect beat with yours." He straddled her small frame and aligned his body with hers. His hand moved along the smoothness of her thighs, leading her into position until she arched her body in pleasure, like she used to do, without checking her temperature or ovulation cycle.

The phone rang and he jerked upward, annoyed.

"Oh, your mother!" Angela said, springing up, pulling the bed sheet over her nakedness.

"My mother?" All the breath left Michael. "Don't answer it."

"I forgot to call her and I promised. I gave her my word that I'd call her the second you came home. She's so worried about you, you know," Angela said.

Michael rolled over onto his side. "She's going to drive me crazy."

"Oh, let me answer it before she has a heart attack." She hurried to pick up the phone. "Hello. Michael just got home. Everything's fine," she giggled, slapping Michael's hand away as he tickled her. Angela hung up on Sylvie, without hearing her reply, and turned her attention back to her husband.

"Michael, you meant what you said about making a baby tonight?"

He pulled her back down onto the bed. "Come here," he said, cuddling her in his arms.

"I bet we just did."

"Why are you crying?" he asked.

"Because, you big jerk. Because I wondered what it would be like if you never came home again." She wiped her tears. "I was worried sick about you. As much as I want a baby, I don't think I could ever live without you."

They remained holding each other quietly in the dark, as if they had made love for the very last time.

Chapter 9

S ylvie walked quickly to the Long Island railroad station in Queens wearing all black in mourning for her son, even though the color was unflattering on her. She assumed it was too early to reach Adelstein by phone and decided to see him in person. *It's about time we meet, especially with all that's going on*

On the train ride in, her mind raced as she saw litter blowing in the wind across the tracks. She thought about what could happen in her family's lives if the art was recovered or restitution was made. *Michael will get the child he wants so much, and maybe more children will come in the future. They could get a bigger house, a fancy car, and Angela could stop dressing like such a poor hippie.*

Sylvie boarded the overcrowded, dirty subway. No one offered her a seat. The subway ride reminded her of that harrowing train years ago; she shook the image out of her mind. The man standing next to her smiled, but she turned away, looking out the graffiti-covered window.

When she exited into the busy station, she felt exhilarated seeing women and men dressed sharply and fashion billboards. *Wish I had gone into design. I would have been ridiculously competent at it.* She imagined herself carrying a portfolio filled with brilliant designs, the envy of the industry. Swept away with the flow of the throng, no one seemed to notice her odd gait, but surely they were admiring her attire, even at her age. *They should have seen me in Holland when I was young and pretty. Without all these damn wrinkles.* She regretted being such a sun-worshipper.

When she reached the Park Avenue address, she snapped her head back to look at the height of the building. *Pretty impressive.* Once inside, she read the list of names next to the elevator and saw *Adelstein, Greenberg, Smith, Attorneys at Law.*

"Oh my God, he's on the thirty-second floor," she blurted.

"Do you suffer from heights?" a young Asian woman on the elevator asked.

"Oh. That's not why I . . . Never mind, dear, I'm fine." She smiled. She wasn't about to explain that the number thirty-two had always been her lucky number—*Spoorstraat 32*—the address of her father's gallery in her hometown.

She stormed into the waiting area, ignoring the perky blonde secretary perched behind a desk. She marched forward, reaching for the knob to the door marked *Private—Harvey Adelstein.* Two secretaries rushed about with folders full of papers, chatting about something.

"Excuse me, ma'am? Ma'am, you can't go in there!"

"And why not?" Sylvie acted indignant, her hand on the knob to Adelstein's office.

"Who are you?"

"Why, I'm Sylvie. Sylvie Rosenberg."

"You don't have an appointment, Mrs. Rosenberg. Please take a seat and I'll announce—"

"It's *Ms.*, and I can't wait for that nonsense." Sylvie never cared before if anyone called her Miss or Mrs., but she wanted to show the girl who was boss.

"Ms. Rosenberg, please."

"What's going on out here?" Mr. Adelstein asked, peeking out from his office door.

"This woman barged in here."

"Mr. Adelstein, how are you? Well, I'm here, the one and only Sylvie Rosenberg." She held out her hand as if a female member of the royal family.

"Ms. Rosenberg, I wish you'd called first. I have to be in court soon."

"Oh, they can wait a few minutes." She took notice of his tailored suit, his shiny shoes, his dapper haircut, and the dimple in his chin, exactly how she'd imagined from hearing his voice on the phone. *A three-piece, vested suit would be better.* "It's so nice to finally meet in person . . . Now, where shall we begin?"

"You have about ten minutes, Mr. Adelstein," the secretary warned.

"Thank you, Elaine. I'll move things along." He winked at his secretary.

After Sylvie explained her son's reaction to the news about his brother's death, she shut up and let the attorney speak.

"So, he's still upset with you?" Adelstein asked.

"*Upset* is not the word. I've never seen him so agitated. He blames me for all those years I never told him his brother existed, all those years that he could have had some kind of family. 'Who knows,' he said, 'maybe my brother could have moved here and lived with us, when we were growing up.'"

Adelstein shook his head.

"And now, it's too late . . . ." She drifted off, looking around the office at the framed plaques and the paneled woodwork.

Sylvie sank deeper into the overstuffed leather chair and took in the view of the skyline behind his mahogany desk. She was overwhelmed with all she had to consider—reclaiming the long-lost family art, divulging truths, facing the past again in a court of law, worrying about the kids and future grandchildren.

"So, let's get on with it, shall we?"

He laughed. "Everything takes time."

"But the other day you said you had good news about the art." Sylvie leaned forward in the leather chair, her face scrunched as if in pain.

"I only meant that the Dutch committee agreed that some of the documentation we presented seems legitimate."

"Oh, that's wonderful."

"Well, it's promising, but it's not a cause for celebration yet, by any means."

"I can't read you, Mr. Adelstein. Lay it on the line."

He smiled. "This whole process can take longer than we originally anticipated. Maybe years. It took the Dutch government years to recover the scattered art from Germany at the end of the war. The art was not only held in museums, it was also lent to embassies and other official institutions . . . some smuggled out of Germany to Austria and South America."

"And now it has to go to the rightful owners," Sylvie huffed. "Mr. Adelstein, with all due respect, these paintings do not belong to the Dutch government. First the Germans stole them and now the Dutch? They belong to my family. *To me!* And if they give me a hard time, I will call the newspapers, radio and television. I will let the public know that in Holland, anti-Semitism still exists."

Mr. Adelstein held up a restraining hand. "You must understand that this is a huge claim, over 200 paintings, and it takes time."

"Time? It seems I've been waiting forever."

"I understand. But we've only begun the process. And it's complex. They have to pinpoint when the paintings exchanged hands. Perhaps the paintings were sold before the Germans could confiscate them."

"What about that *Horsefair* painting from 1633 by Ruysdael we had talked about? Isn't that specific enough? I believe you said it's at the Stedelijk Museum in Leiden."

"Yes, that's one of the legitimate-looking documents." His voice picked up. "It's a hopeful."

"*A hopeful?* Speaking of painting, you're not painting a very hopeful picture here, Mr. Adelstein. Perhaps I should consider alternative legal counsel?"

"Now, now."

"Listen to me. And you listen good. We need to let the world know that these masterpieces belonged to my father. That one Rembrandt alone, if nothing else, saved twenty-five lives, to be exact. Jewish lives."

"Ms. Rosenberg, you know I am a Jew myself."

"You may be a Jew, Mr. Adelstein. But you weren't there."

"And you're going to hold being born too late against me?" He tried to lighten the mood.

"No, what I'm saying is that nearly forty years later, I'm still feeling persecuted."

"There you go; now, that's what I need from you—it's all about the persecution at this point. Where we lack proof in documentation, you must fill in with how you were victimized."

"I have an exceptional memory, and I promise you, I will not hold anything back."

"Yes, I'm sure you won't. That's what I'm counting on. But there's also the matter of—" He paused.

"Matter of what?"

"Well, the question of your father's reputation."

"Reputation? I don't quite follow."

"It's something we may have to deal with. I didn't want to mention it to you yet, but you must realize, they will try to find your father's flaws."

"We all have flaws, but how many of us can say we saved lives?"

"Listen, the Dutch government is not willing to part with these national treasures without putting up a fight. The committee will no doubt resort to making your father's business dealings look . . . corrupt. You were only a teenager at the time. You couldn't possibly have been aware of everything your father did in his business back then. There was a lot of bartering going on when the Germans first invaded Holland. That's why it's imperative that we prove the point of sale. Did he actually give up his paintings? Did he sell them? And if he did sell them, which ones? And at what price? Was it half the market value? We're talking big money here and cannot assume anything."

"As far as I'm concerned, our paintings were stolen from us . . . by the lousy Nazis."

"We have to prove it, Ms. Rosenberg."

"I don't know anything about the numbers," Sylvie stuttered. "If there were any papers signed, it certainly was a sale under duress."

"I don't expect you to know numbers, but in the courts, they'll want to know about the timing, dates, more facts. Again, Ms. Rosenberg, we must prove point of sale, when the paintings changed hands. Concentration camp deportations began in the beginning of 1941. The Nazis didn't begin confiscating Jewish property in Holland until later. It became common knowledge that the Nazis were out to acquire artworks; your father's collection was at the top of their list. The court must determine exactly when the sales took place. As the war and Nazi power increased, the Nazis stopped buying and simply began taking. That timeline is critical to our claim."

"Yes, that's the pressure my father was under. They took it by force. And it's a known fact that the Nazis forged records of ownership. Yet the burden of proof is on *me*?"

"I'm afraid so."

"Ha!" She twisted her torso in the seat. "It's insulting that I have to defend my father's character against these murderers." Sylvie started to cry. "My father, he was a hero." She took a tissue from her purse.

"I know it's unfair," her attorney said. "Life's not fair. Do you know that the Dutch government actually charged the surviving Jews back taxes when they returned from the camps to their homes that were occupied by Germans?"

Sylvie covered her mouth with disgust.

"The Dutch government realizes that they don't own the paintings themselves, but determining who does is proving more difficult."

"Well, one thing I am is determined," Sylvie said. "To right this wrong."

Mr. Adelstein sighed. "Ms. Rosenberg, I want you to know that I believe your story. I think you deserve to recover what was taken from your family. I will do everything within my power to reclaim your treasures."

"Mr. Adelstein, I contacted you almost five years ago to change my name from Beckman back to Rosenberg—thank God. Anyone I ever trusted in my entire life has let me down. Being you're on the thirty-second floor, I'll take the gamble."

He looked perplexed. "So, is that a yes?"

She smiled. "Yes, Mr. Adelstein, you can continue with the case."

The secretary tapped on the door and peeked in. "Is everything all right, Mr. Adelstein?"

"Yes, Elaine, we're finishing up."

He glanced at his watch and stood at his chair. "Very good, then, Ms. Rosenberg. Now, I really must run."

Sylvie stood to leave.

"By the way, I have an international colleague by the name of Van der Berg who's already probed certain areas. He's top notch."

"Thank you. I'm only used to the best," she said, walking out.

Back on the Park Avenue, Sylvie realized how restricted her life was because of the lack of money. *It's always about money. I can't do anything I want to do—the theater, fine restaurants, serious shopping.*

"Ooh, shopping," she blurted as she turned down Sixty-Sixth Street off Park. *Who knows? Maybe when I come into a lot of money, I can move into the city.* On Madison she fell in love with the display of shoes in a store window and pressed her nose against the glass. She spent the next few hours walking, window-shopping and dreaming of what could be.

Instead of getting on the train to go home, she made a hasty decision to go to Atlantic City, and like the old days right after Mitchell left her without alimony and child support, she'd schmooze with the pit bosses and they'd comp her for a nice juicy steak dinner.

First, she'd start out at the roulette table—number thirty-two. *The thirty-second floor—it was a sign.* She smiled at a woman on the bus who was about her age, and the woman smiled back. "Are you going to Atlantic City for fun, or do you live there?" Before the lady had a chance to answer, Sylvie said, "I'm going to win!"

"That sounds like fun," the lady said. "I have no luck in those places. I'm meeting someone there who does all the gambling. I go for the food and the shows."

"I have a feeling I'm going to win the jackpot tonight!" Sylvie clapped her hands together.

"Good for you," the woman said. "That's the attitude."

Sylvie concentrated on the litter outside the window again.

People are so irresponsible . . . Ugh . . . I'll stop gambling as soon as I win enough for me and the kids. Everyone will be happy again—because of me.

When Sylvie stepped inside the casino, her adrenaline shot up like a prize fighter's in the ring. The bright lights and cheering crowds made her bounce on her feet and think of when she was on stage as a child ballerina. After all those years at the ballet barre, she could never straighten out her feet like the other girls who danced with feline grace. She felt unnatural and powerless as a dancer. *Yet here, at the casino,* she thought, *this is where it's at.* She only had a little power left in her purse—about a hundred dollars in cash.

She immediately found a roulette table and almost tripled her money. She then headed for the blackjack tables and got chummy with the pit boss, who promised her a complimentary dinner. Everything was going her way. She loved every minute at the table she picked. The thrill of the dealer shuffling, the splitting of the cards, the doubling-down—it all came back to her. She felt alive again.

People sitting near her were attracted to her energy. "Lady Luck." The gentleman next to her saluted her with his Scotch on the rocks. "Let me buy you a drink," he offered. "My name's Henry."

How soon she'd forgotten that lately she was doing well avoiding her vices. "Oh, what the hell, Henry. I'll take a gin and tonic."

"Thatta girl," he said, politely. "A gin and tonic for the lucky lady," he shouted. "In fact, drinks around the table." She stared at his calloused hands, figuring he was in construction. There was a pack of Lucky Strikes next to his cards. "Want one, uh—?"

"Sylvie," she offered.

He shook the box until she could reach one cigarette if she so chose.

"Nasty habit," she commented. "Sure."

Even though she had quit smoking years ago, she inhaled deeply, as if it were yesterday, and allowed the burn to assault her throat like an old enemy. She directed her exhale into the open space above the dealer. She noticed the generous tip Henry gave the waitress when she came back with the drinks. He whispered in Sylvie's ear. "I don't have to tell you, I'm doing great tonight."

"I think we're bringing each other luck," Sylvie said.

"The thing is," Henry said, "we have to know when to walk away. You know what I mean? Walk away a winner."

"Shall we . . . shall we go now?" Sylvie asked, feeling woozy. "I was comped a nice steak dinner." As they both got up from the table, everyone cheered, thanking them for the winning streak. "Wee, this is fun," she announced, letting Henry spin her around in a circle as they headed for the restaurant.

Henry had nice dimples and was pleasant, but Sylvie wasn't attracted to him. *His cologne is cheap, his shirt wrinkled, and is that a toupee he's wearing?* She realized how easy it would be to get picked up but was only in the mood to make money.

The drinks kept coming all through dinner, and she rode her emotions like a roller coaster, one minute laughing, the next crying.

"I have nowhere else to go, anymore," she blabbered into his shoulder with her runny nose. "My son hates me now."

"Oh, why's that, sweetheart?" Henry asked, rubbing his suit coat with his handkerchief. He flagged down the waiter for coffee.

"It's a long, long story . . . you don' wanna hear it," she said, now feeling downright dizzy.

"Take another few sips," he ordered, stirring her coffee cup for her. "We have to sober you up and be sure you can make it home."

Eventually, she finished her last cupful of caffeine and no longer slurred her words.

"How are you feeling now? Less wobbly?" Henry asked, holding her arm as he escorted her to the bus that would take her back to Queens, New York.

"Much better. You're a nice man." She patted his cheek, twice. *Toupee and all.*

Sylvie went home with almost $5,000. "I'm rich," she said, spreading the money across her bed. She wished she could share the news with someone but couldn't tell a soul. She'd give the kids a few days to cool down, and then she'd call them. Of course, she wouldn't mention where she'd been. *Gambling and drinking.* Such familiar words, like old friends. She laughed out loud. She already picked out a whole new wardrobe in her head.

Although Sylvie had sobered up hours before, Angela thought she sounded funny over the phone. "Mom, are you okay?" Angela asked.

"I'm *grreat,*" she said, spreading her dollars out again, counting them. "Two for me, one for you, three for me, one for you, five for me . . ."

"What are you doing?" Angela asked.

"Oh, I'm playing a card game," she giggled. "I have to play alone, you know."

"Mom, we can't go on this way. Why don't you come for a visit tomorrow? I'll work on Michael," Angela finished.

"I'd like that." Sylvie fought back the tears. "I'd like that very much."

When she rested her head on her pillow to sleep that night, she thought twice about what she had done. She couldn't resort again to a secret life of gambling. There were times when gambling took the food out of Michael's mouth as a child. She'd promised him a trip to Disneyland, which never happened. Gambling had led her to other bad habits, including smoking and drinking. Once, Michael had come home from school and found her laid out on the couch in a stupor, a cigarette still lit in the ashtray.

After Sylvie's sweet-talking, mother and son were on speaking terms again, and she was on her best behavior during her stay at their house. She did motherly things and made herself useful, helping with the laundry, peeling vegetables, making a nice fruit salad, and even dusting the furniture. She was careful not to insult Angela's housekeeping, bearing in mind that Angela worked full time and didn't have a maid at home or staff at work to help her.

Aside from her sudden transformation into becoming domesticated, Sylvie also became extremely complimentary. "Angela, that's your best work yet," she said about the half-finished canvas on the easel of two youngsters running on the beach.

Then she turned to Michael. "I read your article this week. Very interesting, I must say."

Angela commented to Michael, "She's trying so hard." Sylvie pretended she couldn't hear them.

"I like her much better this way," he said.

"And I like your kinder side better, too," she admonished her husband. "Give her a break. I know your mother has her flaws, but she also has a soft, fragile side that makes her forgivable."

After dinner, Sylvie insisted the two of them go out to the movies. "You said you wanted to go see that movie for weeks now—that scary one. What's it called? *Carrie*?"

"Oh yeah." Angela's eyes lit up. "Let's go, Michael. Do you want to come with us?" she asked Sylvie.

"Me? No, I hate scary movies. You two go, and I'll clean up the dishes."

Michael stared at his mother as if he didn't know who she was and finally smiled. "Thanks, Mom." Then he looked at his wife for approval.

"That's a lot better," Angela whispered, as if grading one of her students.

Sylvie was satisfied with herself that she won them over. *Being domestic once in a while isn't so bad,* she told herself. *It wouldn't hurt to help out more often.* She'd surprise them when they got home and saw everything looking so perfect. *I can be a good mother,* she told herself.

After doing the dishes, she tidied up Angela's art supplies and Michael's piles of papers, and went to each room to collect garbage from the trash cans.

She noticed the blanket on Michael's side of the bed had been turned back. *He must have taken a nap today. I hope he didn't have another one of those headaches.* When she folded the crumpled bedspread back and tucked it into the mattress, she felt something stuck underneath. "What's this?"

She turned over the envelope marked *Adoption Money* and sighed. "This is all they've saved? Poor kids. They're going to need some help." For a fleeting moment, she felt guilty about having spent all her winnings on new clothes and jewelry, and quickly rationalized the art money would be coming soon.

Wouldn't it be wonderful if every time I could, I sneak extra money into their envelope for them? She thought about it more.

If I borrow their money, temporarily, I can double it—triple it, even—for them in no time. They won't even know I took it—they probably won't open the envelope until the end of the month again when they cash their paychecks.

❧

Two days later, Sylvie went back to Atlantic City to play her lucky thirty-two, but this time luck eluded her. She had no luck at the blackjack tables either.

"What's going on here?" she asked the dealer, as she busted with a twenty-three. *I lost everything, all the kids' money.* She wanted to cry. She wished the man with the toupee were around to boost her confidence.

"Your luck will turn around," the squatty man next to her commented. "Let me buy you another drink." Sylvie studied his face for the first time and thought he wasn't too hideous. "Sure, a gin and tonic would be nice," she answered, knowing she already had too much to drink.

Later on, they strolled through the casino together and then had more drinks in a smoky lounge, while a comedian entertained them with his slapstick and made her laugh despite her fears of being found out by Michael and Angela. *Oh, I really needed that laugh.* She took another sip of her cocktail.

"You have a nice smile." He touched her hand, and she tried not to flinch.

"Why thank you," she responded.

"Would you like to have a nightcap later in my room?" he asked as he got his wallet out to pay the bill.

She noticed the nice thick wad and tried not to stare as he returned it to his left coat pocket. "Oh, um, that'd be nice." They both stood to leave the bar. "I'm not tired enough to end the evening."

"The evening's just begun," he said, brushing her neck with his stubby fingers.

"Wow, you have the suite, I see." She stepped on the plush carpeting with the busy pattern and entered his ultra-modern room with silver chrome furnishings and king-size bed.

"Only the best," he said. "For someone like you. Do you mind if I get into my robe, to unwind a bit?" he asked.

"No, not at all. In fact, while you're in the bathroom, I'll make myself comfortable, too." She made sure he was watching her as she kicked off her shoes. As soon as he closed the bathroom door and she heard the water running, she quickly put her shoes back on and went to the chair where he left his coat jacket, deftly removing his wallet. After she slipped the bills into her purse, she let herself out of his suite and ran as fast as she could down the hall, past the elevators, to the stairwell. She didn't look back until she was out of breath, boarding the bus home.

A few days after she swindled the guy, Sylvie flipped through the yellow pages and stopped at the ad for Wanda's Wigs located in Queens and wrote down the address on a piece of scrap paper. Her next visits to the casino would have to be incognito.

When she entered the little shop, she heard bells jingling above the door. The sound didn't alert the salesgirl, whose head was resting on the counter. The girl was wearing a crazy black spiked wig, a ton of makeup, and was humming a sleepy song unfamiliar to Sylvie.

"Excuse me, hello?"

"Oh my God, you scared me," the girl said.

"Business is not booming, is it Wanda?" Sylvie said, suddenly feeling sorry for the girl.

"Yeah, it's been slow. Sometimes I fall asleep on the job. That's why I put the bell on the door."

"You didn't hear the bell when I came in."

The girl laughed. "Maybe I should rig a bucket of water over my head, instead."

"So, let me see what you have," Sylvie said, noticing a huge difference in price between the quality of wigs. She made up her mind to help out the girl. "I want to see your best redheads."

"Of course, right this way, miss."

Sylvie already liked her. She called her *Miss*, not *Ma'am*. "That one's really terrific on you," the salesgirl said. "You look beautiful with dark hair," she told Sylvie, smacking her gum.

"I don't think it does much for my complexion, though."

"Really? Then how 'bout trying this one on?" She giggled, holding up a rainbow-colored Afro wig. "No one ever buys this one."

"That would be fun, but it would also attract too much attention."

"What are you, on the run?" The girl laughed.

Sylvie adjusted a red wig on her scalp, admiring herself in the mirror. "You know, I like this one. Sold!"

"Oh, that's a smart choice—one of our finest hairs. Should I put it in a bag?"

"No, I'll wear it now. It's precisely what I need. I'm on my way to—oh, never mind."

The cluster of tiny bells chimed on Sylvie's way out.

Chapter 10

Angela called out, "Oh my God, Michael! Where is it? Where is it?"

Michael came running into the bedroom. "Where is what?"

She was on her knees, reaching her arm nearly up to her shoulder under the mattress. "Where's the envelope?"

"The envelope?" Michael looked wide eyed. "It's gotta be here." He nudged her away and felt for himself. Then he flung the entire mattress off the bed.

"It couldn't have disappeared!" she cried. "I mean, we've been home pretty much all along, haven't we? Except for—"

"Except for when we went to the movies and left my mother here alone," he finished.

She stared at him. "You don't think . . ."

He stared at her. "That's exactly what I think." He sat at the edge of the box spring, cradling his head in his hands.

"There's got to be an explanation for this, Michael." Angela stroked the back of his neck to calm him; he pushed her hand away and stood to pace the room, his limp worsened whenever he was stressed.

"Michael, sit down; you're making me nervous." She watched him hobbling back and forth in their small room. "Michael, stop.

Let's think about this; maybe she moved the money to a safer place in the house."

"Hand me the goddamn phone."

"Michael, don't jump to any conclusions. Your mother has her faults, but I don't think she'd steal from us. Not our baby money."

"Oh no? Give me the phone," Michael barked.

"Not unless—"

"Unless what, Angela?"

"Never mind," she said.

"No. What?"

"Unless . . . she's gambling again."

"Bingo!" Michael reached for the phone. He picked up the receiver, his fingers trembling as he dialed. "Where's the goddamn money?"

"Where's the money?" his mother repeated. "Who is this?" she stalled. "Michael?"

"Our money's missing, Mother. You took it, didn't you? That's all we care about—saving every penny so we can get that baby in our lives. How could you do this to us?"

"Michael, I-I can explain," she cried.

"Don't bother!"

"You don't understand."

"Excuse me? You steal our money, and *I* don't understand? I'm surprised you're not pretending you're having trouble hearing me now," he yelled. "But that would be pretty impossible, wouldn't it?"

"Stop screaming, Michael. I can explain."

"You set us up. You told us to go to the movies. You were the only one in our house. Why? So you could steal from us, your own kids."

"Michael, listen—"

"There's nothing to explain, nothing you can say, Mother. You hurt us bad this time. No more visits."

Angela pulled at his shirt sleeve. "Tell her we're calling the cops . . . We need that money."

Michael shoved her away and continued pacing with the phone to his ear.

"I can't come for my visits?" Sylvie asked.

"We are done with you—*kaputt!*"

"I was only borrowing the money," she said through sobs. "It was supposed to be temporary. Because we'll be getting a fortune soon."

"Oh really, a fortune? A fortune from what? From gambling? Tell me the truth. For once in your goddamn life, tell me the truth. Have you been gambling again?"

"Michael, that has nothing to do with the fortune. I'm talking about a case—"

"A case of what? A case of liquor? You're drinking again, too, aren't you?"

"Will you please let me finish?"

"I think you are finished. Tell me, have you been gambling again? With our money?"

"Well, uh, yes, only so I could—"

Michael slammed the phone down and picked it up to slam it down again.

"Why didn't you demand that she pay us back?"

"With what? You can't squeeze blood from a stone."

"She could take out a loan . . . ask her family in Europe. We can't give up. You should have threatened you'd call the police. Why can't you stand up to her?" Angela burst into tears.

Angela struggled to get through a whole day teaching; she couldn't concentrate on her assignment plan. She dropped a jar of red paint on the white linoleum and started wiping it up when some students walked into the room right through the mess. She snapped, "Can't you see I'm in the middle of cleaning this—"

Paula stepped back. "Oh, I'm sorry, Mrs. Beckman."

Angela was used to the kids calling her Mrs. B. and knew she wasn't herself. "No, I'm sorry, Paula. I'm having a bad day. It's only paint. It can be cleaned up."

Paula got a roll of paper towels and got on her hands and knees to help, directing others to walk around the spill. Angela wished the other messes in her life could be wiped away so easily. She knew she'd only feel worse when at home.

Getting through small talk at the dinner table was excruciating. "So, did Horton say anything to you about being late for work this morning?"

"No one said a thing," Angela said, sullenly, pushing around the food on her plate with her fork.

"I'll help with the dishes," Michael offered, trying to make amends.

"No. Don't. I've got it."

"Then, I'll be in my office if you need me. I have two deadlines to meet for the paper this week." He left the kitchen, knowing she'd probably start crying.

Michael was only at the typewriter for five minutes when the phone rang. "Michael, how are you? Where are you?" the voice asked.

"Oh man, sorry, Dr. Freid. I totally forgot about my appointment. I'm going through a family crisis right now."

"Oh, I'm sorry to hear that. Can I help?"

"No. No, thank you."

"Let's say we reschedule, tomorrow, same time, 7:15?"

"Uh, no, I think I need a break—don't take it personally, Doc."

"It's not me I'm concerned about. You have a lot on your plate."

"Dr. Freid—"

"You can't get through it by yourself."

"I appreciate it. I've gotta go now. I've got to meet a deadline."

"Okay. Feel free to call me, anytime, Michael."

"I'm sure I will, Dr. Freid."

Michael hung up and positioned his fingers over the typewriter keys again, his hands shaking uncontrollably. He massaged them until they were steady.

"Oh my God, I'm losing it," he said aloud. He bit his knuckles and leaned back in his chair, then stood and flung his papers and everything else on his desk with the sweep of his arm.

He heard Angela outside his office. She gingerly tapped on the door without entering. *She's afraid of me,* Michael thought. And for the first time since being in Nam, he was afraid of who he was, too.

"Michael, are you all right?" she said softly.

"Yeah." His voice cracked and tears formed. "I dropped something. Clumsy me." *Oh my God. I can't take this anymore. Maybe Angela's better off without me . . . for a while, at least.*

He got down on his knees and gathered his work, trying to reorganize it. He would finish his articles, even if he had to stay up all night working.

By 2 a.m., he fell asleep on the couch in his office, not wanting to wake Angela.

Things didn't get better after that. Day after day it was obvious they were avoiding one another. Because of the fatigue and the stress, Michael ached all over, and it didn't help that he chose to sleep on the lumpy couch every night, either. His excuse was his novel. He worked on it all through the night and didn't want to disturb her.

"Okay, whatever you've gotta do, Michael," he thought he heard her say, as if she didn't believe him this time.

After missing a few sessions, Michael went to see John, his physical therapist. He dreaded the lecture he'd get for not showing up lately, but needed to connect with someone.

"Hey, where've you been?" John asked, watching Michael head for the exercise bike.

Michael made a face. "You don't want to know."

John studied Michael's expression. "I was ready to call you and demand you report for duty," John joked.

"Well, I'm here now, ain't I?" Michael mounted the exercise bike.

"Ouch! What's going on?" John put his hand on Michael's back, and Michael spilled his guts about his mother and the adoption money and the effect it was having on his marriage.

"You're taking a nosedive right now. Why don't we talk in my office for a minute," John said.

"You sound like a fighter pilot," Michael said.

"Michael, stop pedaling. We need to talk."

Michael shook his head. "I don't know . . . not right now. I'm burnt out."

"Don't say that. You were doing so well," John said, sizing up Michael's posture. "Aside from your emotional health, I'm worried about your physical well-being. I sense muscle weakness, for one thing."

Michael squinted.

"I can see the pain's back?" John asked.

"Yeah, it's back."

"Looks like you've lost some flexibility."

"I've lost more than that," Michael growled. "*Angela.*"

John was speechless. "You and Angela? You guys are soul mates."

Michael dismounted and quickly left the gym. "I'll see you around."

"Will you be coming to your next appointment?" John called after him. Michael didn't answer as he stumbled toward the exit.

Angela threw her valise back onto the bed and unlocked it when she remembered she had forgotten to pack her sandals.

"Are you almost ready?" Michael asked. "You don't want to miss the flight."

Angela tightly held her round-trip ticket to Orlando in her hand, eager to see her parents, who kept telling her about the beautiful guest room they had fixed up.

For weeks she said how eager she was to get away . . . Now, she's probably eager to get away from me. She must really hate me by now;

she didn't even ask if I'd be all right by myself, didn't make me promise not to go surfing alone. She won't even look at me.

In between flight announcements, Christmas music played. "Ten days of sunshine should lift your spirits," Michael said. "I know I haven't made things that pleasant for you lately. I'm sorry. You know how I get during the holidays." He thought back to when he was a kid, visiting his Christian friends, seeing their large families celebrating Christmas.

Angela got teary eyed and grabbed her luggage. "What do I tell my mom and dad about you not showing up?"

"Tell them the truth. Tell them I have a lot of work to do."

"Is that really the truth, Michael?" She couldn't look at him when she asked.

"You'll be better off. Christmas should be a happy time, and I'm only going to bring you down. Maybe by the time you return, I'll be my old self again."

"Well, if you change your mind, you can always book a flight," Angela said.

Michael nodded. He longed for her dimpled smile and hadn't heard her infectious laugh in a while. She gave him a peck on the cheek and was gone.

Elvis Presley was singing about a blue Christmas, and Michael looked up at the speaker. "Oh, shut up." He couldn't get out of there fast enough. He'd bury himself in his writing, not answer the phone or the doorbell. He'd be a total recluse for almost two weeks—dreading it.

After meeting his deadlines for the paper, he worked twelve hours a day, hardly leaving his desk to eat meals. He hadn't shaved, hadn't surfed, hadn't done anything except absorb himself in his words. When he was finished, he read all the revisions he made on his novel and wept. He knew it was good. *It's not just good. It's goddamn great!*

He examined his stubby beard and bloodshot eyes in the mirror and splashed cold water on his face. He'd decided to hand-deliver the manuscript to Mr. Baker. The holiday traffic was horrendous. Eventually, he found a parking spot off Broadway and slid a few coins into the meter. Without realizing his pain, he practically ran the entire way with his cane to the editor's office. He stood at the building and took a deep breath before entering.

The next day he felt both exhausted and wired. He found an old joint in his sock drawer and decided to have a smoke, something he never did anymore. After a few tokes, he startled when the phone rang.

"Hello?"

"Michael, it's Rob Baker."

"Mr. Baker, how—?"

"Michael, my boy, you did it! It's going to print."

Michael let the air escape his lungs, as if he'd been holding his breath underwater.

"Really? You read it so fast."

"I honestly couldn't put it down. It's a bestseller—mark my words."

As soon as Michael hung up, he lifted the receiver to call Angela, but then stopped himself. Maybe he should wait. His first book had bombed; he didn't want to jinx the whole thing. No, he'd wait until she got home and they could celebrate over dinner in that cozy little Italian restaurant they used to go to in East Hampton. They'd also celebrate the advance that would enable them to finally adopt Linh, now a toddler.

There he sat, patting himself on the back that someone told him his work was worthy, yet he questioned his own validity. He questioned his worth. Why didn't he feel totally satisfied? Why didn't he feel fulfilled?

It seemed that overnight everything fell apart—his brother, his mother, his anxiety, his depression, his work, his self-esteem, his dreams . . . and now, Angela—poof! Even she disappeared. She went to a magic kingdom. He wondered if he was still her prince.

Michael stared out his kitchen window after making lunch, mesmerized by the whitecaps on the water. When he saw the mail truck pulling up next door, Michael went outside to hand the mailman his holiday tip envelope.

"Thank you, Mr. Beckman. I hope you and your wife have a nice Christmas."

Michael waved again as he pulled away. "Yeah, Merry Christmas."

As he headed back up the walkway, his heart thumped when he saw the return address on an envelope. Michael let the letter drop from his hands onto the snowy grass.

"Damn it. Why?"

How could he share this news with Angela? If he hadn't been so pigheaded about only adopting this particular child, they could have gotten another little boy or girl by now.

He could hear himself telling her the news: *Well, I failed you again, Angela. They've probably chosen a well-to-do-couple from Danbury, Connecticut, to raise our child, a doctor and his lovely wife who belong to the garden club—pillars of the community.*

Michael bent and picked up the letter, crumpling the papers in anger. Inside the house, he locked the door and got out the photograph of Baby Linh and stared at the face he had grown to love. Then he tucked it away in the same drawer with old photos of his dog Shadow, Tom, his buddy from Vietnam, and the most painful of all—a picture of him with his father when he was only four.

He felt like he was riding a wave of his emotions—good news, bad news, all in one day.

Michael left the dirty dishes piled up in the sink, and went out the back door dressed in his full-body wetsuit and rubber booties.

"At least the surf's good." He grabbed his Hobie and staggered toward the water, buffeted by the icy wind. He paddled fast to where the waves were breaking. The water temperature was forty-four degrees. Crouching on his bad knee to catch a wave made his body shudder in pain. Once he was far out enough past the breakers, he turned around to face his house and noticed it was snowing. It was Christmas Eve.

Chapter 11

A ngela stood back and looked at the rather large mural hanging above her parents' dining room table. The bright-pink flamingo was a bit much, but she didn't want to hurt their feelings. She hoped they weren't able to read her expression; it was probably the most hideous piece of art she'd ever seen. And that fake Christmas tree in their turquoise Orlando living room, *yuk!*

She was very relieved, though, to see a change in her mother's state of mind. Obviously, the warm weather was healing for her folks these past few years. "You guys seem really happy here," Angela said. "I think it's great. Dad's playing golf and you're playing tennis. I can't believe you're the same people." She briefly thought about how hard her parents had worked, and what they lost in their lifetime.

"We sure miss seeing you, though, Angela. We met some nice friends here and enjoy our social life. And you, honey? How are you doing?" She caressed her daughter's cheek. "You're a little gaunt. Let me make you something to eat."

"Uh-oh, I have a feeling I'll be putting on a few pounds while I'm here." Angela also had a feeling her mother knew something wasn't right. Mothers are intuitive like that. But how would she know about that stuff? She wasn't a mother yet herself.

"I'm okay, Mom. Really." Angela paused, and then she burst into tears. She saw her mother's face drop and regretted showing her emotions.

"Oh, honey, what is it?" She handed her a tissue. Angela could depend on her mother to have Kleenex close by. "Is it because Michael couldn't come with you?"

Angela nodded. "I guess."

"I know you're still going through a rough time, with hormones and all."

"That's only part of it."

"There's more? What else?" her mother asked while quickly heating Angela a plate of leftover chicken parmesan. "Are you and Michael okay, you know, together?"

Angela didn't want to tell her mother that Michael was no longer affectionate or about his temper.

"Well, let's forget it. I'm okay, really. I'm sorry I even brought it up."

"Angela Lee, don't pull that on me. I'm your mother, and I know when you need to get something off your chest. What is it?"

Angela paused and then broke down. "His mother stole our adoption money." Angela gritted her teeth and counted to three.

"What? What did you say?" Her mother's jaw dropped. She slapped a hand over her open mouth.

They sat for almost two hours talking about everything they needed to talk about, and then Angela felt overwhelmed and tired. Lately, she often felt fatigued. "I'm going to go lie down for a while now, Mom."

When she carried her suitcase into the guest room, she saw some of her old paintings and stuffed animals from when she was young.

"Mom, you saved my old stuff?" She broke down, crying again. Her mom knew how to make her feel at home. She laid her head back on the lilac pillow, her favorite color. She slipped her shoes off and got under the covers and heard her mother quietly leaving the room. *How can I miss him when I'm so mad at him? Why didn't he threaten his mother to return the money or else we'd take legal action? Why can't he for once in his life stand up to that woman? Maybe I am angrier at him than at her.*

She also thought about the full day she'd have tomorrow, when she'd meet Katie at Disney World. *I can't wait to see her and the twins.*

As Angela waited by the entrance of Magic Kingdom, she saw hundreds of mothers scurrying along with their small children. She observed them like she was watching a movie screen, zooming in on the interactions, the joy and the closeness.

She peeked past the entrance into the park where a mother was making her child pose for pictures. "Cheese," he said. She was surrounded by mothers and fathers laughing with their children who wore Mickey Mouse ears.

"Angela! Angela!" It was Katie, hurrying up pushing the double stroller with Kelly and Kevin dressed as Winnie and Piglet.

"Oh my God, how cute!" Angela screamed and kissed them both. "I missed you guys!"

"Say 'Hi, Auntie Ange,'" Katie prompted them, as if the six-month-olds could talk. "How are you?" Katie asked, and Angela instantly bawled like a baby.

"I'm sorry. I don't know what's come over me." Angela wiped her eyes on her sleeve. "You wouldn't have a tissue, would you?" She thought of her mother handing her one yesterday when she cried. *What is with me, lately?*

"Angela, what is it? I'm getting worried about you. Seems like every time we talk on the phone lately, you're crying . . ."

Angela shook her head. "No, no, it's nothing . . . No, it's everything."

"What is it, nothing or everything?" Katie pressed.

Angela's voice broke. "Is insanity nothing or everything?" She managed a weak smile.

"Come on, let's get into the park, find a nice café, and sit and talk before we battle the crowds."

"Sounds perfect," Angela said, still shaken.

Angela filled Katie in on what had been going on: the family visit from Europe; the family secrets revealed; the death of Michael's secret brother; Sylvie stealing their adoption money.

"I can't believe she'd do that. I mean, that is low."

"Well, she did it."

"What now?"

Angela shrugged. "I don't know. The worst part is because of all that went on, Michael and I haven't been getting along. I haven't said this out loud, even to myself yet; sometimes I wonder if he wants to separate, at least for a while."

Katie looked surprised. "You two are the couple of the century."

"Maybe we were once upon a time," Angela said, sadly.

"Listen, this will all blow over."

Angela wrapped her arms around her stomach and winced.

"What's the matter? You're not feeling well?"

"Yeah, it's probably that time of the month. Cramps."

"Oh, yuck, sorry."

"There's one other thing." Angela hesitated. "A few weeks ago, Michael did something weird in bed."

"You mean, kinky?"

"No, you big goofball. That's why I love you. No one else makes me laugh like you do. I woke up in the middle of the night with Michael's hands around my . . . my throat."

"He tried to strangle you?"

"Shhh!" The family of four sitting at the table next to theirs looked over. Angela lowered her voice. "There was no pressure or anything. He had no idea he was even doing it. He was having another nightmare."

"About the war? And you were the enemy? How'd you ever go back to sleep after that?"

"It's been exhausting anticipating the next time it could happen. We've been sleeping in separate rooms."

"Oh, my Lord. Maybe you guys need outside help."

"He's talking to a counselor on his own. Maybe I'll have to join him soon. I think we just need some time and we'll be fine. With his mother out of the picture, at least he's not throwing things around the house while he's awake." Angela laughed.

Katie didn't smile. "You're not really laughing on the inside, Ange."

Angela looked at the three of them apologetically. "Hey, let's continue this conversation another time. I'm not going to burst anyone's bubble . . . We're in Disney World, for goodness sake," she said with a high-pitched voice.

"The parade's about to start, kids. Let's go find Mickey and Minnie, shall we?" Katie pushed the double stroller faster.

"You bet." Angela ran along next to them. "*Pssst*, Katie, I've gotta tell you one more secret. I'm really in love with Donald."

"Geez, I thought it was another man. But a duck! You always did go for the rebellious type."

During Angela's two-week stay in Florida, there were no phone calls from Michael. Angela had insisted her parents go out to celebrate New Year's Eve without her. The notion of not kissing Michael at the stroke of midnight made her cry, and she had buried the clock under her pillow. Now, as she sat with her parents on her last night with them at the Tiki Inn restaurant, she watched a catamaran glide by on the waterway without a sound. The setting was romantic with thousands of twinkling white lights lining the railing. It could have been a perfect vacation. She told her parents that while they were out, she and Michael had talked on the phone every day and that he asked about them and sent his love.

"I told him about the lovely gifts you'd given me and that I'd be bringing home his wrapped ones. He said you shouldn't have."

She hated to lie, but it almost sounded true to her.

Since Angela had to budget her money, she only had one gift to give them in return. She'd waited, nervously, for the large canvas to arrive that she had shipped to Orlando, right before she left New York. Luckily, it came the day before Christmas. She'd painted a scene she'd never attempted before, with her father in mind. Angela was thrilled that she captured such action and made the canvas come alive with the first stroke of her brush—sailboats in the wind, whitecaps and rough seas.

Her father looked at his wife. "Do you think we can take down that hideous flamingo that my sister-in-law sent us and replace it with this? She's already seen it hanging there."

"Phew!" Angela blurted out. "I'm so glad. For a while I was afraid you suddenly lost your fine taste in art."

"So, how's Michael doing with his writing?" her father asked. "I hope his second book does better than the first."

"Yeah, it's coming along. He's in the revising stage now." She wondered herself how that was going. "He said he was snowed in a couple of days and got a lot done." The lying was getting easier.

"You said he surfs in the winter? *Brrr.*" Her mother shivered.

"Oh, Mom, you're always cold. That's another reason Florida was such a smart move for you."

"So, he must really miss you." Angela's mother exchanged glances with her husband. It reminded Angela of that dreadful monkey-in-the-middle game she played with them, being an only child.

"Michael's been much too busy to miss me. He's under an enormous amount of pressure—his deadlines for work, the novel, Sylvie, the adoption, his nightmares."

"His nightmares?" her father blurted. "I thought they were gone."

"As long as you two are okay with each other, nothing else matters," her mother said. "Everything else will work itself out; isn't that right, dear?" She looked at her husband. "After what we went through, losing Anna, it wasn't easy. We gave each other strength, loved each other through the hard times." Her mother placed her hand on top of her daughter's.

"Hi, y'all." The perky young waitress came to their table with tiny red and green bells swinging from her hair as she spoke. "May I take your drink order now?"

"I'll say," Angela responded. "Three piña coladas, and I'll take one of those little umbrellas in mine."

"You from New York?" the girl asked.

"Long Island. Going back tomorrow."

"Oh, hope you had a nice stay here."

Angela admired the girl's flawless complexion and wished she could blink and erase a few years of worry lines from her own face. She wanted to swing her hair too and hear the jingle of bells like the waitress. She was so festive, so full of life.

"The piña coladas here are yummy. They're like dessert before dinner." The girl giggled and jingled simultaneously as she left to get the order.

"That girl sure has the holiday spirit," her father noted. "Ah, youth." Angela sighed.

Her parents looked at one another and then their daughter, nearly thirty years old.

"Now, where were we?" her mother asked.

"If you're asking if I still love my husband, the answer is yes. As much as the day we met."

The waitress set their drinks on the table.

Angela's father winked at his daughter and wife. "Let's have a toast to that." They all raised their glasses and took quick sips. "And here's to Michael's book, too. I know it must not be easy writing a novel, but pressure from work is not a bad thing. The adoption and Sylvie are a separate issue."

Angela's mother jumped in. "I can't believe I'm going to say this in defense of Sylvie, but I believe, in her heart, that she truly loves you and Michael."

JANET LEE BERG 135

"Taking their money, though, is a peculiar way of showing it," her father admitted. "Forget Sylvie for a minute. I'm more concerned about Michael's nightmares coming back. How long has he been having them?"

"Not too long," Angela answered. "You know how mellow he is. It takes a lot to trigger his nightmares."

"That's a positive thing," her mother said.

Angela tried to joke. "True. Having empty pockets is not a positive thing."

Angela's father put his hand on his daughter's shoulder. "Don't be proud, young lady. Your mother and I want to help you out with—"

"Dad, no, you're not giving me any money." She thought of their little tin full of coupons they save for food shopping. Their retirement money was all they had. "That's not why I told you all this. I love you for offering, but I think things happen for a reason."

"You mean you don't think Baby Linh is the baby for you?" her mother said

"I mean, if she's the baby we're meant to have, then that'll be wonderful. But if not, then we'll have to wait for the one that's right for us."

They sipped their drinks in an awkward silence.

Angela's mother dabbed her eyes with her dinner napkin. "After spending these past couple of weeks with you, I hate to see you go."

"I know, Mom, but you're making me fat! I can hardly button my jeans." Her mother winced. "You know I can come back in the spring, or better yet, you can come to New York. You should see how cute the beach house looks now."

"Spring in New York." Her mother wiped her eyes again. "I have to admit I do miss the change of seasons. And my favorite is springtime—new hope, new growth."

On her return flight, Angela thought of the empty pink room. She pictured the other rooms, too, how cute she and Michael had decorated them; the soft colors they'd chosen to make it feel homey. They'd even worked on the outside of the house before winter set in. Everything looked picture perfect to anyone passing by—newly painted sage-green trim and window boxes, a pine wreath on the front door. Suddenly, she felt misplaced with the whole façade. She couldn't forgive her husband so easily for not calling her while she was away. She imagined the ride home from the airport in New York would be a quiet. She'd simply tell him she was tired. And she was tired, tired with the whole thing.

Once back home in New York, Angela felt out of sorts. She hardly had the energy to hang her 1980 equestrian calendar on the refrigerator with the Palomino magnet while she was thinking about the news Michael finally had the nerve to share with her—the rejection letter for the adoption of Linh. *What a way to start a new year,* she sighed.

Angela stepped on the scale and gasped. "Six pounds?" Ever since she allowed her mother to overstuff her with her good cooking down in Florida, she felt bloated and unattractive. Just a little extra weight on her small frame made her feel uncomfortable. *Emotional overeating,* she thought.

She knew lately, though, that their marital problems were partly her fault. Unlike Michael, she lost her enthusiasm to work on the relationship.

Chapter 12

At a stoplight Michael gawked at the sports car revving its engine. He was envious. Not because of its sleekness or bright-red paint job, but because it looked like a mother and son enjoying a ride together on a sunny winter's day. The guy driving opened his car window and yelled to Michael.

"Hey, Beckman, is that you?"

Michael recognized Andy Reese, the star basketball player from high school.

"It's great to see you. How's it going, man?" Andy asked. He pointed to the older woman sitting next to him. "This is my date, my mom. It's her birthday, and I'm taking her out to lunch."

"That's great, Andy. Enjoy your birthday, Mrs. Reese." Michael waved as the light turned green and both cars pulled away, the red car way ahead. Michael hadn't seen his own mother since she spent the weekend with them and stole their adoption money to feed her gambling habit. *Maybe it's time.*

Sylvie answered the door wearing her bathrobe and silly elephant slippers they'd given her the year before for her birthday. She wore no makeup, and her hair was unkempt. The first thing he thought upon seeing her was that she'd aged. They stood for a while staring at one another on the threshold, and then Michael stepped inside.

"I'm sorry, Mom. I should have let you explain things to me. You must have had a good reason for—"

Sylvie tried holding back tears. She pulled her head back to get a better look at his face. "What's the matter? I know something's wrong. Why are you here? Do you have bad news to tell me? Is it Angela? Is she okay?"

"Mom, stop. She's fine."

Sylvie whispered, "Oh, thank God. I've missed you. I knew you'd show up eventually. Come in and sit with me."

"I missed you too. I had to let go of some of my anger before I saw you again."

"And it's gone? The anger's gone now, Michael? No more anger?"

"I've been really good. Now, it's Angela's turn."

"What do you mean? Angela's angry?"

"Why don't you get dressed. I'll take you to lunch. I'll fill you in on what's been going on."

Sylvie's face lit up like a happy child. She continued to ramble on from her bedroom as she went to get ready. "I'll wear my roseate pantsuit even though there's still a chill in the air."

Michael laughed to himself. She popped her head back out her door again. "By the way, any news about your book yet?"

"Mom, please get ready, and I'll fill you in on everything over lunch."

He picked up one of the many framed pictures of him and Angela lining the shelves. She lived for the two of them. He knew that. He felt a lump in his throat thinking how he'd punished her long enough. They would talk as long as it took for him to understand this woman, his mother. And perhaps, as long as it took for her to understand her only son.

Scanning her small apartment, he saw how reclusive she'd become. There was a pack of Lucky Strikes on the table. *Smoking again? Another reason her skin has aged so much.*

Suddenly, Michael no longer felt intimidated by his mother. For the first time in his life, he had power over her. Maybe it was because now he felt the time had come that he had to take care of her, not the other way around. He picked up the newspapers collected on the chair, stacked the unopened mail on the counter, and gathered dirty dishes from every corner of the room.

Michael knew he'd come a long way since he was able to open up with some intense therapy with Dr. Freid. Magically, the inner peace he'd always had before Vietnam returned. He was no longer angry at the world. The only thing left to work on was his relationship with Angela.

Soon he'd make everything right again. First he'd talk to his shrink about his wife rejecting his affections. They'd stopped trying to make a baby months ago, right before Christmas. And he understood her reasoning; it became too much like a chore, not at all pleasurable. He couldn't blame her for being cold when he recently tried to show her some tenderness.

Michael had found it difficult to restrain himself from calling Angela while she was staying with her parents, but Dr. Freid had told him he needed to reach his crisis point—rock bottom—before asking his wife to again trust him; he wanted to be there for her again, be the same man she married.

He was getting ready to go on his book tour. She knew he was going away but was unaware of the details. Wait until he had to tell her how long he'd be gone—close to four weeks—starting in San Francisco, then on to Tucson, Dallas, Chicago, Philadelphia . . . working his way back east to New York. He wondered whether his absence would make her heart grow fonder or if it would cause their marriage to spiral downward.

After seeing his mother, Michael decided to stop at the department store and pick up a box of chocolates. Like his mother, chocolate made Angela happy. She'd been complaining lately about putting on some weight, but to him she looked more beautiful than ever. Her skin seemed radiant.

Making his way through the mall, he paused at the jewelry store window and spotted a silver bracelet with seashells and starfish. *Angela will love that. I'll have them wrap it up nice, too, in her favorite color—lilac.* He bounced happily down the aisle between the glass cases.

After his purchases, Michael bumped into a woman near the food court. He was suddenly distracted by what he saw.

"Oops," Michael apologized as he studied the couples seated at small bistro tables with shopping bags at their feet, taking bites of their sandwiches in between conversations. He did a double take at one of the couples dining. He quickly stepped back behind a wide pole. *Is that Angela?* He blinked hard, trying to focus. She told him she'd be having lunch out; he didn't know it would be at the mall. And he certainly didn't know that it would be with a man.

He'd never seen the guy before. Nice looking, solid build under his blue sports coat, thick wavy hair and dark, prominent eyes. He was smiling. *What guy wouldn't be smiling,* he thought, *sitting with her?* The scene was surreal. The two of them were laughing. They leaned into one another as if sharing secrets.

What secrets? Is she sleeping with him? How long? Does she love him?

Michael felt nauseous. At first, he wanted to approach them, but found himself running in the opposite direction into the blur of people coming in and out of stores. He stopped suddenly to wipe his hand over his wet eyes.

He bounded out the nearest exit door, carrying the gifts for his wife. It didn't matter. *A couple of gifts won't change her feelings.* He'd have to do a lot more than that. Stepping outside into the strong breeze, he felt disoriented. He hobbled around the parking lot like an old man, his leg throbbing as he searched desperately for his car.

"Where'd I park? Where's my car?"

Michael wished he could lie on the asphalt and give up. *Maybe she deserves someone better.* Oddly, he wasn't angry, despite being perturbed, confused and hurt by what he had seen.

She'd always tell me she missed my calm. It was one of the reasons she fell in love with him on that first day they'd met at the beach. The two of them watched the seagulls overhead as the waves lapped up onto the sand. They discovered one another like treasures washed up on the shore.

Michael knew what he'd have to do to win her back. He'd have to prove to her that he was his old self again, no matter what it took. He hoped it wasn't too late. Finally, he found the car. He sat in the driver's seat for a long time, thinking about his strategy. He wouldn't mention that he'd seen his wife with that guy. He'd have to prove he loved her more. Then he remembered the book tour. *Oh man, the book tour. The timing couldn't be worse.*

Michael moved around the room in jerky motions until Dr. Freid persuaded him to relax.

"Michael, we had our session yesterday morning. Why the urgency to meet again today?"

Michael looked at him, unable to catch his breath. "Sit. Please." The doctor gestured toward the chair.

Michael took a seat. His breathing was rushed, almost as if hyperventilating. "There's been a new development after I saw you."

"Sorry."

"Slow down. Take your time."

Michael gripped his armrest.

"Are you able to continue now?"

"I think Angela may be cheating on me," he uttered quickly.

"What makes you say that?"

"I saw her." Michael rubbed his face. "With another man. At the mall."

"The shopping mall? That's hardly a place to have an affair. Perhaps she ran into an old friend."

"Well, they gave me the impression that they were pretty connected, as if they knew each other very well."

"I don't think you should jump to any conclusions. What did she say when you asked her about it?"

"I haven't asked. And I don't intend to."

"Why not?"

"Because I'm afraid."

"Afraid of what?"

"Afraid of making it too easy for her to end it with me. I don't want to give her an easy out while I'm trying to improve. You know I'm much better now, right? I just need some more time."

"I agree, but don't hide from what the reality is while—"

"What? You think I'm only prolonging what's meant to be? I want to be the best husband I can be for her."

"Will you still feel that way if she is cheating on you?"

"Lately, I've been an asshole. She deserves better."

"Maybe you're being too hard on yourself."

"Maybe I deserve it."

"How do you plan on winning her back?"

"That's the hard part. I only have a few more days until my book tour starts."

"And you're worried about leaving her alone? Worried she'll see him again?"

"I'm worried sick."

"Unless the time you're apart will be good for your relationship, give her time to rethink."

"Yeah, I've already thought out the absence makes the heart grow fonder thing. I plan to call her every night, send her notes and flowers, and—"

"Best laid plans of mice and men."

"You sound pessimistic, Doctor."

"I'm only saying if you try too hard, she won't buy it, no matter how sincere you are. Didn't you say she already berated you for cleaning the house too much?"

Michael leaned forward, resting his elbows on his knees, and his head in his hands. "I can't lose her, Doc. I don't know what I would do without her."

As soon as Michael walked in the door, he hung up his jacket and got to work folding the laundry, vacuuming the rugs, organizing paperwork. He was sweeping the back deck with a wide broom when she walked in.

"What's with being Mr. Clean? You feeling guilty about something?"

Michael thought he should be asking her that question, but he didn't. "I also breaded the flounder for dinner. I'm on a roll . . . my way of burning up nervous energy."

"Seriously, why are you doing all this?"

"I'm trying to make up for being such a jerk these past couple of months. It's my way of saying I'm sorry."

"Well." She threw her hands in the air. "You may have earned yourself a gold star, but you're still sleeping on the couch tonight," she said, leaving the room.

He followed her like a puppy. "Ange, you've gotta cut me a break. I also want to tell you about some good news. I went to see my mother. I took her out to lunch at Jade's—her favorite Chinese restaurant—and we talked about everything."

"So, now everything is all better, is it? You put another bandage on the boo-boo?"

Michael was surprised by Angela's resentment. "I thought you'd be glad about that." Angela didn't respond. *Maybe she's thinking that my mother will interfere again, cause even more trouble.*

"Angela, she looks terrible, pathetic, really. She's pale and thin, as if she's not eating at all. Her voice is raspy as if she hasn't used it in a long time."

Angela remained stoic. "I wish her well, Michael. Don't you remember how you were so mad at your mother and weren't ready to forgive her?"

"Yeah, of course I remember."

"Well, that's where I'm at now. At the time I was afraid either you'd explode, or she'd have a heart attack. It took a while for me to digest everything. I'm still not able to forgive her. And you know what? I no longer . . . oh, never mind."

"No longer, what? No longer care?" he asked with hurt eyes.

"I care, but I wish everyone would leave me alone. Goddamn it, just leave me alone!"

When she slammed the bedroom door and went to bed without dinner, he realized this was exactly how he had treated her. He'd wait until she found her old self again, too.

The next morning, he had to share the inevitable with her. "Well, you may get your wish," he started, "about being left alone." He gulped and placed his itinerary on the table before her. He watched as her eyes widened.

"I wish you a lot of luck on your book tour, Michael," she said like a distant acquaintance.

Chapter 13

S ylvie picked through her messy nightstand drawer looking for the Chanukah card the kids had sent her during the holidays. She sighed, thinking she'd finally lost Angela, her daughter-in-law. Michael did say she was having terrible mood swings, lately. *Maybe it'll pass, like menopause. That put me over the edge.*

"Oh, there it is." She recognized the card with the blue dancing Stars of David zigzagging across the front and opened it. Her eyes watered. The holiday had come and gone after the whole adoption money fiasco.

She took the two tickets to see *Guys and Dolls* on Broadway out of the card. At first Sylvie had scoffed at two tickets, knowing she'd most likely be going alone. Coincidentally, the timing worked out well. Her friend Cynthia was in from California visiting.

At the matinee, they sat dead center, third row and whispered to each other throughout the show until they were hushed by a woman sitting next to Sylvie and flashing dirty looks.

"Being so close to the stage, I'm sure she's not missing anything. I'm half deaf, and I can hear what's going on. She's being a crotchety old bit—"

"We'll have to wait until we go to dinner after the show." Cynthia smiled.

"Is that your stomach growling or mine?" Sylvie asked, and they both giggled.

Sylvie and Cynthia had known each other for twenty years. They met while working in sales at a major New York department store. After Cynthia moved west to be with her daughter, the two stayed in touch regularly by phone.

At the end, the audience gave a standing ovation and waited for the final curtain call, until the applause died out. "The music, the singing, was all incredible and very exciting. Thank you so much for sharing it with me," Cynthia said as they stood to leave their row."

Once outside, Sylvie pulled Cynthia to walk arm-in-arm, talking about the play and how much they enjoyed each other's company.

"The play was funny, wasn't it?"

"And romantic, too," Cynthia added.

"Romantic? Aggh, what do I know about romantic?"

"Sylvie, we all have some romance in us. Isn't it Valentine's Day tomorrow?"

"Oh, what a bunch of nonsense that is. This is the best day I've had in a long, long time. Let's not ruin it talking about such foolishness."

"We should be able to talk about anything, shouldn't we? What are friends for?"

"I know. You're right. I'm not used to talking about romance. You're my only friend."

"I understand. I don't know if I will ever meet anyone again at this age. I'm almost sixty. Vinny's been gone a year already. It feels like forever. I married him when I was only eighteen. I have no interest in meeting anyone, but you, you're younger, and you've not been with a man for how long now?"

"About twenty years, since Michael was a little boy."

"And do you ever wish—?"

"You aren't only my friend, you're my psychiatrist, Cynthia." Sylvie wiped her wet face. "I used to wish. I used to dream. But that's all it was, wishing and dreaming."

Sylvie wiped her face again.

"Hey, crying is good for us women, sometimes. Are you okay?" Cynthia cupped Sylvie's cheeks in both her hands. She had a way of penetrating through Sylvie's eyes directly to her soul. "Tell me, honestly, how are you really doing? Talk to me, my friend."

Back in Holland, Sylvie's best friend at the Jewish school, Hana, had always referred to her as "my friend," too. Sylvie felt heartbroken that she had been the one to survive. Hana's entire family was most likely slaughtered at the camp.

"Let's talk over lunch." Sylvie pulled her along by the hand down the sidewalk until they reached a small out-of-the-way restaurant that served Greek food.

"Ah, Greek? You remembered, Sylvie, how much I love Greek food."

"Of course. Moussaka for two?"

"And we can't forget the grape leaves."

After they put their order in, they lingered over wine and chatted away.

"You know, I really needed that talk. I didn't know how much until now. Life, who can figure it. You're the one whose husband died, and I'm the one who's a mess. After you moved to California I was in a slump. Between worrying about Michael's health and his marriage and money problems, I'm afraid I had gotten myself into some deep trouble."

"Trouble, what kind of trouble?"

"Oh, little things, like addiction—gambling . . . stealing."

"Is that all? You should have nudged me in the theater during the gambling scenes. Maybe they would have given you a part."

They both laughed.

Sylvie went further into detail about her problems, and it made her feel better to get it out. She loved Cynthia for never judging her, always making light of what really hurt her heart.

"I hope you are finished with all that trouble these days, Sylvie. Are you?"

"I'm doing better. I finally dug myself out and dug myself deep inside my apartment. Too deep," she sighed heavily. "I'm starting to see the light again. Michael made me promise to get out more. And I try to go once or twice a week, you know, go into the city to see a show or go to Central Park. Actually, tomorrow I may go to the Metropolitan Museum of Art."

"Oh, it's about time you showed an interest again. Art was your life at one time. I bet a lot of memories will come back to you."

"That's what I'm afraid of."

"I wish I could go with you. You know I'm leaving tomorrow."

Sylvie choked up. "Another time. It was so refreshing to see you again, Cynthia. You seem pretty content now."

"My life as *Grammie* in the suburbs is boring in comparison, but it's fulfilling to watch three grandchildren every day. I'm deep into diapers and storybooks, a safe life."

"I only wish I could have such a safe life," Sylvie added.

"Your babies will be coming."

"You'll be the first to hear the good news when that happens . . . if that happens."

"I have a funny feeling it will happen sooner than you think. I'll say a prayer for you."

"You know how I feel about prayers."

"I know; I should feel that way, too. After praying my heart out, I still lost Vinny, but somehow it helps me stay sane. I had no choice but to go where my daughter was. I'm glad you have your son not too far away. It's the children that keep you going."

"He was a good man, Vinny. He usually had something nice to say when he stopped by the store. I suppose it's even harder to lose someone you had loved so long."

"And I suppose I was lucky to have him that long. I feel your pain that you never met the right man, Sylvie."

"And I never will."

"Oh, don't say that. You never know. When you least expect it . . .

Well, my friend," Cynthia said, "I predict that when I come again next year to see my sister, you'll be sharing a lot of news with me. You will be telling me you fell in love. And that you are a grandmother. I don't care what you say, I will still pray for you."

Sylvie wondered if Cynthia remembered the conversation they shared one day in the cafeteria at work when Sylvie told her how she had stayed up nights praying for her best friend who had been taken away during the Holocaust. Now, she couldn't remember the words to those prayers.

The ringing sound of the cashier and clatter of dishes and trays came back to her as Cynthia sat there, unable to answer Sylvie's questions: *Why would God answer some prayers and not others? Is there a right way to pray? What about those stuck under the rubble for days after an earthquake? Or sick infants incapable of praying and they die without ever having lived? Or the elderly and senile hooked up to oxygen, suffering alone in pain? What about those who are mentally handicapped? Is God half deaf, too, like me?*

Cynthia pushed away her half-eaten Greek cuisine and waved to the waiter for the bill. "I'm getting this," she told Sylvie, grabbing the check.

"Thank you. And thank you for your good wishes and for being such a good listener. I'm grateful that you are now living a boring, safe life with your family."

They both smiled as they walked further away from the Greek restaurant, locked together with pretzel arms. They hugged and said goodbye at the corner. With one last wave, Cynthia called out to Sylvie, who turned back to look at her. "Enjoy the art tomorrow, my friend."

Goodbye again, Hana.

Sylvie reached from her queen bed and pulled back the curtains. Morning sunspots speckled above her on the wall. She was relieved the drizzle from the night before had ended. If it had been raining, she'd easily make an excuse to Michael and put off her visit to the art museum where she'd immediately be drawn to the Dutch masters exhibit. It's not that she didn't already relive her past every single day since the age of fourteen. She feared stirring up memories she had shared with her father when they bonded over his most precious art.

She studied her face in the bathroom mirror and turned her head sideways. Some days she still saw youth in her face, and this was one of them. *Maybe it's because I spent the day with my friend yesterday. Cynthia was so complimentary. About my figure, my clothes, about everything. She makes me feel confident about myself. Not too many people do that for me anymore.*

For that reason alone, she applied very little makeup and wore her hair plain, tucked behind one ear. *Hmm, maybe just a little blush and a tad of lipstick.* She shimmied herself into her lime-green and pale-pink cotton shift and wore low beige pumps with a matching bag.

"Good morning," her nosy neighbor Mrs. Lenhart said as Sylvie fumbled with her keys, locking the door behind her before continuing. "Don't you look lovely and fresh in your pastel colors." The woman peeked out her door like clockwork, whenever she heard someone in the hallway. She was more alone than Sylvie, if that was possible. Even her fat cat had run away. Sylvie thought about replacing it the next time she came upon a stray.

She stood on the grand steps at the Metropolitan Museum of Art and gazed up at the detail in the carved friezes above the Corinthian columns. After paying, she stepped further inside and saw a tour guide directing a group of a dozen or so high school students into the modern art exhibition. She didn't care for modern art. "Rubbish," she mumbled under her breath.

"Where's the real art?" she interrupted the tour guide in front of everyone.

"I beg your pardon?" he said, indignantly.

"The Dutch art. Where's the Dutch art?"

The students laughed as he pointed to the Leham wing with an incredulous look on his face. She heard one of the girls say that she hated modern art, too, and then an argument started among the kids.

She went off in another direction, and when she stepped into the Dutch room, she was overwhelmed with her father's presence. She felt his touch on her goose-bumped arm and could swear she smelled his cigar smoke.

Chapter 14

A ngela hugged Michael's bed pillow to her face, smelling it and plumping it with her hand to make it look like he'd been there sleeping beside her and he only got up to use the bathroom or to get something to drink in the middle of the night. He would be gone two more weeks, and every day dragged by slowly. She wondered what he was doing. Maybe he was dreaming. At least he hadn't been having those horrible nightmares anymore. *Seeing Dr. Freid was a good idea after all. At least I did something right*, she thought, smoothing out his pillow again.

As she swung her legs out of bed to get ready for work, her nagging indigestion returned. *Oh, give me a break. I haven't even eaten breakfast yet.*

When Angela walked into the faculty room, an older teacher looked her up and down. "Hey, are you okay? Your skin color's kind of . . . green."

Angela twisted her mouth. "It's this sour stomach of mine lately, Grace."

"Weren't you complaining about that last week?"

"Yeah, a little, I guess, when I started worrying about Michael going away on his book tour." No one knew she was having marital issues.

"Now that he's gone it's turned into a full-fledged tummy ache?" Grace inquired. "Honey, I think you should go see a doctor. Why don't you ask Mr. Horton to find someone to cover for you and leave a little early?"

"Why, I look that bad?"

"Actually, aside from today, you've never been more beautiful, sweetie. Isn't it better to double-check these things? Once, I waited too long after my appendix burst and the poison spread—well, never mind; you don't need to hear the gory details."

Angela put her hand on Grace's back as they left the faculty room and headed for their classrooms. "I'll tell you what's really gory. Working with acrylics that dry too quickly. The stuff is so unforgiving."

"Ah, talk about unforgiving—I have to review their notes on dangling participles." The two teachers split up, moving toward opposite wings of the building.

Angela panicked for a moment. *What if it is something serious?* She heard about what happened to the art teacher she replaced who had been diagnosed with a rare blood disorder. She shook it off. *This is ridiculous. A little upset stomach. What next, have Horton call an ambulance? I'm fine*, she thought, entering her classroom and hitting the light switch.

"Now, let me get out all those damn acrylics."

As soon as she walked in the door after work, Angela plopped herself down on the cushy chaise under the window and kicked off her shoes, noticing a splatter of blood-red paint on the soles of the black leather. The uneasy feeling in her stomach subsided hours ago. Now her feet ached. *Hmm . . . seems I'm aching everywhere, lately.* She rubbed her toes and closed her eyes, and leaned her head back.

"Is that the doorbell? You're kidding me." She pulled herself up out of the softness of her seat and, passing the kitchen window, saw the van with large bold letters: *Ocean Floral.*

The delivery boy standing outside the front door barely looked old enough to drive, and she assumed he must have pulled into the wrong driveway. She opened the door with hesitation, ready to direct him elsewhere. His one hand was posed, ready to knock; his other held a huge bouquet.

One whiff and she knew. "Lilacs," she said softly, her heart melting on the spot.

"Yeah, I think so," the boy said.

"So, I guess you do have the right address."

She totally forgot about her aches and pains while she moved toward the kitchen, searching through cabinets for a vase. "Perfect." She snatched up the chartreuse and violet vase she'd delicately painted with intricate sprigs of baby's breath. It brought back the romantic memory of when she had worked on it, so happy in love that first year. Michael sending her flowers when she least expected them.

Quickly, she reached for the card and read the words: *Angel Face*, the endearment he used to call her when they were dating. "I remember the days when you wore lilacs in your hair and that day at the park, lying in the grass, studying the clouds."

Oh my God, of course I remember, too. It was like yesterday.

Angela remembered that day vividly. It was the end of the first summer they met in 1969. She and Michael were kissing, laughing, and sharing short-lived memories of Woodstock. They were so young, disallowing negative thoughts about Sylvie trying to separate them for being "different" from one another.

They remembered how Hendrix had turned his electric guitar into a bomb-making machine, not knowing that Michael would end up in Vietnam. Michael's head was on her lap. His body was relaxed. He had no war scars yet. He drifted off to sleep as she stroked his soft hair. Angela felt her body go limp thinking of his touch.

She especially remembered studying the one cloud with the wings. It reminded Angela of her sister, Anna, who had died unexpectedly. She would tell Michael about Anna some other day.

Angela often thought about her sister, while she was in the ocean; long tendrils of hair flowing among seaweed, how her mother must have felt when the child let go of her hand at the water's edge. Angela had to shake the image of Anna's red pail moving back and forth with the waves.

Angela sat alone with her TV dinner balancing on a wobbly snack table, watching a game show on television. With an artist's eye, she sorted the colors of the food on the tinfoil tray—the pink ham in the center, the green peas to the left, and the red potatoes to the right. *I'd much rather do a painting of this mush than eat it. All I need is some linseed oil.* The phone rang.

"Hi, I'm checking up on you. Are you okay?" her mother asked.

Angela knew the idea of her being alone at the beach house while Michael was on his book tour didn't sit well with her mother. And she also knew her mother was curious if she'd heard from Michael.

"Michael sent me a beautiful bouquet of lilacs," Angela offered right away.

"Aww, see, he's still a romantic." Her mother sounded emotional, a tell-tale sign that she had been worrying about them. "You know, I wanted to tell you something, or ask you something . . . Hmm, funny I forget now what it was. Probably not too important. Finish your dinner, honey, and I'll call you back if I think of it. Or else I'll call you tomorrow after my card game."

They hung up simultaneously.

Immediately, the phone rang again and Angela quickly picked up.

"Hi, Mom," she giggled. "You remembered?"

"How did you know it was me?" Sylvie asked.

Angela swallowed hard. Without letting herself think, she hung up on her mother-in-law. The black phone rang again and again until she finally picked it up.

"Please, please let me talk to you, Angela," Sylvie pleaded. "You don't even have to say a word, okay? . . . I hear you breathing. I know you're still there, so I'll just talk."

Angela could hear her blowing her nose, probably because she'd been crying. Sylvie was a calculating crier. Angela hadn't talked to the woman since that night the money had disappeared.

"I need to explain myself. I know you think I'm a despicable person. Who could steal from their own children?" she started. "Especially if it cost you the adoption you were counting on."

Angela covered her uneaten TV dinner with the foil and leaned back into her chair, knocking over the snack table. "Shit."

"I know. I know I'm shit. I'm sorry," Sylvie said.

Angela couldn't help but smile. The way she said *shutt* instead of *shit* with her Dutch accent, the way she misinterpreted things. She let Sylvie go on, thinking it was probably the same explanation she had told Michael over lunch recently. And how she had tried to win the money back, but failed.

"I hope you're still listening, because there's more. Michael doesn't even know. And I don't want him to ever know."

"Know what?" Angela snapped.

"I overdosed on sleeping pills a couple of weeks before Michael came to visit me."

"And you want me to forgive you for that, too?"

"You don't believe me, do you?"

Angela breathed into the phone, disgusted. "You're telling me you planned this?"

"Yes, it was deliberate."

"I believe you. I believe you, Sylvie, goddamn it . . . because it's another selfish act on your part." Angela shifted in her seat, trying not to get too emotional.

"I know. And I don't want sympathy. I want you to know why I changed my mind when it was almost too late."

"I don't care, Sylvie," Angela managed to say in between silent tears.

"It was because of you."

"Me? Oh, brother. This is getting really interesting," Angela sniped.

"When I started having trouble breathing, I was coming in and out of sleep. I felt too weak to pick up the phone, yet somehow I did and managed to dial. I called for help. In the distance I heard sirens, thought I was hallucinating. I heard the voices of the emergency people ... were they really referring to me? 'Shallow breathing, weak pulse, cold, clammy skin ... did you check her pressure, her reflexes?' Something about pumping my stomach ... Then I slipped away and I saw your face. You were happy. You were holding something. Then I heard the baby cry."

"It's only a dream, Sylvie."

"Then, I felt a stethoscope. Where was I? I was shaking, having a seizure, I guess. I almost went into a coma. The doctor later told me that my heart had almost stopped."

"Okay, enough. I get it ... it's my fault," Angela said through tears. "I'm supposed to feel guilty. Well, damn it, Sylvie, didn't you know I really loved you all along, no matter what?"

Sylvie burst into tears. "I don't blame you. I'm a terrible person, that's what I am. May I come see you? May I? I know Michael's away and you must be lonely."

Angela looked at the lilacs and softened. "When are you thinking of coming?"

"Tomorrow."

"Tomorrow?" Angela winced.

"Wouldn't that work out for you? It's Saturday."

"Actually, I'm going to a Tupperware party in the neighborhood."

"You call that a neighborhood?"

Angela grimaced. She knew Sylvie was right. There was a limited number of women anywhere near her age on that street. Most of them were wealthy and had renovated their beach cottages into two-story mansions.

"How about Sunday?"

She couldn't believe she was agreeing to this, but she knew how happy this would make Michael.

"See you Sunday, then. And by the way, I wouldn't mind a cake holder."

Barbara showed their neighbor Gail where everything was set up in the dining room. "Hi, Barbara," Angela said. "I'm a few minutes late."

"Better late than never," Barbara commented.

A Tupperware representative was jotting down items selected in her notes and rang up totals on her calculator.

"Okay, girls, let's finish this up and go enjoy that delicious-looking dessert."

Angela was the last one in line. When she saw how much the cake holder cost, she went to put back the items she was going to get for herself.

"Is that it, then?" the woman asked, obviously annoyed. "You changed your mind on the mixing bowls? They're only twelve dollars and they'll last forever."

She dug deeper into her pocketbook.

The woman leaned in closer to show Angela the total on the calculator. "If you get both the mixing bowls and the cake holder, this is what it comes to—"

"Oh. Gee, I forgot about the tax," Angela rubbed one shoe against the back of her leg, embarrassed she couldn't afford more. "Sorry, I don't have enough."

"You're putting them back?" The woman flipped her calculator closed and stood.

"Those cream puffs are scrumptious," a buxom woman interrupted. "And how are you, Angela? I haven't seen you in quite a while. Have you put on weight?"

Angela put back the cream puff she had on her plate. The only other choices were cheesecake, chocolate éclairs, and brownies. Not a carrot in sight.

"Where'd Barbara set up the coffee pot?" she asked, changing the subject.

"In the kitchen next to the fridge."

She headed toward the aroma and saw that the pot was blocked by a group of women adding sugar and cream to their cups.

"Oh, Angela, we were just talking about you." Yvonne poked her lightly with her fork.

"You were?" Angela said, forcing a shy smile.

"Yes, we're all wondering whatever happened with that adoption thing?"

"You mean, she still can't get pregnant?" Angela heard someone whisper.

"Shhh, she'll hear you," one of the gossipers said.

"So, tell me, Judy, how is that little one of yours?" Angela asked.

"Oh my God, he's the light of my life. Pictures . . . I have lots of pictures," she said, retrieving them from her purse. "He's already nine months now. The time is certainly zipping by."

Angela placed her empty coffee cup on the counter and then slipped out the back door. She was glad she had chosen to walk to the party, happy to breathe in the fresh salt air and escape the cattiness. She wept the whole way home.

Ahhh, how I love the sea air. Then she thought of Sylvie coming the next day and cried even harder, talking to herself out loud. "Ahhh, Sylvie. Sylvie and her stupid cake holder," she moaned, with the plastic item bumping into her leg with each step.

For some reason, her mother-in-law seemed different. *Could she have finally changed for the better? Finally grown up a little?* Regardless of whatever happened, Angela was grateful their time together was peaceful. It was comforting having "family" nearby.

Sylvie didn't bring up anything that would annoy her daughter-in-law. They dragged their wooden chairs closer to the shore and spent a lovely day together, sitting by the water with a thermos of hot tea and pastries filling Sylvie's new cake holder. Sylvie even let sand get in her shoes. They moved stiffly in their jackets.

"What are these chairs called, again?" Sylvie asked.

"Adirondacks." Angela breathed deeply, her face pointed up at the sun.

"Oh, *adri-onicks*. I knew that," Sylvie said.

Angela laughed and felt a sudden closeness. Sometimes she really loved this woman. But it wasn't easy.

Chapter 15

Michael read from his book, peeking up at the bookstore audience in between words. Some in the crowd were Vietnam vets wearing their hero medals.

He read passages about nature, about the boy, Tsan. He noticed one girl in the front row who had dark eyes like his wife's. He wondered if Angela had gotten the flowers he sent, wondered if she was thinking about him. Or was she thinking about that other guy?

He read an excerpt through blurry vision.

"I ran through the trees, holding the boy on my back with his bony frame weighing less than my knapsack. We didn't run in fear that day. I was his playmate. For only a few minutes, we tried to forget what was going on around us. He trusted me, a strange man from a strange land. We were prey, like two animals in the jungle, yet one entity as God had planned, soaking in the rays of sunshine that filtered between the dense leaves.

"We spoke few words as we ran in and out of the river, splashing one another, hiding behind tree trunks, jumping out in surprise . . . the same places I had poked stiff bodies with the end of my bayonet.

"He grabbed my hand and looked up to me. 'Mikeel. I like playing with you very much. Can I go be with you to America?' he asked.

"I looked at his spirited face, wearing the Mickey Mantle T-shirt I had given him. Maybe I misled him into thinking that the world was a good place, at least where I come from. I neglected to tell him it's also a world of false hope.

"'We will always be friends,' I told the beautiful boy. 'No matter where we are.' I think he knew what I meant by that. We continued playing, both pretending that anything was possible.

"'You and me, we go to the Yankee Stay-dum.' 'You bet,' I answered, patting his head. Someday.

"Playtime was over. Two animals left the fantasy behind and, together, watched the jungle transform into hell again."

The days of being on the book tour had passed slowly and been excruciating for Michael. As he dialed his home number, it occurred to him how empty Angela must have felt down in Florida during the holidays without him. It didn't matter if he was ready to be there or not—he should have at least called her. He'd apologized, but there was so much to make up for because of his post-traumatic stress.

I've been so wrong about so many things. She didn't deserve my mood swings. No wonder she needed someone else when she was lonely . . . I pushed her into his arms.

"Michael, thank you again for the lovely bouquet of lilacs." Angela let the phone rest on her neck. "This is the third time now. I wish you weren't wasting so much money."

"Flowers for you are not a waste. Besides, sales are great. The people are great. Everything's great. Except that you're not here with me . . . Ange, I can't tell you how much I miss you."

Angela took in all his affection with every phone call, yet did not reciprocate. He was glad he had to work for it. Late at night he'd reminisce with her while they both lay in their separate beds, miles apart, talking mostly about the past, sharing their joy over nature, the beach, the gulls and the ocean spray.

Then, somehow, he let it all out—how much he loved her. How sorry he was. How he couldn't blame her for finding someone else. "I saw you, you know."

"Saw me? What do you mean, saw me? When?"

"At the mall a few weeks ago. With another guy."

"Huh? I wasn't with . . . ooh," she said, stunned. "Michael, oh Michael, did you think—?"

"Are you still seeing him?"

"Do you know who that was?"

"No. Should I?"

"That was Katie's brother, Billy. We ran into each other. We talked about old times, about—oh my God, no wonder—"

"Really?" He was glad she couldn't see his tears.

"How can you think that even for a minute? We've always been true blue to one another. Whenever problems came up, we still got through them. Nothing can take that from us."

"Yeah, I shouldn't have doubted you, you're right. I don't deserve you." Michael shook his head. "I remember when my mother tried to separate us, and you gave me the same lecture—about our faith in each other."

"You should never forget that, Michael. *Never!*"

After she scolded him, he said he was sorry in the smallest voice that came from the deepest place within him.

"These days apart have been helpful for us. And not just because of all the flowers, either," she joked. "It's mostly because I was afraid I lost you—your quiet mind. You slowly found your way back to me by calling every night before going off to sleep . . . talking about the things we used to feel before—you know, before all our heartache. I missed the old you."

"Yeah? Well, I missed him, too. He's back now. He came to his senses."

"Don't feel so bad about your outbursts of temper. It showed me who you are and how passionate you can be when life throws you those curves."

"I think you're trying to tell me that you forgive me."

"There's nothing to forgive. I fell in love with you because you're real in every sense of the word. And I know you. I don't need some perfect man, perfect husband. What is that?" she scoffed.

Michael laughed. "Yeah, we're not perfect by any means."

"I'm glad because I only want your honesty."

"That's not asking too much," he apologized.

"I fell in love with you because you're a dreamer," she added. "And I only know how to love dreamers. Dreamers who know what matters in life. You encouraged me to fly, to see the world. You made me believe that nothing is impossible. When I look at you, I recognize my own dreams. I see myself. You let me know who I am."

"Wow. I did all that? You sure are boosting my ego."

"Yeah, yeah, I know. Keep calling me angel face and I'll say and do anything you want."

"Anything?" he asked.

"Michael, you should know that I could never stop loving you. I wish you were here."

"I wish I was home, holding you," he said.

He thought about the day at the beach, when they were reunited after he'd returned from Nam. It was the first time she'd seen him in his wheelchair, and he felt like less of a man. She had come up behind him, wordlessly, and as if expecting her, he pulled her onto his lap. Both of them holding on to one another like they'd never let go. His eyes watered and she told him there was nothing sexier than a man that allowed himself to cry. And he did.

There were times they had cried after that, too. They cried over no life in their freshly painted nursery. But there, they mostly cried separately, neither facing the other one's pain; if they had cried together, it would've made their loss real.

"I can't wait to see you," she whispered. "I saw your mom, by the way."

"Seriously?"

"Yeah, and I let her explain everything and I forgave her. Hmm, maybe I am an angel." She laughed.

"You are," he said.

"Well, I must admit, she was on her best behavior."

"She's sweet when she wants to be sweet," he said. "But she's no angel."

Chapter 16

S ylvie skimmed the Art section of the newspaper with her finger to see which Dutch masters were showing this week. She'd been in a joyful mood ever since she saw Angela. All seemed forgiven.

As soon as Michael gets home, the three of us will be back to our old selves. He'll be happy to hear that I listened to him, and I'm getting out more. He won't believe how I got back into art so quickly. How I remembered so many facts. At the museum, standing in front of those paintings, I heard Papa's voice, felt his breath on the back of my neck . . . I felt hope. Hope for what, I don't know.

Sylvie stood before one dark piece of an interior scene with light peeking in from a small corner window, typical style of the Dutch artist. At first she was unaware of the man standing next to her, also admiring the artwork. Then she sensed something about his closeness. She nervously twisted the strap between her fingers on her shoulder bag.

"Did you say something?" he asked.

"I . . . I don't know, did I?"

He paused, stroking his chin. "You said something about what happens when they close the museum at night."

"Oh, I thought I was saying that to myself."

He laughed. "We all do that sometimes."

Sylvie liked his profile as he continued looking at the artwork. His starched white shirt had cranberry pinstripes, and he wore neatly styled salt-and-pepper sideburns. He was older than her, she guessed maybe by ten years.

"So, what happens when they close the museum at night?"

"Don't laugh," she said. "I imagine all the people—the peasants, farmers, gypsies, to the dukes and earls and kings and queens— stepping out of the canvases they've been stuck in for centuries."

"At midnight, of course," he said.

"Of course." She smiled and felt a sudden shyness come over her. Something fluttered inside her chest.

"I especially enjoy the Dutch depiction of everyday life."

"It's incredible, isn't it?" Sylvie moved toward the scene, pointing out more detail. "They were influenced by the Italians, especially Caravaggio."

"Really?" He seemed impressed. They discussed the genre at length and then began walking in the same direction.

Sylvie was disturbed when they stood in front of a boat scene battling rough waters; the artist captured pure fear on the faces of those aboard ship. She played a moment over again in her own head, gagging from the stench of fish on the boat she had escaped on.

"Are you all right?" He reached for her elbow but withdrew his hand.

"Yes," she said, instantly shaking off the mental image as she searched the depths of his eyes. "I'm fine."

"I can see you really study the artist's interpretation. Are you an artist? A professor of art?"

"Me? No, I'm just a lover of art."

"I am, too," he said. "I'm not nearly as knowledgeable as you. Sometimes I join the guided tours, sometimes I bring my own books on the subject. I come here every Friday, yearning to learn more."

"If you have such a strong passion for something, you will get what you want from it." She didn't tell him she was thinking of when she was a kid, studying books on art to impress her father.

"Well, perhaps we will meet again in this very spot." He looked into her eyes, turned away, and they went off in different directions.

"Perhaps," she said to the empty air.

On the way home, she felt a skip in her step, like she was sixteen again.

A few days had passed. Sylvie looked at the calendar. Michael would be coming home soon. She felt anxious, ready to do something. *Anything but shopping*, she thought, now that she was actually trying to save money. *Saving* was never a part of her vocabulary until she came so close to losing the kids forever. She had to think of them first, and soon, she would have enough money to pay back what she had taken from the envelope under their mattress.

She couldn't shake that man at the museum out of her head. She wondered if her friend Cynthia was right about having romantic feelings again in her lifetime. Seemed impossible. She almost picked up the phone to call her, but she knew if she did, Cynthia would ask a million questions. Sylvie hadn't even asked him his name. *And what did he say? He goes to the museum every week? What day of the week? Did he mention what day of the week?*

She paced her living room thinking about him, trying to talk herself out of such foolishness. Then she remembered, heard his voice in her head. *"I come here every Friday, yearning to learn more..."*

"Oh my God, it's Friday. Today is Friday."

She took a quick shower, reached inside her closet and grabbed the first skirt and a sheer ivory blouse that complemented her complexion. For a split second, she realized that it didn't matter what she wore—not to someone like him, whatever his name was. *He was really looking at* me *that day, not at what I wore. And he listened to me talking about the art, as if he respected me.*

Even stranger than that—Sylvie heard him, too. She was actually listening, and that was something she was never proficient at—

whether a result of her hearing loss or not. There must have been a reason she was tuned in to this stranger.

Sylvie craned her neck, searching for him. She tried to recall specifics about his appearance that day, mostly recalling his chiseled profile. There was that moment, though; they seemed to stare into each other's eyes. She shivered, started to panic that she would never find him again. She looked hard at a man about his height, also with salt-and-pepper hair.

"I thought you were someone else," she said.

"People say that all the time," he laughed. He looked her up and down, and it gave her the creeps. After a couple of hours passed, she was almost ready to give up and leave the museum; then she stopped in front of a sensual-looking painting by Peter Paul Rubens called *The Union of Earth and Water*. She sighed.

Was that her father's breath again at the back of her neck? "Do you think they're lovers?" A man's voice startled her.

Sylvie jumped. "It's you."

"Sorry."

She was right about his eyes. They were deep and sensitive.

"What did you ask?" She felt a wide smile about to cross her lips but held back, not wanting to appear too anxious. "Do I think they're lovers? Hmm, being such a romantic, I believe they are, yes." *Cynthia should hear me,* she thought. "Do you? Think they're lovers?"

"Not a doubt in my mind. I've studied this work before—her gentle curves, her pale white figure connected to his darker figure."

"Yes," Sylvie said. "Do you see the way Cybele looks at Neptune, the god of the sea? Her posture is so relaxed. She looks at him as if nothing in the world matters but him. I love the swirling composition and placement of the flowers and fruits, the way the cloth drapes across their nakedness. Rubens idolized the Venetian artists—it shows in his work."

Sylvie realized she was talking too much and abruptly stopped to study his face as if it were another canvas hanging on the museum walls. She watched his lips moving and imagined what it would feel like to have them lingering over hers.

"I'm sorry . . . maybe because you're not answering me, I am being too presumptuous."

"What?"

He cleared his throat. "I asked if you would like to join me for coffee later."

"You did? I didn't hear you . . . that's because you're on my left side and that's my—" She decided not to tell him about her bad ear; it would only age her.

"If you have somewhere else to go—"

"No, I would love coffee. I would love lunch even more."

"That's what I was going to get to next. I guess I should ask what your name is, first." They both laughed. "Mine is Roger."

"Roger, I'm Sylvie." She extended her hand.

Together, they left the museum and talked over coffee, lunch, dinner, and visited the top of the Empire State Building, which Sylvie insisted was the most romantic place in all of Manhattan.

"So, I can't believe you're Dutch. That's cheating a little, you know," he teased, as they looked out over the twinkling lights of the city. "You're cold. Here, take my jacket."

Sylvie wasn't really cold, but it felt heavenly when he slipped his suit jacket over her shoulders and gave her a squeeze. They talked about everything as if they were running out of time. She did not and would not tell him about possibly getting back any family artwork. She wanted him to like her for who she was, finally beginning to understand what Michael had preached over the years about what's on the inside.

They spent the next week together at lunch and dinner.

Sylvie couldn't dial Cynthia's number fast enough. "His name is Roger."

"Sylvie? You sound so excited. Everything alright?"

"Oh, it's very exciting, and you were right. I'm in love. And his name is Roger. We've been seeing each other now every single day."

"That's wonderful. For how long?"

"Nine and a half days."

"Oh."

"Cynthia, it doesn't matter how long. I feel something. I haven't felt this something in a long, long time."

"*Mazel-tov*," Cynthia said. "I'll pray this works out for you. So, what is he like?"

"Well, he's an architect, lives in Manhattan, a widower with one grown child, a daughter who lives in Virginia where he was born and raised. He has seven brothers and sisters, loads of nieces and nephews all living there. He's tall and has broad shoulders, his hair is speckled with gray, and he usually wears a bowtie."

"A bowtie?"

"Yes. He's not into designer anything. He has his own style."

"Hmm . . . maybe a cure for your obsession."

"Funny you should say that. I'm going through a little withdrawal, but I am not shopping much anymore."

"Ha, that'll be the day, my friend."

"I mean it."

"Wow. This does sound serious."

"And he loves music, plays the harmonica."

"The harmonica, really?"

"Yes. The blues. Also, he knows a lot about art. I met him at the museum. He also reads a lot and belongs to a book club. He devours mysteries. He's a big fan of 1940s noir films. And, oh, how can I forget—he recently became a grandfather."

"This is great news, Sylvie. Next, you'll be calling me about your grandbaby."

"Oh, how I wish that for the kids." She hesitated. "I have to share a secret with you. I've been praying, praying for them to have a baby.

Every night when my head hits the pillow, that's what I ask for in my prayers—for their baby. And for the first time in decades, I'm sleeping soundly. Who knew? Praying is a cure for insomnia."

"God must be in a state of shock since—*Wait!* Don't touch that outlet!" Cynthia yelled to her grandchild. "Why is it that they always go for electricity?"

"They do?" For a second she wondered how Michael survived as a toddler.

"Gotta go, Sylvie."

"And one more thing about Roger. He's—Hello? Cynthia?"

Chapter 17

Angela sat on the family room couch reading *To Kill a Mockingbird*. Her concentration was broken by a rustling sound near the front door. She set down her book and retrieved the baseball bat she kept hidden under the couch in case of intruders.

She tiptoed to the front door to sneak a peek out of one of the stained-glass panels flanking it and spotted a brown cardboard box on the ground with a pretty, lavender bow. No longer frightened, she put the bat down and opened the door a crack. "What in the world?" She squealed as she looked into the box. "A puppy!"

She picked up the shaggy-haired pup and cuddled it to her neck, stroking it. The puppy licked her neck and cried.

"Aw. Where did you come from, little fellow?" She held the dog up to her face and noticed the feminine color of its collar. "I mean, little girl?"

"Michael, I know you did this," she called. "You're the only one around here who knows my favorite color. Where are you?"

He stepped out from behind the bushes. "I wish you saw the look on your face when you opened the box."

"Oh my God! I'm so happy to see the dog. And see you." She wanted to jump in Michael's arms, but didn't feel spry enough to do it at the moment, especially with the weight of the puppy in her arms.

"I'm so glad to see how happy she makes you."

"Where did you get her?"

"At the pound. She's pure mutt. Isn't she a great dog? Look at the size of those paws. They say she's not even a year old and she's housebroken. Her owner was evicted or something and they were about to put her down and—"

"Shut up," she said, grabbing Michael and kissing his lips."

"Wow. If this one little dog makes you so happy, there's cages full of—"

Angela started crying.

"Are those happy tears?"

"I'm so happy you're back and so happy about the puppy." She stalled. "But I haven't been feeling well. I took the day off tomorrow to go see a doctor."

He took the dog from her. "What's wrong? And why haven't you told me this?"

She placed her palm along her lower abdomen. "I'm having a lot of pressure, here, like a brick. I didn't want to upset you while you were away, so I figured I'd wait for you to come home and then tell you."

His face paled. "I bet it's some kind of a stomach virus you picked up from the kids at school again. What time's your appointment? I'll drive you there."

"No, I'm not making you go with me. You have so much work to catch up on, don't you?"

"You're my wife. You come first."

"Are you sure? The appointment's at ten. What about the newspaper? And what about her?"

They both looked down at the puppy, who stared up at them with contentment. "What harm could she do?" he said. "It's not like we have valuable furniture or anything, if she decides to chew on something."

"True," she said, considering the pretty floral pillows on her couch. "Hey, what should we name her?"

"We have a lot on our minds tonight. We'll come up with a name for her tomorrow."

While driving to the doctor the following morning, Angela said, "I've got it!"

"Got what?" Michael asked.

"The collar that she came with. The color. Let's call her Violet."

"I like it. Sweet little Violet."

"There." She pointed. "That must be it, on the right—the brick building. Peconic Medical."

"Okay," he said, pulling into the parking lot. "There's a spot right by the entrance. How are you feeling, hon?"

"Ask the butterflies in my stomach." She grimaced.

After filling out the paperwork and dealing with the usual tension of the waiting room, Angela's name was finally called. "Please don't take offense, Michael, but I'd like to talk to the doctor alone for a few minutes about my symptoms. I'll forget what I want to say because you'll make me too nervous."

"Me? I make you nervous?"

"Well, we make each other nervous. We're very much alike."

"True."

"If it's bad news, you won't be able to hide what you're thinking and it'll make me crazy."

"Okay, don't forget to call me in as soon as you're done with your talk with the doctor."

Angela was led to the examining room door by an unsmiling frumpy nurse who handed Angela a white paper gown. "You can get undressed and the doctor will be in shortly."

The nurse re-entered. "I'm going to take your blood pressure now," she said. "Pressure's on the high side." She stuck a thermometer in Angela's mouth. She made a few notations in Angela's chart and removed the thermometer. "Normal."

"Really? That's not what my friends tell me."

Still, no smile. "Get on the scale, please."

"Oh, not the scale," Angela said in a dramatic voice, trying to get a reaction.

"You have something against scales?"

"Only since I gained ten pounds," Angela said.

Dr. Hirsch entered the room.

"Good morning, Miss—excuse me, *Mrs.* Beckman. How are you? I'm Dr. Hirsch."

"Good morning, Doctor." Angela said nervously. "My friend at work recommended you."

He smiled. "I see on your chart that you've been feeling fatigued, with stomach pain, and your feet ache? So, what's up?"

"I'm an art teacher. I'm on my feet all day." The nurse rolled her eyes, unsympathetically, and left the room.

"Uh-huh." He pulled down her lower eyelids and flashed a small light into them.

"Sometimes I ache everywhere." Angela's eyes started welling with tears. "Sorry," she said, holding her hand up. "Did you write that down, too? That I laugh and cry at the same time?"

He motioned for her to lie back on the exam table. "Rest your head on the pillow. I'm going to press down, so let me know if I hit a tender spot."

She felt his fingers kneading her stomach like a circle of dough. "That's where the brick is. What is it? My appendix? Gallbladder?"

"Hey, who's the doctor here?"

She sat up again.

"Your blood pressure's a little high. Aside from that, all your vitals are good. I could run a test or two, but you know what? I feel this is a gynecological issue and I should send you to see a colleague of mine. He's got a great reputation. After you get dressed, we'll talk. By the way, is that your husband climbing the walls in the waiting room?"

"Oh, Michael? Um, tall, sandy blond hair, madras shirt, green sneakers?"

"Yeah, pretty sure about all that, except for the shoes." They both laughed.

"I'll tell him to come in," he offered.

Angela's mind was racing as she got back into her comfy blue jogging suit. She was relieved she wasn't dying but wondered why he was sending her to a colleague for a "female issue."

Michael and the doctor entered at the same time. "Is my wife okay, Doctor?"

"Michael, I'm fine." Angela reassured him.

"I was telling your wife that I'd like her to see a colleague of mine. In fact, I'll walk you there. His office is right down the hall."

"Oh boy," Angela sighed. "Two doctors in one day."

"No offense." Michael grinned. "Angela doesn't like anything to do with doctors or hospitals or blood—that sort of thing."

"Sometimes I feel the same way," Dr. Hirsch joked. "Follow me," he said and led them down the hallway to a glass door marked OB/GYN.

"I'll go in ahead," Michael said, "and put your name down."

Angela grabbed the doctor's arm. "It's not a tumor, is it?"

He put his hand on her shoulder and gave her a paternal look. "No, I'm sure it's nothing to worry about. You'll be in good hands with Dr. Fisher. He is somewhat reserved. From Germany—very meticulous."

Angela turned the doorknob and entered the office, joining Michael, who had already started filling out more paperwork. "I got as far as your name and address. After that, I'm clueless."

She smacked his arm. "You're no help." She took the pen and answered the same questions she had answered many times before at other doctors' offices. "If they graded us on this stuff, I'd ace it."

"Something to aspire to, heh?" Michael teased.

As they waited in the gynecologist's office watching pregnant women of all sizes coming and going, they didn't say much. Instead of feeling her usual pang of jealousy around mothers-to-be, Angela was giddy and started to laugh. The other women in the room ignored her and kept their eyes on the magazines they were reading.

"What's so funny?" Michael asked.

"I thought of Violet. We gave her such a calm name. I sure hope it suits her. Maybe she's the destructive type and we should have named her Beast."

Michael tried to shush her, but then broke into laughter himself. "I can see it now—the lamps and tables are upside down, the pictures are off the walls—"

"And the stuffing is hanging out of the couches . . ."

A few minutes later a receptionist called for Angela.

"Good luck. I love you," Michael said.

Angela shook her head as she came back into the waiting room. "Dr. Fisher didn't have much to say, the usual probing and testing," she said, taking a seat next to Michael's. "He was quite thorough, though."

"Not fun, heh?"

She twisted her mouth in agreement. "Not fun at all. They'll call me back in soon and suggested you come, too." She inhaled deeply. "What if—"

"Promise no more with the *what ifs*. Let's just get this day over with."

Dr. Fisher glided into the room, his stethoscope hanging over his clinical white coat, and immediately shook Michael's hand. "Nice to meet you, Mr. Beckman. Why don't you both have a seat?"

"How's Angela, Doctor? How's my wife?"

"She's fine," he said. "They're both fine."

"Both?"

"Your wife and the baby," the doctor said, jotting down something in his pad.

"*Baby?*" Michael and Angela responded in unison.

Michael toppled into the tall glass jar on the counter, knocking cotton swabs onto the floor, catching the jar before it came crashing down. "Sorry." He attempted to pick them up and replace them.

"Leave them; it's okay. I'm guessing you two didn't know you were expecting?"

Michael and Angela looked at each other. "It's impossible," Michael said.

Angela didn't make eye contact with her husband, and for a second wondered if he thought she really was having an affair. Then she directed a question to Dr. Fisher. "How can that be? We haven't been, you know, together, in a while."

"Maybe you're further along than you think. These things happen," he said, going on in detail with a scientific explanation as the two of them sat there, open mouthed, holding hands.

"Dr. Fisher." The nurse stepped into the room. "Dr. Meyers is on line two."

"Excuse me for a minute, please."

They were both speechless alone in the room. Michael touched Angela's tummy and stared into her eyes. "Oh my God, Angela." Angela covered her quivering lips with one hand, her eyes filling up. Michael wiped her cheek dry, and then his. "You've never been more beautiful."

"I don't know what I'm . . . no wonder I've been feeling this way, the nausea, the weight gain, the crying." She laughed. "I didn't know being pregnant can make you turn into an insane person."

"This is what we've dreamt of, Ange. I know it's hard to believe, but it's finally happening."

"I don't quite understand. I hope everything's all right."

"Everything is all right," Michael said. "In fact, it's perfect."

❧

They practically floated on the car ride home, talking about the furniture they'd pick out for the nursery. "I think we should look for a honey-color wood, which will work for either a boy or a girl."

"You can buy whatever you'd like for the baby. And then we'll have to start saving for his or her college soon, too."

Angela lightly slapped his shoulder. "Oh, Michael, let's not rush his little life away."

Angela and Michael walked into their house, thinking the worst. Violet was sitting on the couch, with its stuffing still in place, paws crossed, and relaxed.

"Aw, what a good dog," Angela said. "Everything's intact. Oops! Is that your belt, Michael? Or what's left of it?"

Michael tossed the belt aside and scanned the room. "At least she is housebroken. Now, I want you to rest and put your feet up." He pointed to the couch and Angela took a seat next to the dog.

"Funny," she said. "Out of nowhere, we're going to be a real family, not just in a house, but in a real home with a dog and a baby."

Michael went to make her a cup of hot tea as she relaxed on the couch. She picked up the telephone to share the news with her mother.

"I don't know exactly how to interpret the doctor's explanation. He said sometimes this happens, especially when women under stress miss their periods as much as I have. They may not know they're pregnant for the first few months. That and also because I ignored the symptoms. I thought I was suffering from bad indigestion and was irritable because I was worried about Michael going away."

"You need to get plenty of rest, honey. How far along are you?"

"Almost five months, and I had no idea! Can you believe it? The doctor said this sometimes happens to women; it's a condition called amenorrhea."

"Oh, Angela," her mother cried. "This is so wonderful." She heard her mom call her dad into the room to share the news. He got on the phone and said, "We're going to be grandparents? This is the best news I've heard in a long time!"

"Yeah, Dad. Get your tools ready. You have a lot to teach him or her in that special space you go to—where you fix things, where you create—"

Her father choked up. "Now you're the great creator," he said. After hanging up, Angela reached for the phone again, with Violet lying across her lap.

"Now who are you calling?"

"I can't wait to tell Katie. Then we'll call your mom."

When she was on the phone with Katie, she provided a little more information that she had withheld from her mother. "The doctor said the baby's small and inactive and is toward the back of my uterus. That's another reason I didn't know I was pregnant. I'm kinda worried that—"

"Angela, I know you. Please don't go worrying yourself into a frenzy."

"You're right. I'll try to keep positive about everything. However, I'm not so sure about this doctor because he's not very talkative. Without saying much at all, he sent me home with a bunch of baby literature."

"Are you thinking of switching doctors?"

"I don't think it's a smart idea to find a new doctor, because I'm already getting a late start. I think I'll just stick it out with him. How bad can he be?"

Chapter 18

Angela stroked Violet's coat, talking to the dog as she did almost every morning after Michael left for his job at the newspaper. Between stepping up his hours at the job and promoting his new book, he was gone more, and she was grateful for the dog's company.

"You were meant to be," she said. "We rescued each other."

Her folks had come from Florida and stayed for a week, leaving the day after Mother's Day. Emotions ran high for all of them because as Angela began her seventh month, she started to bleed.

"We'll turn right around and come back to New York," her mother insisted. Angela told her she'd rather wait for her to return as soon as the baby was born. "I'll need your help more later on, Mom."

Following Dr. Fisher's orders, she had taken a medical leave from teaching and intended to stay on complete bed rest for the remainder of her pregnancy. Grace called once in a while to fill her in on any school gossip; aside from that, she was completely cut off. And she didn't care. Her whole world would be the love she could give to her child, a life full of laughter and hope, and yes, dreams.

With so much idle time on her hands, Angela got inside her head a lot—"an inward journey," Michael called it. She would be responsible for raising her child as a Jew or a Catholic. She and

Michael had discussed which religion to raise their child, but since neither of them had practiced their own religion, they agreed to raise the child in a more spiritual way with kindness and finding the beauty around them. She didn't feel God's presence in a church or a temple. She reminded herself that Jesus Christ himself was against organized religion.

Soon, they'd teach their own creation about the spirit of God by simply encouraging him or her to be a good person. Every day, they'd remind their child that God was all around them . . . the leaves on the trees, the butterflies in the wind, the foam on the waves.

She closed her eyes and dozed off.

After her nap, she flipped through the high-risk pregnancy books again. She hated being labeled as "high risk." *Everything will be fine with my baby. I know it*, she thought. Like the puppy, she believed this baby was meant to be.

She started reading about complications, which included an article by Dr. Gloria Kingsley, titled "Don't Be Alarmed, Mommy." By the end of the chapter, however, she was scared silly by all the things that could go wrong. She ripped the page out of the book, crumpled it into a ball, and threw it across the room, missing the wastepaper basket. She looked at the accumulated pile and sighed.

Aside from the intermittent bleeding, Angela was also at risk because of a few other factors, including an unusually small uterus. She did her best to stay still, but the bed rest was pure torture, and she constantly turned from side to side. Her doctor had warned her that if she didn't comply with his rules, she could end up in the hospital.

With the exception of trips to the bathroom, Angela remained horizontal. Michael left a cooler filled with snacks beside her bed whenever he knew he'd be out for hours at a time. "No excuses," he warned her. "You and the baby must stay put."

He even installed a doggie door for Violet so Angela wouldn't have to bother letting her in and out. From her bedroom window, Angela could see the dog romping on the beach, running and splashing in the waves, digging in the sand, and basking in the sunshine. She imagined how all four of them would do that on the beach when summer came.

The minute hand on the clock seemed to be going backward, and the ticking got louder. The best part of her day was watching Violet outside where Angela longed to be. She sketched the dog running back and forth with her tongue hanging out one side of her mouth.

Michael called almost every hour from the paper; sometimes he had to go on the road. On those days, he'd arrange for a retired visiting nurse to check up on her. He was concerned whenever her blood pressure was high. The RN would also check for blood clots in her legs as the weeks progressed.

"You should massage them whenever you can, to keep the circulation going. I know this isn't easy, sweetheart," the nurse had said. "Bed rest also helps decrease pressure on the cervix and increases blood flow to the placenta."

She felt squeamish at the word *placenta* and suppressed thoughts of labor and hearing herself scream. She'd have plenty of time to study up another time. She marked the calendar, checking off how many days were left until her projected due date. Michael used to tell her how he had marked off the days on his calendar when he was in Vietnam. He had told her that every day he put another check mark, he was closer to going home. Every day that Angela checked off, their baby was closer to home, too.

While on the phone with Katie, Angela confessed her fears.

"I'm really getting scared now. In fact, I'm an emotional wreck."

"Normal," Katie told her.

"I'm feeling twinges."

"Normal."

"Is that your answer to everything?" Angela asked.

"When I was pregnant, I questioned every little thing. And it's all normal. Do yourself a favor and stop worrying. I'm sure your doctor is taking good care of you."

"Hmm." Angela didn't sound convinced.

"What else?" Katie read into her sighing.

"I had a bad dream," Angela divulged. "I didn't tell anyone about it, but I'm telling you."

"Go on," Katie urged.

"I dreamt the baby was stillborn."

"Oh, Ange. That's your subconscious dealing with your fears."

"See, that's not so normal, is it? I should be having delightful dreams now, shouldn't I? I mean, I've been waiting for this baby forever. Why should I be thinking negatively? It's because of all these damn baby books. I stopped reading them, yet they're still haunting me. Why can't they give us the books we had as kids, when the stork delivered babies?"

"I know all that information can make you crazy," Katie agreed. "Once I dreamt the baby was born with two heads. Now that I think about it, I guess that meant twins."

They both laughed.

"I'm coming to visit you as soon as I can get a babysitter to handle the two of them. I had to fire my last sitter."

"Why don't you bring them? I can't wait to see them again."

"Are you kidding? They won't let you get much rest, believe me. They have tons of energy. I love every minute with them. You'll see. You'll love every minute with—what's his or her name? Come on, give me a hint."

"Honestly, we haven't picked a name yet. We want to meet him or her first, then decide on a name that fits. The baby will let us know somehow." Angela yawned. "I'm getting tired. Maybe names will come to me when I go off into la-la land again. Bye, Katie."

"Sweet dreams, little mama."

Angela woke up when she heard a noise. The dog turned her head and whimpered at the figure standing outside at the back of her house peeking into Angela's bedroom window. Angela was startled when she saw Sylvie waving and pointing to the back door, mouthing the words that she would let herself in. "Is the back door locked?"

"Oh my God, this woman is impossible!" Angela sighed. "I'll get up."

"No, don't get up. I'll figure out a way in."

Angela yelled out. "I bet you twenty bucks you can't get through the doggie door."

Sylvie casually entered the bedroom.

"How did you get in? Through the doggie door?"

"A bet's a bet. Good thing I could squeeze my skinny ass through the dog's entrance."

Angela was flabbergasted. "Get my purse over there and I'll pay up."

"Nah, my betting days are over," Sylvie said, dusting off her culottes.

Angela hadn't laughed that hard in days. "Well, it proves you have a skinny ass. I guess it also proves Violet's not a watchdog."

"What? No, she was watching me. She loves me. In fact, she started licking my face when I was about halfway through the door flap. I have dog biscuits in my pocket. Oh, and I brought you some breakfast cakes—*ontbijtkoek*," she said. "I know Michael said not to come bother you, lately, but I figured he'll be at that writer's thing for hours. The city's so far away and you are so far along. Not a brilliant idea, if you ask me. Who can you turn to for help? One of those Tupperware people?"

Angela did her best tolerating Sylvie's hearing problem and bad behavior because her feisty mother-in-law did make the time pass by quickly. It was unnerving, however, the way she sat beside her on the bed, staring at her, as if waiting for something to happen. Angela grew more uncomfortable until her anxiety kicked in and she let out a groan. "Oh . . . "

"What is it?" Sylvie asked.

"I don't know. I have a pain, that's all." She stroked her belly in circles.

"Where? Where's your pain?"

Angela gave her a look.

"Are you okay?"

"Yes, I'm fine."

After sitting in silence for a full minute, Sylvie stood and noticed the magazines and books on the chest of drawers. "What, no fashion? Where's *Vogue*?" She leafed through one of the pregnancy books and gasped at a vivid picture of a baby emerging from the birth canal. "Oh, *Scheisse*! Now, that's a sight."

Angela groaned again.

"Do you want me to call your doctor?"

"It's Braxton Hicks."

"I don't care what his name is, I'm calling him now."

"No," Angela said, shaking her head. "Braxton Hicks is false labor. My doctor's name is Fisher."

"Oh. Fischer? He's a Jew?" She grinned widely. "Jews make good doctors. And lawyers, too. Not so good at plumbing or—"

"No, he's a Ger—"

"What?"

"I said, he's a gem. A *gem* of a doctor."

"Jewish doctors are the best," Sylvie repeated.

"Sylvie, really. You're rambling on, and it's making me nuts."

"I'm sorry, sweetheart. You do have to admit, I took your mind off the pain, didn't I?" She picked up the phone and started searching through Angela's address book. "Should I make the call, or should I boil the water first, you know, like they do in the movies?"

"You are joking, I hope."

Sylvie winked. "You know I'm kidding. I never knew what they boiled the water for, anyway."

"I don't want you to call the doctor. I already told you I'm fine. I wish you would calm down."

Sylvie put the phone back down. "All right. We'll wait and see." She looked out the window at the ocean. "This room is so cozy and relaxing—*gezellig*. You and Michael ever think about doing *zwangerschaps* yoga—you know, the 'natural' way?"

Angela was impressed Sylvie was up to speed on the modern concepts of childbirth. Angela's own mother was old-fashioned.

"I didn't have much time to think about it, actually. And now that I can't leave my bed, I don't see how."

"I know when you are in labor you have to focus on something." Sylvie held up her heavy necklace on the gold chain with the letter *S* inset with diamonds. "How about this? If you have a girl, you can name her Sylvie and keep the necklace."

Angela winced. Not because of the pain, but because she pictured the sweet little naked infant's body wearing the large gaudy letter.

"You're still hurting?"

"Some discomfort in my back, that's all." Angela tried to play it down.

"I thought you said it was in your abdomen."

"It moved," Angela said.

"Lift up the back of your nightgown. I'll give you a nice massage." Sylvie came at her with a bottle of lotion.

"No, really, that's all right."

"Don't argue, young lady." Sylvie applied the lotion to her hands and tugged at the nightgown. "It will do you good. You know, you could be having back labor."

"Back labor?"

Angela exhaled and gave in, letting Sylvie rub away at her lower back with the cold lotion. *I hope she's not right. I can't have the baby yet. I'm only starting my eighth month.* Angela felt uncomfortable with her mother-in-law on her back and watched the clock on the nightstand. Sylvie started singing a song in Dutch.

Angela knew that whenever Sylvie reverted to her native language, she was usually nervous about something.

Sure enough, Sylvie stopped dead. Angela turned to see her biting on her bottom lip. "Sylvie, do you have something on your mind?

"Well, I never knew you had such small hips."

Angela pulled the back of her nightgown into place. "Wow, thanks, I feel much better now," she said, attempting to sit up. "Ouch!"

Sylvie grabbed Angela's hand. "It's okay, honey. Pant like a *hondje*."

Angela shoved her hand away. "A what? What are you talking about? What's a *hondje*?"

"A dog." Sylvie looked at Violet, lying on the carpet with her ears perked up. "You know, I hear that if you get on all fours like a dog, it makes for an easier delivery."

"Jesus, Sylvie. I am not getting on my hands and knees. It was only a paintbrush." She held up the brush to show Sylvie. "I rolled over on it. I'm not going into labor. Any other ideas?"

"Yes. Anneke swore that drinking red clover tea, as hot as you could stand—it helps. I can't remember what it helps, though."

"Who's Anneke?"

"She was a crazy neighbor in our *dorp* . . . sorry, our village in Dieren."

"And why would I want to do what a crazy person does?"

Sylvie reached for one of the books. "In case the baby has other plans, let me read some of your *bookhandel*. You got these books from the doctor's office?"

"Yeah, don't—"

"Oh my." Sylvie's eyes widened.

"What is it?"

"It says you can also bring on labor if you have sex."

"With who?" Angela was getting more irritated.

Sylvie looked out the side window. "Too late, the mail truck just went by."

"You want me to have sex with the mailman?"

"Of course not. But I did hear that a bumpy ride in a truck—"

"Can you please stop talking now? I have no more back pain, just a wicked headache."

Sylvie lowered her head. "You're tired again. Why don't you take a nice nap now and I'll go into the kitchen and make myself a cup of tea and have another one of those breakfast cakes. And then, I'll be going because Michael's on his way home from the city and it looks like Braxton is gone."

Angela pulled the covers over her head and listened to Sylvie banging around in the kitchen. She was probably spilling the sugar all over the counter, her yearly calling for bringing ants into the house. She pictured Sylvie slathering the sugary breads with loads of butter, like she usually did.

In a way, Angela enjoyed hearing someone clanking around in the kitchen. She could take Sylvie in small doses—and from a distance. If she ever did go into early labor while alone, she'd panic. At least Sylvie could drive her to the hospital. She thought twice of Sylvie's heavy foot on the gas pedal and the way she changed lanes without signaling. *Oh man, how will she ever drive my child anywhere? How can I ever trust her with my child at all? What kind of a grandmother will she be?*

Twenty-five minutes later, Sylvie told Angela she'd be heading back to Queens. "I can see tonight's not the night after all, sweetie, so I'll be going now. Besides, Michael will be back home soon—unless you want me to stay longer?"

"No! That's okay. Really," Angela said, weakly.

Sylvie came to her side and gave her a hug. "Thank you."

"Why are you thanking me?"

"Because I know you'd much rather have your own mother here, but you'd never let me know that. You made me feel like you're my real daughter today, like we're family."

"Oh, Sylvie." Angela smiled and turned over to her side under the covers.

Sylvie watched her daughter-in-law as she fell asleep in the glow of the nightlight. She started walking out of the room and then turned back as if she'd forgotten something. She hovered over Angela one more time, kissed her own fingertips, then touched them to Angela's forehead, before leaving the beach cottage with a full heart.

Chapter 19

When Michael got home it was almost dark. He entered the house through the side door in the kitchen where he knew Violet would be waiting for him to come home. He hoped she wouldn't bark and wake up Angela.

"Hey, girl," he said, placing his keys on the key rack hanging on the wall. The first thing he noticed was grains of sugar and cake crumbs all over the countertop and the bakery box, still open.

"My mother was here?" He knew she wouldn't be able to stay away, even though he had warned her not to bother Angela. *She'll probably say she didn't hear me . . . again.*

In a way he was glad she had kept Angela company; he had worried all day about her being alone. And as it turned out, every time he left the conference room to find a phone, there seemed to be someone using it.

Violet couldn't wait another second to get her greeting. Michael bent down to give her a hug as she wiggled her whole body along with her wagging tail. He loved the way dogs greeted you as if their whole meaning to life was that you'd be coming back again to give another one of those hugs. He thought of Shadow, his dog and his best friend growing up, and how that dog was always there for him when he was feeling lonely.

"What's this?" he asked the dog while opening a brown paper bag on the counter. "More of my mom's pastries?"

He opened his mouth when he saw wads of assorted bills in rubber bands. "Oh, wow." He read the enclosed note in his mother's handwriting:

> *To my children,*
>
> *For the first time in my life, I know I'm doing the right thing. I'm sorry you had to wait so long for me to realize that and I want to thank you for forgiving me beforehand. I promise, in my lifetime, I will make it up to you. Because I love you more than you will ever know.*
>
> *Mom.*

He neatly folded the note, and tucked it into his pocket, thinking it was a keeper. When he thought about it, his mother seemed like a different person lately. Still crazy, yes, but happier, warmer.

Michael kicked off his shoes in the corner of the living room and tiptoed into the master bedroom guided by the dimness of the nightlight. He wondered if Angela was nervous about being alone after his mother left. *At least having Violet around probably made her feel protected.* He watched his wife sleeping for a minute, enjoying the rhythm of her breath, the fluttering of her lashes as she dreamt. He sat on his side of the bed.

"Oh, you're home?" She stretched her legs long.

"Shhh, sorry, go back to sleep. I didn't want to wake you."

"Are you kidding? That's all I do is sleep and yet I'm so exhausted. I want to hear about your day. How'd the conference go?"

He kissed her cheek. "Great. I met some interesting people from all over the world who are on board to help sell my book, internationally. I'll tell you about them another time when I'm wide awake. It's been a long day."

"Uh-oh, that probably means you'll be going abroad next."

"We'll talk about it tomorrow."

"I bet you're tired, huh?"

"Tired's not the word."

"Well, I'd get up and fix you something to eat—but I'm not allowed," she said.

"You must be going stir crazy, heh? I'm guessing my mother's visit made things move along quicker."

"How do you know she was here?"

Michael smiled, rolling his eyes toward the kitchen.

"Right, your mom. My kitchen must be looking a little crumby."

"Don't worry, I wiped the counter clean. No ants."

"She means well, I guess. But man, she's a bundle of nervous energy. She had me thinking I was going into labor."

They both laughed.

"Can you imagine my mother playing doctor?"

"Oh, you have no idea about some of the funny things she said and did. Yet, somehow, she was kinda lovable. Do you know how she got in our house? Through the doggie door."

"Maybe I shouldn't have installed the large-size doggie door. What makes my mother funny is that she has no idea she's funny."

"Yeah, how'd you keep your sanity all those years?"

"I escaped when I went away to college. Somehow she always makes her way back." Michael looked at Violet. "Speaking of old faithful, how'd our doggie do today?"

"Michael, she's such great company. She's going to be a great friend to our baby, too."

"There's so much to look forward to, don't you think? We're in a happy place again," he said. "And once this baby comes, we'll be in an even happier place."

"Yeah, I'll be the happiest when I get this baby out of me."

"How are you feeling?"

"I had some sharp back pain today, but it passed."

"You're handling it well, then?"

"No. I'm not that brave, Michael. I'm blocking out everything that could possibly go wrong." Angela pointed to the wastebasket with the crumpled papers she tore out of the pregnancy books. "Some scary literature I'm afraid I can't face. I don't want to know anything that has to do with the hospital. I wish we could have the baby right here," she said, gazing at the half-moon outside her window. "Maybe then I'd feel more in control. I'm sorry we didn't take the Lamaze class."

He gave her a worried look. "Aww, angel face," he said, putting his arms around her. "I'm sorry I wasn't here today to help. Staying in this bed for so long has got to be getting to you. From now on I won't be traveling that far. I'll only be going into town or to the paper. That's it."

"I know you're always here for me," she said, touching her heart. "Now, you can turn the nightlight off and get the rest you need."

"By the way," he said in the darkness of the room. "Did you know that my mother returned our money?"

"Really? She did?"

Michael knew Angela was smiling in the dark. And so was he. He embraced her when she began to cry.

Michael slowly placed the phone back down, still in shock. Then he went into the bedroom with two mugs of hot tea where he found Angela sitting up in bed, sketching more poses of Violet, who was outside her window burying a tennis ball in the hole she had dug. The dog's rear end was sticking up in the air, and once in a while, she'd peek her head up, looking at the bedroom window as if she knew Angela was drawing her. Her eyelashes, mouth and nose were covered in sand.

"Who was on the phone?" She turned the sketch toward Michael to see.

"Love the pose," he said, holding the drawing. "You're not going to believe this; my mother is taking a ride out east to Montauk Point for Memorial Day weekend. But get this, she's going there with a 'boyfriend.'"

"Oh, cut it out," Angela said. "I spent the entire day with her and she didn't mention a word about a boyfriend."

"Strange, isn't it?"

"After all these years, Sylvie has a boyfriend. Well, I think it's about time. Your mother is still very attractive."

"She told me they've been seeing each other for quite a while now and didn't want to tell us until she was ready for us to meet him."

"Wow, this sounds serious."

"She also said that she loves him." Michael sat at the edge of the bed, digesting it. "I told her she can pop in for a couple of minutes since she'll be passing this way. I made her repeat after me, 'Only for a couple of minutes.'"

"Oh, I'm glad you told her to come. I wouldn't miss this for the world."

"Yeah, I've got to admit, I'm curious myself about this guy."

A couple of hours later, there was Sylvie's loud, incessant knocking on the front door. Michael was sitting on a chair next to Angela working and jumped in his seat. "Geez, that's got to be her," he said. "At least she's come to the human door this time."

Angela laughed at him. "Michael, you're barefoot. You want to make a good impression, don't you?"

He slipped into his lucky green Keds without tying the laces. "I'll be right back with my mom and God knows who."

"It'll be invigorating to see a new face. Not that there's anything wrong with yours." She winked.

Leaving the room, Michael noticed how pretty and pink Angela looked. *Have I told her that lately?*

When Michael re-entered the bedroom with his mother and the boyfriend behind him, he watched Angela's complexion turn a deeper shade of red.

"Angela, this is Roger Davis. Roger, this is Angela, and the small world she now lives in." They all chuckled on key as Roger handed her a box of chocolates.

"It's a pleasure to meet you," Roger said. "I hope we're not intruding. Sylvie insisted it was okay with you that we stop by and say hello before going on to the end of the island."

Angela hesitated while looking at him. "No bother. It's not like I had to bake a cake or anything. Believe me, I wish I could bake. I'm not even allowed to put up a pot of coffee. Michael, why don't you put up a fresh pot."

"No, we've already had coffee," Sylvie interrupted. "I wanted you all to meet."

"I hear you'll be breaking out of here soon?" Roger smiled.

"That's up to the baby." Angela brushed back her long hair out of her eyes. "I must look dreadful."

"You look radiant, doesn't she?" Sylvie interjected. "Maybe today's the day?"

"Mom," Michael said, "let's not start that again. One false alarm is enough. She still has over a month to go."

Sylvie patted Angela's hand. "Sorry, I'm so overanxious." Sylvie noticed Roger's eyes go to Angela's sketches scattered about the bedroom. "See, I told you she's talented, didn't I?"

"You did these, Angela?" Roger asked, taking his time, perusing each of the sketches. "They're lovely, full of life."

Violet came to his side and whined as if she knew he was talking about her.

"I see your subject is cooperative."

"Oh, she's a ham," Angela said. "When I show her the finished product, she barks in approval."

"Ha ha, that's wonderful," he said, petting the dog's head.

"Are you an artist, too?" Angela asked.

"Who, me? Oh no, I'm an architect, but work much less than I used to."

"What kind of architecture do you work on?" Michael asked.

"Design projects, you know, dealing with building codes, etcetera."

"That takes a combination of skills," Sylvie boasted. "Science and art."

"Semi-retired, then?" Michael asked.

"You could say that," Roger answered.

"How did you and my mother meet?" Michael turned to his mom, who seemed unusually quiet, and then back to Roger. Maybe she thought they were interrogating her boyfriend.

"Didn't she tell you?" Roger tilted his head at Sylvie.

Sylvie winked. "I wanted to be sure you liked me, and that I liked you, before telling them anything."

"And the verdict?" he asked, putting his hand on her shoulder.

"You know," she said, with a coy expression.

"Anyway," Roger continued. "We really hit it off, your mother and I. She's intelligent, funny, interesting, all rolled into one . . . and nice to look at, too."

"And Roger isn't chopped liver," she said. They all laughed. "Well, we better get moving on. Thank you both for letting us come by. I talked about you two so much that—"

"That I feel like I know you," Roger finished.

"Please, feel free to come back with Sylvie after the baby is born," Michael said. Then he leaned into Roger like a father would to a teenage boy his daughter was dating. "I can see you're making my mother very happy lately. Thank you."

"It's mutual," he said. At the threshold Roger turned around one last time to Angela. "You will be blessed with a beautiful child who will be very loved."

Angela waved with a smile, settling her body back onto the bed.

"Oh my God," Michael gasped when he returned to the bedroom.

Angela sat up more erect. "I know." She shrugged. "Who knew?"

"He's black." Michael grinned.

Angela covered her mouth, laughing. "This is great."

"My mother never ceases to surprise me. Although it would have been even more of a surprise if he was German."

They both went hysterical.

"He's such a gentleman and so handsome. Sidney Poitier-ish."

"They look like an ideal couple, don't they?"

"Like a salt and pepper set."

"Holy shit, did I ever have her pegged wrong." He shook his head. "All these years, I always thought my mother was prejudiced.

"Makes me think of something Otto Frank said," Angela said.

"Who?" Michael asked.

"You know, Anne Frank's father. I'll never forget reading a quote of his. After reading his daughter's diary, he said when it comes to our children, we don't really know who they are. I guess we don't really know who our parents are, either, do we?"

"That's scary," Michael said. "Let's make sure we keep an honest and open communication going at all times with each other. And our children."

"You said children. You think someday we'll have another child?"

Michael rubbed his hands together, obviously gratified. "Who knows? Life's certainly full of surprises, isn't it?"

"Yeah, Roger sure is some surprise. I like him. He's so, you know, down to earth."

"Exactly. What does he see in my mother? My grossly materialistic mother."

"You know, I haven't seen your mom wearing any new things lately. And her shoes are even starting to look kinda scuffed, like mine."

"Wow. She's taking a giant step now in those scuffed shoes. Guess he's good for her."

Sylvie walked alongside Roger on the sidewalk, conscious of her turned-in feet, trying to straighten them out as she kept up with his long strides. He was a big fellow—six foot four, while she was only five foot four. Yet he made her feel equal to him in every other way, which she never felt with other men. He let her know that she was sensitive and entertaining, and very intelligent, every chance he could, which made her feel genuinely satisfied with herself for the first time in her life. He couldn't entirely rid her of all her exorbitant desires that she'd wanted to fill her life with; it was like breaking a drug addict. He made sure to expose her to another world, too; in his world he not only loved art, and reading, he also loved music. He loved the blues and soul and went to out-of-the-way places to find raw talent.

Being Jewish, being black—neither have ever been easy, she thought. She looped her arm through his, and after dinner, they stopped at a little dive of a place with great music and a pool table.

"Memory Motel," Sylvie said. "I like the name. I hope we build a lot of memories, together, you and I."

"You can count on it." They clinked their glasses while sitting at a bistro table, each holding a glass of red wine in their hand, watching three guys near the bar as they performed a few riffs. Roger's eyes lit up to a Muddy Waters tune. He pulled a harmonica out of his pocket. "This is my instrument of passion," he told her. The guitarist stopped strumming and motioned for him to join them. "Nah, I don't play in public."

"Aww, go on, Roger," Sylvie coaxed.

"I didn't know you were into the blues," he said.

"I'm not. They're into me."

Other patrons clapped for Roger to join in as they did an intro to "I'm a Man."

He closed his eyes and moved his lips over the harmonica, inhaling and exhaling with great intensity as Sylvie cheered him on. When he sat again with Sylvie, she said, "You certainly are."

"Are what?" he asked with a smile, slipping his harmonica back into his pocket.

"A man."

"Oh, Sylvie Rosenberg," he said, placing his hand over hers. "You're making a black man blush."

They talked about everything on their walk back to the motel, about the present and the past. She purposely didn't share her family history with Roger about escaping the Holocaust. *There's a time and place for everything. Not quite yet.*

An ambulance raced by on the main street, and she had to shake off bad thoughts invading the good place she was in—the loud sirens signaling curfew, the screeching of wheels on the cobblestone, the flashlights circling brick walls. She shook her head and reached for Roger's hand.

Sunday morning, they skipped breakfast. Roger told her he had the whole day planned—except for one stop at a church with its doors wide open. Sylvie realized she was beginning to see some things that her son had continually tried to tell her, things that he learned and felt while he was on the road, like the day he stumbled upon a congregation of worshippers entering a gospel church down South. Beset by the crowd of strangers, she felt closed in at first, remembering when the doors closed on the train. When the people held hands and sang out in harmony, their gospel voices rising up to the rafters in their humble house of worship, she felt supernatural.

Sylvie looked around her—the mix of ethnicity letting her know how welcome everyone was inside these very small quarters. It was certainly not what she knew while growing up so long ago, so far away. As the day went on, she realized she didn't have to go cross-country like Michael to discover more about people and about herself—only cross-island, Long Island. How odd that it was Roger, this new person in her life, who showed her more about her own son.

Roger and Sylvie walked along the beach. She took off her shoes and let her toes sink into the coolness of the sand, forgetting about her pedicure. They had packed sandwiches they purchased from a local deli and watched the waves rolling in until the sun set. They talked about so many different things, and Roger seemed pensive as he pointed out a brown hawk overhead, which also reminded her of what Michael used to write about during his travels, how he wished he would one day work for *National Geographic* and write about nature. "So, we never really talk about it, but you don't have a problem with me being bla—?"

"Black? I hardly noticed."

He laughed. "You see the looks we've been getting, haven't you?"

"I'm a Jew. Sticks and stones have broken all my bones. When I'm with you, I feel myself healing."

"That's a nice way to put it."

"My son will be indebted to you forever, Roger."

"Why's that?"

"Because you opened my eyes." She tilted her head back, gazing at the open sky, and studied the flight of the brown hawk, too. "Something Michael's been trying to do for years."

Chapter 20

M ichael couldn't stop laughing. "Ha! How do you like that? My mother's hanging out in the same bars as the Rolling Stones now."

"You haven't stopped laughing ever since she told you about going to the Memory Motel. It's great seeing you in such high spirits lately. Promise me one thing."

"What's that?" he asked, examining her face.

"That we'll keep our home a happy place—for the baby. A good sense of humor is so important."

"You got it." He opened one of the windows in the bedroom. "Stuffy in here, right? Want me to open the window more?"

"No, that's enough. Mmm . . . I love the fresh air. There's a nice cool breeze today coming in off the water. I wish I could go run on the beach," she sighed. "I think I'm done with all this waiting."

"We're coming down to the home stretch now." Michael came up behind her. "Want me to give you a back rub?"

"No, today the pain's moved to my front."

"Oh? When's your next doctor appointment?"

"The day after tomorrow. Only five more weeks to go," she said. "If it weren't for that I'd lose track here in prison. Hey, is it Tuesday? Isn't it your deadline day, Michael? Why aren't you hitting away at the typewriter keys?"

"Scoot over." He got in the bed next to her, gently rubbing her tummy. "I now have Nelson covering for me at the paper, 'til after the baby comes at least."

"Oh my God, really? Can he do the job?"

"I've been showing him the ropes over these past few weeks." She rested her hands on top of his. "The reality of this baby actually being in this room with us, in this house—just hit me."

"I know. Hard to grasp, huh?"

Later that same night, Angela poked Michael in the ribs. "Hon, wake up."

"Yeah, what is it? You okay?"

"I'm ready."

"Ready for what?" He sprang up, throwing the blanket off the bed. "How do you know?"

"Believe me, I know. This shouldn't come as a shock anymore. I've been up for the past couple of hours, keeping time."

"You mean you've been having contractions?"

"*Oh* yeah!"

"Why didn't you tell me?"

"I'm telling you now."

"How many minutes apart?"

"Like every seven minutes."

"All right. All right," he said in his sleepy stupor in the blackened room. "Don't go anywhere, don't move. I'll call the doctor."

Michael stood and tripped, almost smacking his head on the wall. "Oh shit!"

Angela laughed. "Please. I don't want to have to drive you to the ER. Take it easy."

"Right, right . . . I'll tell Dr. Fisher to meet us at the hospital."

"Michael, can you please turn the lights on so I don't trip?"

"Oh, yeah. Yeah, smart idea." He laughed. "Remember, Ricky and Lucy. You made me promise to keep a sense of humor, didn't you?"

"We're not on TV. This is real life. Please, get me to the hospital."

"I've got this under control, Ange. I even have the suitcase by the front door, the car's pointed outward, the—"

Angela forced a calm voice. "Michael, please shut up. Don't pull a Sylvie on me."

"Yeah, got it. Oh man, what happened to my lucky Keds?" he said, putting one low-top sneaker on his left foot and tying up the many laces. "It's ripped . . . and where's the other one?"

"Michael, stay focused!"

"Sorry." With one shoe on, one shoe off, he went for the phone. "That's odd."

"What now?"

"There's no dial tone." He peeked out the window at the streetlight. "It's not stormy out. It's not even windy." He looked down at Violet whimpering at his side with the chewed telephone wire hanging out of her mouth. "Violet! What did you do?" The dog dropped the wire onto the rug and howled, something she'd never done before. "What is it girl? She must sense something's up, huh?" Michael stared into space, still trying to come out of his deep sleep.

"Michael—me! Pay attention to me. This is not the Lassie show."

"Right. We'll have to drive to the hospital and call Dr. Fisher from there. Don't worry, I got through a war; I can get through this."

"Good. You do that." She opened her closet door to find something appropriate to wear to the hospital while leaning against the wall. "I wish I could take a shower, but I think I'll have to settle for washing up, and brushing my teeth and hair. Then we better go."

He looked down at his feet. "I'm ready, but I still can't find my other sneaker." Then he spotted it upside down on Violet's dog bed—more torn than the other. He moaned when he put it on and his toes stuck out.

Angela moaned, too. "Hurry! It's getting more intense."

"Ready, let's go."

"You can't wear those."

"I'm not going anywhere without my lucky sneakers. I have a feeling no one will notice my feet, hon." He looked at her tummy. "Screw the shoes—let's go."

"Well, they don't look so lucky to me."

Angela got into the passenger seat, rubbing her belly and trying to hold back an occasional scream for almost the entire way. It seemed forever before Michael pulled up to the front door of the hospital. He ran around the car and helped her out, leaving the car door wide open.

"Michael, the door."

He turned around and kicked it shut with one of his open-toed sneakers.

Once inside, Michael turned in circles. "Where is everyone?"

Angela looked distressed that the halls were empty.

"I'm here." A receptionist stood up from her desk behind the tall counter. "It's two thirty in the morning." She yawned. "Where you tink they are, sweetie?" she said, with a strong Caribbean accent.

"We need to call my wife's doctor. Dr. Fisher. She's having a—" He stopped, to catch his breath.

"A baby?" the receptionist finished, looking at Angela. "You're lucky. Docta's here now—with some kind of... situation." She checked some paperwork. "Uh-huh, that's right. Docta didn' check out yet. He's still with those twins—those twins dat turned out to be triplets. I know this docta's good, but he can't be in two places at one time."

"Please, can you see if there's another obstetrician on call for my wife?"

"We have to wait and see if Docta Fisha's done with those three babies, first, before we go callin' in another docta."

Angela swallowed.

"Now, don't you go worr'in your pretty head. We're gonna get you all set up, okay? And if he's not done, we'll find you a doctor who will help you deliver that little chil'. Ain't that right, Ed?" she said to a man walking by in a green jumpsuit. Ed pulled along his mop and bucket on wheels and gave a wink.

Angela whispered into Michael's ear. "Oh my God, Michael. Oh my God. I don't want this doctor or that doctor or the damn night janitor delivering my baby!"

"Listen, miss," Michael said sternly, "we need—"

She eyed his toes sticking out from his sneakers. "You can call me Puddin. That's what everybody calls me."

Michael scrunched up his face, sizing her up, thinking she must have at least 100 pounds on him. "Puddin? As in Jell-O?"

"*J-E-L-L-O.*" She spelled it out.

"We can't wait. Can you call a nurse in maternity and see if they know if another doctor is available now?"

"*Michael?*"

He walked to his wife, who was being put into a wheelchair by an orderly. "I'm right here, hon." Angela squeezed his hand.

The orderly patted her shoulder. "You look like you're freezing."

Angela attempted a smile. "Must be nerves."

"We'll get you a nice warm blanket, and then your husband can join you upstairs after we get you nice and comfortable in a bed." He looked at Michael. "Why don't you finish with Puddin and give us about thirty minutes before you come up to see your wife."

"I'll be up soon, after I fill out the forms down here, okay? I love you, hon."

Her voice came out between chattering teeth. "I love you, too," she said as the elevator doors closed.

He went back to the reception desk, and Puddin handed him the forms and a clipboard and pointed to the double doors that led into the waiting room.

He grabbed a pen while scanning the paperwork. "Geez, all these?"

"No rush. The first baby takes a while."

Michael walked on shaky legs across the lobby through the

double doors marked *Waiting Room* where there were hard, metal, beige chairs. He had so many questions and no one to ask. He wanted to kick himself for at least not leafing through the baby books Dr. Fisher had given them.

With the clipboard in hand, Michael threw open the double doors and ran clumsily to the reception desk again in his open-toed sneakers, tapping his cane impatiently. "Excuse me, is there a phone nearby?"

"Oh, it's you again," Puddin said. "Who you waking up at this hour? The pope?"

"Well, uhh."

She went back to the magazine she was reading.

"My mother—I'm going to call my mother." He brushed his fingers through his messy hair and repeated himself in a loud voice. "The telephone?"

She pointed, not bothering to look up. "It's in the lobby—that red ting near the counter with a great big dial on the front."

"Sorry. I don't mean to be rude. I'm just a little tense, you know." He headed in the direction of the phone. *Maybe she should be sitting with Angela with her sense of humor,* he thought, as he attempted to dial. *Damn! Someone's jammed something in the coin slot.*

Again, Michael frantically returned to Puddin's desk.

"You back? You been waitin' for your wife to have that baby, what— ten minutes already? I told you, those first babies, they take forever."

"Puddin, cut me a break." He stared at her phone. "The pay phone in the lobby's out of order."

"Really? Ed was supposed to fix it after his dinner break."

She slapped her hand over Michael's as he reached his hand over her desk. "Oh no, can't use my phone. Hospital rules. They're still getting your wife all prepped. Docta's been paged. He does one baby at a time, sweetheart. Now, you gotta rest and save some of that energy for when you get the baby home. They poop every hour and they keep you up all night long. You'll see." She laughed hard.

"Okay, I'll take your advice and wait a little longer before I make my call . . . You know, even when you're arrested, you're allowed one call."

"Why don't you go to the waitin' room near Maternity on the fourth floor and use that phone?"

"There's another waiting room—closer to my wife? Why didn't you tell me that?"

"I was gettin' around to it. Like I said earlier, there's plenty of time before that baby's ready to meet his daddy. Back in my country, I worked with a midwife helpin' women have their babies for years. You better calm yourself down, darlin', or the docta's gonna wanna sedate you."

Once in the horizontal position on the hospital bed, Angela started to hyperventilate. She stared at all the equipment around the room. "Can you please tell me what you plan on doing with that?"

Two nurses, one short, one tall, were at her side, motioning what they'd be doing with the razor blade. She suddenly thought of herself as a delinquent student who didn't do her homework.

"What else don't I know?"

"Looks like she's having a panic attack," one nurse said to the other."

"Don't talk about me like I'm not here."

"Okay, you're having a panic attack. Please, take it easy," the taller nurse directed her. "You're not the first one having a baby around here."

"And *you* should take it easy with your bedside manner."

The shorter nurse spoke up. "What about false teeth? Partials?"

"Excuse me?" Angela raised her voice.

"If you do have false teeth, they'll have to come out," the taller nurse added. "You don't want to choke, now, do you?"

"Why, why would I choke? And, by the way, these are not fake teeth." She pointed to her mouth. "Why are you strapping me down?"

"It's a fetal monitor, to keep track of the baby's heartbeat."

"I-I don't like the way that feels—it's getting tighter and tighter."

One of the nurses gently pushed her back down again onto the hospital bed. "That tight feeling is a contraction. Your body is getting you ready."

"Where's Dr. Fisher? Where's my doctor?"

"The doctor will be here soon."

"I've heard that before." Angela squeezed one of the nurse's hands. "I want my husband." She regretted the ordered bed rest that prevented her from taking the Lamaze classes with Michael. She wished it was his hand she was squeezing.

"Oh my gooood-ness—*Ohhh*."

"You're doing great, dear." The nurse patted her arm. "The baby's coming faster than we anticipated."

"How am I to know when I'm supposed to push?"

"Oh, you'll know, believe me."

"I don't like the way you said that."

"Calm down. Soon you'll be given something to relax. Have you ever heard of twilight sleep?"

"No, it sounds peaceful." Angela sniffled.

"You won't know what's going on once that stuff kicks in."

"Can I have some now?"

"Let's see how much you've dilated. Then, when the doctor gets here, he can order the drugs."

The other nurse took her hand. "Try some breathing exercises. You know, like a dog . . . *hee hee—hoo, hee hee—hoo*."

"My mother-in-law told me that very same thing—about the dog."

Michael hit the button a few times and waited for the elevator doors to open. He walked into the maternity ward, and the head nurse stopped him. "Are you Mr. Beckman?"

"Yes, my wife—"

"Your wife's fine. I'm sorry, it seems things got moving a little faster than expected and you cannot join her in the delivery room, unless you're Lamaze certified."

"Oh, man." He started to perspire . "Can I watch a video real quick on natural childbirth?"

She shook her head. "Sorry. We'll keep you informed, don't worry. She's in good hands."

He found the waiting room on the fourth floor and was happy to see another father-to-be there. Unfortunately, he was using the only payphone in sight. As soon as he hung up, Michael quickly started a conversation with him. "So, is this your first?"

"No, no." The man immediately started dialing again, without asking Michael if he needed to use the phone. "My sixth. The twins we were expecting turned out to be triplets and we already have three at home—all under the age of seven. Hello? Sorry, you'll have to excuse me." He made one phone call after another.

Michael went back to the elevators, down to the lobby, and hurried to the reception desk, again, the rubber soles of his tattered lucky Keds screeching to a halt. Puddin peered over the high counter above her desk and looked down at his feet. "I tink you should oil those things." She went back to what she was reading before he interrupted her.

"Please, the phone?" He pushed a Snickers bar that he'd gotten out of a candy machine closer to her.

"Mmm . . . hmm. You bribin' me now?"

He winked at her. "Please? The triplet dad is using the one upstairs."

"I don't see a ting. I'm just gonna do some filing over there." She walked away, unwrapping the Snickers, and made herself look busy at the file cabinet.

"Thanks." He looked over his shoulder to the right and then to the left before he picked up Puddin's phone. "Mom, it's me."

"Who is this? Michael, is that you? It's the middle of the night."

"Mom, which ear are you listening with?"

"My right ear—my good ear. Oh my God, it's Angela. It's time, isn't it? She's not due yet."

"We're here. At Southampton Hospital. Angela's in the delivery room. The baby is coming prematurely, Ma, and I'm out of—"

"Breath?"

"Out of time. I have a few questions I never thought about asking anyone before. Being you were—I mean are a mother, well, you might be able to answer them."

"I'm on my way." Sylvie hung up.

"No, Mom?"

Puddin *tsk*ed, shaking her head at him. "How long a drive does your mother have?"

"Two hours. I guarantee she'll be here in one."

Chapter 21

Michael started to doze off in a chair in the upstairs waiting area when he felt someone tapping his shoulder. "Excuse me, Mr. Beckman?"

"Yeah?" He jumped when he saw the head nurse standing over him and rubbed the bags under his tired eyes.

"No, relax. It's not the baby yet. Puddin called to inform me that there's a woman in the lobby who claims to know you—your mother?"

"Thank you." The nurse left the room quickly. Michael stepped into the elevator and pressed the button for Lobby. *Oh, this is just great.* Michael didn't know what he was thinking, calling his mother. Angela had warned him ahead of time—she didn't want Sylvie to come to the hospital until after the baby was born. The last thing Angela needed was his mother making her more anxious.

The second the elevator doors opened, he could hear her. Whenever she was overexcited, her hearing got worse, and her voice got louder.

She grabbed her chest, dramatically. "Where's the baby room?"

Puddin's large brown eyes bulged at Michael. "You're right—one hour. Please, everyone, hush up. We have sick people here."

"*Shhh*, please, Mom."

"I'm sorry, sweetheart. How are you doing? Are you okay? You look terrible." Sylvie was oblivious to the woman behind the counter as Michael escorted her toward the waiting room.

"The baby's not here yet, Mom. Why don't we go over to this waiting room, close by, and I'll bring you upstairs after you calm down."

She made a face, tapping the hard chair with her knuckles. "Here," she said, handing him a paper bag. "I brought you a doughnut from home. You look like you need it."

He took a bite of the doughnut. "You don't look so good yourself—you're really pale. Maybe you should try breathing slowly into this bag."

Sylvie took the bag from him, unwillingly. "It's like a morgue in here."

"That's right, place it over your mouth and nose." He looked at her—the hems of her pajama bottoms and her bed slippers were now fully exposed.

"Mom, you drove in your elephant slippers?"

"No, I *drove* in the Caddy."

She looked back at him, her eyes peering out over the bag bellowing and deflating, her hair sticking up in all directions. "Yes, the cop thought they were funny."

"The cop? You got stopped by the police . . . again?" She nodded and held up two fingers.

"You got stopped twice? Did you get a ticket?" She held up two fingers again.

"You got two tickets?"

Sylvie nodded shyly.

"Mom, I called because I have questions. Were you early when you had me?"

She squinted as if thinking about the births. "You were born exactly on your due date. Not your brother, though. He was born early."

"And how was your labor? Frightening? Painful?"

"You don't need to know. It's a woman's place. The only thing you can hope for is that someone treats her with compassion." She looked off in another direction.

He shook his head. "I'm afraid I don't know who's with her now—the last I heard, the doctor was with another patient."

"Who, Dr. Fischer? The Jew?"

"You know him?"

"We're all related."

"Mom, what are you talking about?"

"We need to find out what's going on . . . we need more information how our Angela is doing."

Michael felt his mother's sincerity. "No one's giving me any information."

"That's ridiculous. Let me talk to someone about this."

"No, Mom. They have their rules." He held her down in her seat.

"Rules? Rules are for fools."

Sylvie got up and walked past the two small windows of the double doors that led out to the lobby. "Who's the *schvatza?*"

"Mom!"

"What, Michael? Roger and I kid about that word." Michael peered out to where his mother was looking.

"That's Puddin. She's from Jamaica."

"Jamaica, really?"

"No, Mom. Where are you going?"

"To get me some Puddin."

Michael jumped up after her.

Sylvie tapped her long, painted fingernails on the countertop.

"May I help you?" Puddin slowly lifted her head up from the movie star magazine she was engrossed in.

"You think you can find out what's happening with our Angela and her baby?"

"Sorry, my mother is extremely nervous." Without his mother seeing, Michael circled his finger at the side of his temple, indicating that his mother was crazy.

"A-ha. I see what I can do," Puddin said. "I'm startin' to want this baby more than you!" Puddin smiled at him, sympathetically, and called the Labor and Delivery floor.

"No, no baby yet. They said 'soon.'"

"I know where you're from! Jamaica!" Sylvie clapped her hands together. "I knew I recognized that accent. I love the Jamaican people! I lived there, near Kingston."

"Kingston? Dats where I'm from."

"Tell me, is that old Mr. Brown's Clam Shack still there?"

Puddin smiled. "My sista says it is. I used to go there all the time. And you know the church up the road wit the prity arch windows? Still there."

Sylvie told Puddin she was Jewish. "I lived at Camp Gibraltar there, at the refugee camp for three years. "

"I remember hearin' my mother tell me stories 'bout the refugees livin' there."

"We were exiled to paradise, people used to say. Hah! I shopped in town, bought a lot of hand-woven jewelry at a little market around the corner from Mr. Brown's."

"Oh my sweet Lord," Puddin hollered. "That was my uncle Willy's place. I have so many relatives over there."

Sylvie and Puddin laughed, and Michael shook his head as they continued exchanging stories about Jamaica. When his mother tried, she could be charming.

"Mom, why don't we go to the upstairs waiting room now where it's more comfortable. Maybe we can even get a little sleep, okay?"

In the upstairs waiting room, Sylvie sat close to Michael and put her arms around him. He hadn't gotten a hug like that from his mother since he was a small boy. He laid an arm over hers and enjoyed the embrace, and they both fell asleep.

❧

"Happy Birthday, Baby Boy Beckman," Angela thought she heard a voice say as she was coming in and out of her twilight sleep.

An aide marked the baby's weight on a chart. "Five pounds on the nose," she said. "Length—19 ½ inches."

Shortly after, the aide gently shook Angela's shoulder to wake her. "Congratulations, Mrs. Beckman. Would you like to hold your baby now?"

Angela looked into the face of the aide she hadn't seen before. *It must be the morning shift,* she thought, seeing sunshine out the window reflecting off the roof.

"My baby? He's here? Is he all right?"

The aide placed the infant in Angela's arms, and immediately, Angela felt engulfed in a massive wave of love for this tiny new person. She'd never felt this kind of love before.

"How soft and warm you are," she whispered, her skin next to his, wondering if he knew, from her motherly touch, the love she felt inside.

"Your husband's on his way."

Angela stared starry-eyed into her son's eyes; she'd never seen anything more beautiful in her life. "Is this the daddy?" the nurse asked, winking at Angela.

Michael stood in the doorway, unable to move. He stared at his wife and child. "Our son," he said, as tears welled.

"Yes, yes it is," she said, tearing up. "Would you like to meet him?" Michael walked toward them.

"Where's your cane?"

He looked down at himself, then around him, as if he'd lost an appendage. "I have no idea." They both smiled—two miracles, simultaneously. Angela lifted the baby into his cradling arms. He stood speechless for a few minutes and then broke down. "Wow! Look what we made."

Michael sat next to Angela and watched her kiss the baby's closed eyelids. Then she kissed her husband's.

"Won't you wake up to say hello to your daddy?"

"My mother came, too. Sorry. I left her sleeping in the waiting room. A nurse said she'd wake her up in a few minutes. Believe me, she needed the rest. I just wanted to spend some time alone with you first."

There was a sudden commotion coming from the hallway. "Ma'am, do you have a pass?" a man's voice said. Sylvie stood at the threshold with the security guard at her side. "Do you know this woman?" He winked.

"Well, let me think about that," Michael teased.

"Michael!" Angela slapped his arm. "Yes, we know her. She's—"

"I'm Grandma," Sylvie announced and entered the room in her pigeon-toed walk that made the elephant trunks of her slippers bounce inward.

"So much for the alone time," Michael whispered to Angela.

Sylvie shook as she stood next to her son—holding his son. Her eyes turned to liquid. "Sweet Lord, thank you for answering our prayers."

"Would you like to hold your grandson?" Angela asked, smiling.

Sylvie's legs wobbled. "Candy. I need a piece of candy. I'm feeling dizzy. I must be having a sugar-withdrawal thing."

Michael quickly pulled up a chair for her, and she sat and unwrapped a caramel she found in her purse, and then searched for a tissue.

"Mom, I didn't know you were such a softie."

"I knew," Angela said. "She's your mother, isn't she?"

Sylvie reached out to hold the baby, but then retracted her arms. "You know, I think I will wait until he gets home before I hold him. I don't want to drop him in case I faint." She leaned closer to her grandson. "He's so beautiful. He has my eyes."

Angela and Michael suppressed their laughter. The three of them watched the baby cooing and sleeping for hours. Sylvie fell asleep in a thick padded chair in the corner with a smile on her face. The new parents stayed cuddled on the bed until Sylvie awoke.

"Have you decided on a name yet?"

They looked at one another. "We'll think about names all day, I'm sure, and by the time we leave the hospital, you'll be the first to know, Mom. You have a spare key to our house. Instead of driving all the way back to Queens, why don't you sleep there? I'm going to stay here a couple of nights at the hospital with Angela. You said that chair's pretty comfortable. And I have a gym bag in the car with a change of clothes. If you'd feed Violet, I'd appreciate it. Get some rest and stick to the speed limit."

"And tell Roger to come, too," Angela called after her.

From the doorway Sylvie looked back at the three of them in a halo of love and peace. "I'll drive extra careful . . . I have a lot to live for."

Chapter 22

Sylvie woke to see the dog's face next to hers on the pillow. "Oh, you are the spoiled one, aren't you, Violet? I'm afraid it's not for long, though. You'll have to make room for the baby coming, you know."

She took a quick shower and got dressed in a casual outfit. Roger would be coming soon, and they had a lot of work to do before the kids got home. She made herself a cup of coffee and sat out on the back deck overlooking the ocean in the early morning sunshine. It struck her how odd it was that her heart was now beating happily, when not too long ago, she felt it had almost ceased.

Roger arrived early, like he promised, and they ate a quick breakfast and drove to a local paint store. Roger placed the two small samples of blue paint and the two large gallon cans near the register.

"Why two of each?" Sylvie asked.

"I'd like to see which one looks better in the natural light in the nursery. I'll put both sample colors on the walls and we'll make our decision before opening the gallon cans."

"Good plan."

"Uh-oh." Roger hesitated. "What about the dog? Will she get in our way? I'd hate to see them have to rename Violet 'Blue.'"

"That Violet is a wonderful puppy. She slept on the bed in the guest room with me last night. Tonight, she will probably try to squeeze in between the two of us."

"As long as she doesn't take my pillow."

When they got off the main road, Sylvie looked differently at the homes, imagining the families that filled them—mothers cooking scrambled eggs, fathers doing the bills, children chasing one another around the house. She tried to remember the words to the Dutch lullaby she knew as a child, so she could sing it to her grandson.

Roger looked at her, and they both passed smiles back and forth; there was so much to be grateful for. He had often told her how great it was to be a grandparent. Soon, she would meet his daughter, Lila, and her four-year-old son, Bryan, and the rest of his Virginian family. He had told them his relationship with Sylvie was getting serious and promised they would drive down South over the summer so they could meet her.

"I wish we could be there when the kids get home tomorrow and see the baby's room is no longer pink. They'll need their privacy, so we should leave early, before they come home."

Sylvie used her spare key to Michael's beach house and unlocked the front door. "Isn't it a cute little house, and so near to the beach," she said to Roger, who carried the heavy cans of paint. "The baby furniture was delivered a few days ago, and of course Michael didn't have the time to change the wall color."

Roger glanced at the corner of the room that contained the honey-colored changing table, chest of drawers, and the rocking chair. "Where's the crib?" he asked.

"Oh, did I forget to tell you? It's still in the box. After we are done painting, maybe we can put it together."

"We? I didn't know you were handy, Sylvie."

"Umm. A little bit."

"Great. You can start reading the directions on how to assemble the crib while I cover the furniture with the drop cloths and test out the colors. Then you get to decide which one you like best."

Roger got busy prying open the lids with a screwdriver while Sylvie opened up the pamphlet of instructions, turning it in circles, to find out where to begin.

"What? The instructions aren't in Dutch?" He looked at her. "Trouble?"

"Well, I may have exaggerated. I'm not really handy. At all."

Roger laughed. "I wouldn't say that. I know you have exquisite taste." He stood back, examining the samples. "So, which color do you prefer?"

"That one." She pointed to the one on the right, closest to the window. She read the label on the can. "And I love the name of the paint color. True Blue."

"Come here, and I'll show you how to paint the moldings." He spun her around in a circle. "I got this handy dandy work apron for you," he said, placing it over her head and tying the string behind her back.

"Do you hate me now because I'm not handy?"

"I love you for trying."

"You said you love me for trying."

"Yeah, I did say that, didn't I?" he teased.

"I love you, too."

"Now, let's start the worst part—the prep work. Do you think you can put the tape around the moldings?"

"Yes, sir. I think I can handle that. Where's the tape?" She looked around the room.

"In the pocket of your apron."

She reached inside her pocket and gasped. "What's—?"

He smiled broadly as she held the ring with the small diamond in her fingers.

"Roger, it's a ring!"

"That it is."

"Oh my God, Roger, are you asking me to—"

"Marry me?" He got on one knee. "Yes, I am, Sylvie. Will you marry me?"

She slipped the ring on her finger and jumped into his arms, spilling the paint can; she quickly set it upright, but not before getting True Blue paint all over her fingers. She grabbed his face in her hands and playfully streaked both his cheeks. Still stunned, she asked, "Do you know who you are, Roger? You are the one. You are my Prince Charming."

"I think that's a yes?"

"Yes, yes, and yes," she said, kissing him.

Roger opened all the windows in the baby's room to let the paint fumes air out overnight. He and Sylvie were exhausted, and they were grateful they didn't have to drive back to Queens. In the morning they would place the assembled crib and new furniture where they thought it should go, and slip out of the house before the kids got home.

Shortly after sunrise Sylvie nudged Roger. "Let's get out of here early, so the three of them can come home and enjoy their little family."

"I'm wide awake," he said. "Let's hit the road."

Her eyes grew moist as she locked the front door behind them. "I can hardly wait to get back here and finally hold my grandson."

Angela was escorted down to the lobby in a wheelchair, holding her baby boy, with the proud father at her side. Unlike the night before, there was a lot of activity around with nurses and incoming and outgoing patients and visitors. Michael walked past the receptionist desk and saw a stern gray-haired, bespectacled woman sitting in Puddin's chair.

She had the phone tucked under her chin while filing, writing something down on a chart, and never noticed the new family exiting. Michael wished it was Puddin to say a final goodbye.

He drove with their precious cargo, as Angela called the baby. "Isn't this surreal?"

"I don't want to ever leave his side," Angela said. "I don't know how I'll ever go back to work. Who will watch him? I don't know anyone around here who I'd want babysitting him."

"Hey, what about Puddin? She said she only works part time at the hospital on the late shift."

"Yes, of course. She's so knowledgeable about newborns."

"She certainly loves babies. Oh, I hope she'll say yes."

They both looked at their son. "Hard to believe how happy this little baby is making us, huh?" Michael made the turn onto Dune Road. "I wonder about Linh."

"Oh, Michael. I bet she's with a nice family," she said in a dreamy voice. "They have a charming little house in the country with geraniums in the windows."

"With a big yard to play in."

"And a picket fence."

"With a dog."

"And a garden."

Michael turned into his driveway. "I wonder if I call the adoption agency, if they'd give me any information about her at all."

"You'll never forget Linh, will you?"

"I think this little guy will make it a lot easier," he said, turning off the engine. "My mother's car isn't here. She said she'd be leaving before we'd get home."

"Phew," Angela sighed. "I love your mother, but we need to relax, don't you think?"

"You can say that again. We'll have enough excitement to deal with when we introduce the baby to the dog."

"It's funny how the waiting seems forever, yet you're still not prepared when the time comes. I'll have to remember he likes surprises." Angela felt slightly shaky getting out of the car and handed the baby to Michael. "Remember, support his little head. He's very fragile."

"You're like an eggshell," he announced to his son, raising him up to his own face to nuzzle him. "I'll come back out to the car for our stuff," he told Angela. "Let's get you two into the house and settled."

Violet wiggled and cried happily as soon as they walked in the door, but seemed to be afraid of the little bundle they were holding. "She'll get used to him soon enough. Then you'll be sketching the two of them, before you know it."

"I can't wait; there's so much to look forward to, Michael."

He walked slowly beside Angela to the couch in the family room, and once she sat down and put her feet up, he placed their son in her arms.

"I want you to relax for a while. I'll go put up a pot for tea, and get the rest of the things out of the car. After I'm done putting the crib together, I'll make us some grilled-cheese sandwiches."

"Oh, Michael. You have so much to do."

"It's okay. I don't want you moving a muscle. You're going to need your strength tonight when he wakes up screaming."

The tea pot was whistling when he got back inside with the bags. He took the baby momentarily from Angela and propped him on a pillow in her lap and handed her a cup of chamomile tea. The baby was still wearing the little cap on his head with yellow and orange ducks that Puddin had given them as a gift.

She leaned her head back on the couch pillow and let out a long breath.

Michael started toward the baby's room and stopped in the hallway. He called out Angela's name. "You've got to see this."

"What is it?"

"I can't believe . . ."

"What is it? . . . Oh my God, how did—?"

They both said "Sylvie?" at the same time.

"Well, I'm sure it was her idea, but my mother's never done any manual labor in her life. Poor Roger must have gotten roped into the job."

Angela walked around the baby's room. "What a beautiful shade of blue, isn't it? The furniture fits perfectly. And look, they put the crib together. Now you don't have to."

"That's a relief. Should we put him in his crib?"

Angela gently placed him down, and Michael felt a pang in his heart when he saw the tears on Angela's cheeks. "Oh, I thought the hormone thing was over now that the baby's here."

She punched his arm lightly. "I'm over-tired, that's all. I've never felt so happy."

Michael felt the walls with the flat of his hand. "What a great paint job he did. Not a speck of pink to be seen."

She picked up the music box sitting on top of the changing table that Sylvie had given them when she found out they were expecting. She admired the colorful little windmills hand-painted on the lid and opened the box, letting it play a Dutch lullaby called "Slaap Kindje Slaap":

Sleep little child, sleep.
Outside a sheep is walking.
A sheep with white feet
It drinks its milk sweet.

Angela's hiccups started right before dinner, and Michael surmised that something was making her nervous.

"It's our first night alone in the house with this little living creature swimming in that oversized crib and—" She hiccupped. "And I'm afraid he'll drown."

"Oh, sweetheart." Michael held her close to him. "You're thinking about your sister, aren't you?"

She burst into tears. "Yeah, I didn't even know I was, until I realized how much I love our baby, and if anything ever happened to him—"

"All right, honey, now stop."

"I'm sorry. I'm an idiot for even thinking that. I guess my mother's pain losing Anna is really registering with me."

"It's too sad to think about. You need to have pleasant thoughts . . . Your parents want that for you, and you know, so would Anna."

She nodded. "I know. You're right."

"I'm sure all new parents are a little frightened on the first night home with their new baby. My mom's coming with Roger tomorrow morning. She'll let us take breaks, and then your parents will be coming the next day."

"They'll be so helpful. My mother sure loves to cook. And I think your mom will be much calmer with Roger around. He's such a positive influence on her. I know she can hardly wait to hold the baby. My mother's so excited, every time I talk to her, she can't stop crying," Angela added. "Oh man, we're gonna have a nuthouse, aren't we?"

Angela fed the baby, and Michael leaned over her and kissed the bridge of her nose. "He's a lucky little guy having you for his mother."

"Yeah, you think I'll be a good mommy?"

"It's written all over your face," he said, heading for the front door.

"I have to say—" She bit her lip, holding back her emotions. "I never felt so fulfilled."

Michael winked. "Me either," he said.

Sylvie didn't knock. She didn't ask if the baby was asleep; she came running through the house and headed straight for the baby's room. Roger followed, laughing at her.

"Sorry, she's a ball of fire, that one. Ever since she quit smoking, she's even feistier."

Angela shushed Sylvie outside the door to the baby's room. "No, lower than that," she told her. "Listen to how quietly I whisper." Sylvie tried to mimic the volume of Angela's voice, yet was incapable of whispering.

"I'm too excited," she said loudly.

"*Shhh!*" Angela covered her mouth with a finger, but it was too late. The baby woke up, wailing, to Sylvie's delight and Angela's dismay. Michael and Roger joined them and followed Sylvie as she abruptly opened the door to the blue room and called out, "Grammie's here, sweetheart."

They all looked at one another. "Grammie?"

"Sit, Mom," Angela ordered her, pointing to the rocker. "I'll hand him to you, and it will be your job to stop him from crying."

Angela leaned over the crib and picked up the infant, his lip quivering from crying so hard. "Here you go, Grandma Sylvie. You finally get to hold . . . *Samuel.*"

Sylvie froze at her daughter-in-law's words as she took the crying baby into her arms.

"Mom, what's wrong?" Michael's voice was full of concern.

"How could you have known?"

"Known what?"

"The baby's name." Sylvie gently rocked back and forth, lightly patting her grandson's back as his chin rested on her shoulder.

"What about the baby's name?" Michael asked.

"If you don't like it, please don't tell us, because we're not changing his name." Angela smiled.

"You couldn't have known."

"Known what?" Michael repeated.

"That's what I had named my baby in Jamaica. Your brother—his name was Samuel. I named him after someone I cared about very much, left behind when we escaped the Nazis. It was a secret that I kept to myself. You couldn't have known. I never told a soul, not my mother or father or even Gretta or the midwife."

Michael leaned against the crib. "It's a coincidence."

"There are no coincidences in life, Michael." Sylvie's face was serious as she softly stroked the baby's downy hair.

"I think you're right. It's like my brother was here with us, spiritually. He gave my son his name."

Angela rubbed both her arms up and down with her hands. "I've got the chills."

Roger's expression showed he was already getting used to this captivating family.

The baby cried harder, and Sylvie stopped talking to the adults and gently rocked him, staring into his eyes, as if they were the soul of the universe. "I love you, Samuel."

The baby stopped crying and looked at his grandmother with an attentiveness the others couldn't help notice.

"I think he loves you, too, Grandma," Angela said.

"What about Grandpa?" Sylvie asked.

Angela and Michael looked at Sylvie, inquisitively.

Sylvie held out her hand and showed the engagement ring. "Roger's asked me to marry him."

"Oh my God, that's wonderful," Angela said.

Michael smiled at Roger, patting his back. "Don't worry, you don't have to call me Dad or anything," Roger joked.

"Now I will tell you what our plans are. We'll be going to Holland on Thursday and—"

"Holland?" Michael raised his voice. He was not sure why he felt such disappointment with her news. If it were a year ago, he would have loved her to take off. Did he feel she had no right to go so far away, now that she was a grandmother?

"I know you're probably wondering why I'd want to go at such a time, now that Baby Samuel is here. It won't be easy to leave him, but there are two reasons I must go. One reason is because I would like my sisters and brother to meet Roger and give their blessings. We will be married by a judge and have a nice wedding dinner out somewhere in my hometown. I'm so pleased after we got everything out in the open, and that Gretta can go back to Dieren. Perhaps when we return, we can have a party in your backyard?"

"We have a lot to celebrate," Angela said to her mother-in-law, holding Samuel. "We can invite my parents and our friends we grew up with in Massapequa, and—"

"And Roger's family from Richmond."

"I'm going to get a kick out of this party," Roger laughed.

"While I'm in Holland, I want to look up my two closest friends— Hana and Samuel."

Michael and Angela looked at Roger to see his reaction. He held up his hands. "Don't worry, I understand that we all have unresolved things in our lives, especially as we get older."

Sylvie touched Roger's arm. "You have nothing to worry about." She put her hands over his. "I already told you—you're my Prince Charming."

"How sweet," Angela whispered, touching Sylvie's shoulder.

"Now that all the secrets are exposed, I can finally have closure and peace with my Dutch family."

"Amen," Michael said softly. "What was the other reason? Didn't you say you have two reasons for going to Holland?"

Tears fell from Sylvie's eyes as she looked at the sleeping baby. "You must wait to find out the other reason."

Chapter 23

The wheels of the KLM airliner touched the ground with precision at Amsterdam Airport Schiphol. Sylvie and Roger arrived in the land of tulips and windmills where they'd soon wed. Her sisters had arranged the time and place for her in Dieren where they had spent their childhoods. Gretta knew the judge who would officiate at the wedding from earlier days when her father dealt with his losses and, then later on, when she had to arrange her mother's institutionalization.

Roger took Sylvie's hand and gave it a squeeze. "Can you believe the day after tomorrow, we'll be married?"

"I can't wait for my family to meet you."

Roger looked a little apprehensive. "Do you think they'll accept me, being—"

"Being what? Being too good to be true?" She touched her fingers lightly over his. "Funny, I was always the biased one. You have nothing to worry about with them."

And she was right. They seemed to love Roger almost immediately. Gretta looped her arm through one of his, and Ruthie did the same with his other arm. They strolled along the cobblestone street, chatting and pausing to point out buildings they remembered until they stopped before their childhood home in Dieren. A hush fell over all of them.

Gretta and Ruthie let go of Roger's arms as he stepped closer to the house and studied the gables.

"So, this is where you grew up? It's quite an impressive house."

"And he should know," Sylvie added. "He's an architect."

"This is true," Wilhelm said. "All of Europe has so much art you would appreciate."

"Oh, I know," Roger said. "I studied in Rome and Paris when I was in college, but I've never been to the Netherlands until now."

Ruthie was quiet, looking at the house. "I can't say I remember it like this. Did they paint the trim a different color? Put on a different roof? Has the house shrunk, or is it just because I've grown?"

"It looks pretty big to me," Roger said. "You lived on three floors?"

Ruthie craned her neck to see through the iron gate at the side yard by the service entrance. "The shrubbery's also grown, dwarfing its size. I'd love to go around back and see those magnificent gardens Mama and Papa kept. Maybe we can just knock on the servants' door and they can give us some information."

Sylvie closed her eyes, the inside of their home coming back to her. In her mind, she already was in the foyer. To the left was a small hallway that led into the sitting area for guests to wait. The walls were made up of many partitions tiled in blue-and-white delft with sprigs of green. There was also a divan in the corner. *Was it green toile?*

To the right of the large foyer was the living room filled with small groupings of artwork on either side of the delft-tiled fireplace. She could almost hear the patter of thin leather soles as she tiptoed on the parquet floors when she had sneaked around the house eavesdropping, to find out the latest news since the Germans occupied her country.

If she went straight from the foyer toward the kitchen, she would pass the dainty wallpapered powder room and massive linen closet, stacked neatly with fluffy white towels. It was also where the maids hung their uniforms. She'd forgotten some of their names, yet recalled the feel of their skin and the smell of their aprons: lemon, vanilla, and almond.

The pantry door, usually closed off to the children, was right before entering the spacious, sunny kitchen. There was a long central marble countertop beneath a rack of well-polished copper pots and pans. Oma used to roll out the dough there for her various breads and desserts. The tall white cabinets were clear glass with wooden grills, displaying the everyday blue-flowered dishes her family had used. The memory of the times when they were blessed with an abundance of delicacies made her stomach rumble. *Guilt? Again?*

If she turned her head to the left while walking down the long hallway that led from the foyer, she'd enter an archway into the dining room, with its dark cherry furniture; the sideboard where Papa kept his radio that brought them such joy, listening to lovely music of Mozart or Handel, or the reading of poetry, until it changed into a dreaded thing in the room that spewed terror from Radio Oranje to the BBC.

On every wall there were heavy-framed paintings: a river scene by Ruysdael, a portrait by Maes, a winter landscape by Goyen . . . One by one, she saw the masterpieces as they were hung before they vanished from her home.

Sylvie answered Ruthie. "For goodness sake. I think we should knock on the front door. It was our house, first. If they don't give us a tour, at least we'll be able to peek inside the foyer."

"Are you sure that's a good idea?" Gretta hesitated. "Now that happier days are here, shouldn't we just forget?"

"Oh, come on, Gretta," Wilhelm said, "We've gotten through it all. The ghosts are gone now."

They knocked several times, but there was no answer to their past.

Sylvie, excited about everything, stayed up for hours, jotting down her thoughts. She'd remembered so many of the paintings that had hung in her house, but didn't share her thoughts with her family; they'd find out in a few days about her attempt in the courts at reclaiming the art.

She dressed quietly at dawn, foregoing the noisy bangle bracelets, watching Roger as he slept. The time change had worn him out, and she knew he'd be sleeping for a few more hours. Her plan was to slip out for a while and trace her old tracks of years gone by. Sylvie was determined to visit one last ghost—Samuel Nowakowski—her first love. She would tell him she'd forgiven him—that she understood, that she had no hard feelings toward him, and also share that her first grandchild carried his name.

She took a trolley through town to the countryside, and when she stepped off she realized she remembered the names of all the back roads. Set on acres of land, she saw his farmhouse in the distance and, beyond that, a red barn. She wondered if that was where he had promised to hide her and her family.

There was so much to talk about, to get through, and move on from; so much to try to forget. She couldn't get there fast enough. She quickened her pace as she hurried closer to the house, and then when she reached the front door, she knocked firmly. When a woman appearing a few years younger than Sylvie opened the door, she saw Samuel's eyes in hers and choked back her tears.

"May I help you?"

"Hello. Miss Nowakowski?"

The lady nodded, cautiously.

"You may not remember hearing about me," Sylvie said, out of breath. "My name is Sylvie Rosenberg. Your brother and I . . . were . . . friends."

"Samuel?" The girl's brow furrowed.

"Rosenberg. Does the name ring a bell? Your father was the curator at my father's gallery in Dieren."

"Oh. Oh my, yes." She put her hand to her mouth. "Of course. My father spoke highly of him. My name is Ava. Won't you come in?"

She extended her arm inside the homey setting crowded with burlap bags of fruit and vegetables. "Excuse the mess," she said, pushing the bags of cucumbers, tomatoes, and apples to the side. "We only picked these this morning and the delivery truck will be passing by soon to—oh, you don't need to hear—tell me, Sylvie, how are you?"

Sylvie entered the humble home, remembering when the family from Poland had first moved in and worked the farm.

"Come, into the kitchen. After your long walk, you must be parched. May I offer you a cold drink?"

"A glass of ice water would be fine, thank you." She told Ava a quick history of her father's trade, their escape, the three years at Camp Gibraltar, and about life in America.

Ava squeezed her eyes shut. "How terribly frightening for you. Someday, I would like to go to America." She refilled Sylvie's glass. "I'm sure you want to hear more about Samuel."

Sylvie nodded.

Ava poured herself a glass of cold water. "I'm sorry to tell you he's no longer alive," Ava said gently.

Sylvie shook her head. "No!"

"Yes, Sylvie, it's been almost forty years since he's gone. Come, let me show you something." Sylvie followed Ava into a small, sparsely decorated room. Ava went straight to a corner cabinet and pulled a cloth box from the shelf. "Samuel had many regrets after your family parted. He kept some memorabilia from the gallery. He loved working there, you know."

"Yes, he talked about being a curator like your father when he got older." She sat on a hard wooden chair and slowly went through Samuel's keepsakes—his stamp collection, a small brass key, a pen engraved with his school's logo, an old gold locket probably belonging to his mother or grandmother, and at the bottom, a photograph of the interior of the Rosenberg gallery.

"Oh, there's the doorbell," Ava said. "They're here to pick up the produce. Take your time, Sylvie. Perhaps you will find something that the two of you shared from those days."

Sylvie stopped and stared closer at the photo of the gallery. There, on the far wall, she squinted at the painting she and Samuel had sat under, the one with the girl in the ruffled blouse he had compared to Sylvie. On the back of the photograph was a drawing of a heart that Samuel had made with their initials written inside.

She was crying when Ava returned. "I'm sorry. Maybe I shouldn't have—"

"No, no. This is a good way to finally say my goodbyes." Sylvie wondered if Samuel too carried any kind of guilt all these years. That was not something she wished upon him.

"Tell me, did Samuel ever marry?"

"No, only two years after you were gone, he joined the underground, trying to help other Jews—what was left of them. He was with a small resistance group, and they managed to save some people. He especially made an effort to rescue children, to send them to homes, passing as Christians. It was not easy. By mid-1944, Hitler's orders were to shoot on sight."

Sylvie cried, reaching her hand out to Ava's.

"He was captured and lined up in the square with the others. They were all shot."

"Oh my God, I don't know what to say."

"My brother died doing what he had to do—the right thing."

Sylvie dabbed her eyes. "Only days ago, my son and his wife had their first baby, my first grandchild, and I must tell you that the name they've given him is Samuel—a hero's name, for sure."

Ava reached for Sylvie's arm. "You once loved my brother?" Sylvie dried her eyes and nodded, a delicate smile creasing her lips.

They talked about Ava's family, all doing fine, and about other acquaintances Ava thought Sylvie might recall, but since they went to different schools, they didn't have the same friends. Ava knew nothing of Hana's family. Sylvie didn't want to know. She wanted to think of Hana being alive and well and not know the truth anymore.

She could hear her friend's voice in her head, how she went on about the boys and about their future becoming ballerinas or movie stars.

Sylvie finally revealed her past to Roger. She told him and her siblings that she'd be going to court in a few days trying to reclaim their stolen art. She felt a sense of relief sharing the news, and they all commended her for seeking justice.

"Unfortunately, I will not be able to attend the hearings with you because of business," Wilhelm said.

Ruthie spoke up next. "Oh, and I'm committed to attend seminars for work. They've been arranged for months. Had I known—"

Sylvie smiled forgivingly. "Please, don't feel you have to be there. I'm sure it will be long and drawn out."

Gretta cleared her throat. "I will be there, Sylvie. That's a promise."

Sylvie hugged her older sister, tightly, recollecting how they bonded on the train the night of their escape. In the pandemonium, Wilhelm had been accidentally herded out of the boxcar with others being transferred to Belgium where a truck waited for them to go to a death camp. The whistle started to blow, and she screamed his name and pleaded with the guard that taking him was a mistake. He was reunited with the family, and when they continued their journey, Gretta looked at her in a different way. She shared a portion of her food with Sylvie, as if paying her back for saving their brother. Sylvie feared the tenderness Gretta showed her, thinking it was because this was their ending.

The evening before Sylvie and Roger were to wed, they spent a romantic night alone in Amsterdam, hiring a canal boat that took them along the many channels. They had dinner by candlelight on the boat and talked intimately about what they believed made them who they were—who they had become. "They say wisdom comes with age." Sylvie let out a small laugh. "I don't know. I think of my regrets, big and small."

"We're human. Aren't we supposed to have regrets? I regret my wife's car hit a tree and overturned. Maybe I should have been the one going to pick up our daughter from her school dance that night. It was a rainy, foggy night, and I got home from work late. My wife offered and I let her go. It could have been me, instead, being scraped off the road like—"

"Oh, Roger." She wrapped her arms around his neck. "We can't control our fate."

"What about you?"

Sylvie turned to face the open water. "I have many monumental regrets having lived through the Holocaust as a Jew that I can only focus on small ones most of the time." She pointed her chin up at the sky, as if searching. "Silly, when I think of that last night in our house when we had to make our escape, I regret not opening my birds' cage and setting them free."

Roger touched her cheek. "Their freedom, so symbolic."

"They were my love birds, so sweet. I have a recurrent dream that I forgot to open the cage door—that the Nazis killed them in a cruel way." She buried her face in the crook of his shoulder, wondering if it was possible to kill in a kind way.

Sylvie wore a simple ivory mid-length chiffon dress and a pair of low pumps. The only jewelry she wore was her Jewish star. She noticed that time had taken the edge from the sharp points; they were duller as she pressed them into her fingers. Roger looked elegant in his ivory linen suit and Frank Lloyd Wright cufflinks, Sylvie's wedding gift to him.

Aside from her nieces and nephews, Sylvie was shocked to see her elderly aunt Chelley there, and two Christian neighbors from the old days whom her sisters had invited as a surprise. The guests gathered at the top of the hill, inside the quaint windmill restaurant filled with dozens of potted tulip plants. When the judge asked everyone to take their seat, Sylvie noticed Ava and her father entering the tavern and joining the crowd. Mr. Nowakowski took both of Sylvie's hands in his, and his eyes welled up.

The judge slowly studied everyone's faces before speaking a word. "I have known the Rosenberg family since I was a young man. Sylvie's parents, Josef and Helene, were honorable people, always ready to give to their community, to those less fortunate. This is a very special and happy occasion for me, as I am sure it is for all of you. I feel such a positive energy from each and every one of you. I want to share with you something Sylvie and Roger told me upon meeting today." He glanced at the couple for permission, and they both nodded to continue.

"Sylvie said that she and Roger are very different people in every possible way—they were night meeting day."

The small crowd mumbled.

"Yet one without the other has less meaning, doesn't it?" the judge asked.

Almost everyone nodded in agreement.

"We are gathered to unite this man and this woman in marriage, which to both is an institution founded in nature, they tell me. With hearts full of love and abiding will."

Sylvie and Roger stepped forward and faced everyone. "We want to thank you all for coming here today. Being in my hometown with you again and sharing our wedding with you means the world to us. Roger and I stayed up late last night writing our wedding vows, which we both would like to read at this time."

Roger: Love one another with each breath to the fullest without suffocating the other.

Sylvie: Let our roots grow together as a flower, with separate petals of beauty.

Roger: Love one another's laughter and tears, without fears of it as a duty.

Sylvie: Share all of our senses in the warmth of the sun—separate entities, separate rays.

Roger: Celebrate our differences, without losing mutual peace.

Sylvie: Stay friends through it all with time, never allowing the romance to fade.

Roger: Let the stream flow as one from our hearts, converging souls when we must part.

After their vows were read, the judge stepped forward to speak.

"Sylvie and Roger, may your steps of marriage as husband and wife be as simple and natural as love should be, and with all this joy, may you forget all your past sorrows and feel as one, but so free. I now pronounce you husband and wife."

They kissed, and everyone flocked around the newlyweds, anxious to talk to them.

Roger whispered in Sylvie's ear how beautiful she looked. And she realized that she never felt more beautiful on the inside, even in her younger, richer years.

Chapter 24

Sylvie arrived at court at ten sharp to learn that a decision had been made. "Is that a good sign or a bad sign?" she asked Mr. Van Der Berg, the Dutch lawyer. His expression was not encouraging.

The first judge entered the courtroom and everyone stood. Sylvie thought of Michael and Angela waiting for her phone call back home in America; she wondered about their reaction. The judge made eye contact with the barrister and the attorneys and then asked Sylvie to take the stand. Sylvie's knees buckled beneath her skirt as she made her way to the front of the courtroom, not daring to make eye contact with anyone, not even her sister or her new husband.

The judge cleared his throat. "*Mevrouw Rosenberg, hoe gaat heet met u?*"

"*Met mij gaat het goed . . .* I am fine, Your Honor."

The judge concentrated on Sylvie's face. "Ms. Rosenberg, after extensive research I'd like to read the following to you: According to the London Declaration of January 5, 1943, regarding Forced Transfers of Property in Enemy-Controlled Territory, it warns that any transfers or dealings, direct or indirect, are considered invalid which have come under the occupation or control. This warning applies whether such transfers or dealings have taken the form of open looting or plunder, or of transactions apparently legal in form, even when they purport to be voluntary effected. After much deliberation, and upon the evidence and testimony heard in this room, the committee has reached a decision.

"It is determined the Rosenberg family business had operated under extreme duress. After years of extensive research, the court has made a decision strictly regarding voluntary sales versus forced sales between the dates of August 2, 1940, up until your family escaped on October 20, 1942."

The dates and transactions for each individual painting and the name of the artists would be held on record, and provided accordingly. The judge ruled in favor of the heirs.

One at a time, people in the gallery stood to applaud.

Gretta and Adelstein hugged Der Berg, thanking him.

Sylvie touched the microphone, and it made a shrill sound. "I would just like to say . . ."

Everyone standing quickly sat back down to listen as Sylvie leaned in closer to the microphone and, finding her mouth suddenly dry, wished she had a hard candy. She quietly cleared her throat, shut her eyes to think, and gently exhaled.

"My entire family would like to say *dank u* to the esteemed committee and the honorable Dutch legal system for this overdue but welcome justice. These paintings—my father's life's work—brought so much joy and beauty in his lifetime. I hope to donate some of this good fortune towards educating future generations about Holocaust awareness."

Sylvie rummaged in her pocket for a sweet. She'd settle for a Lifesaver.

"Were we blessed to have my father here today, you could see for yourselves what his artwork meant to him. And for you restoring them to his children. I thank you on behalf of my beloved father, Josef Rosenberg."

Sylvie dabbed at her eyes with a hankie. She glanced at Gretta for moral support. A momentary flight of fancy allowed Sylvie to imagine what a delight it would be to tell her father that the artwork would be passed all to Michael, the grandson he never knew, and great-grandson, Baby Samuel. And that because of her father's educated eye for art and his business acumen, her son and his family would enjoy the benefits of these masterpieces. It occurred to her that Michael would also want to save the world with their good fortune.

Sylvie was at once drained yet energized with the outcome of this arduous lawsuit. She composed herself and glimpsed Roger, whose smile reminded her how lucky she was. With a final nod to the panel of judges, she stepped down, her feet straight, no longer turned in like a spoiled child. Her heart swelled the size of a prima ballerina.

Hermann Goering and Hitler admiring confiscated art

Marianne and
Benjamin Katz
"OMA and OPA"

Nathan and
Benjamin Katz,
art dealer
brothers with
some of their
antiques

Rembrandt painting,
Portrait of Raman,
(later renamed *Dirck Pesser*)
traded to Nazis in exchange
for 25 Jewish lives

The only painting the
Dutch government
returned to family
in US.

Man in a High Cap
by Ferdinand Bols
1616-1680
(a student of Rembrandt)

Second and third, L to R: Benjamin Katz and Brother Nathan Katz
(other two, unknown)

Schilderjen-Antiquiteiten Firma Katz Gallery in Dieren, Holland

Interior of the Dieren Katz Gallery, 1936

Katz Art Gallery

Refugees at Gibraltar Internment Camp, British West Indies

Marques de Comillas, the boat they had escaped on

Escapees: Vogue Katz Berg and 6 year-old-Alma, Mother and Sister
with Baby Murray born at the Camp, siblings of Bruce Berg

Acknowledgments

I had always thought of Rembrandt as my favorite artist . . . and then along came Mary Vettel, author and book doctor who shaped my book like a sculptor with clay. Additional thanks to the Koehler team.

I am grateful: to my family who believed in me over the arduous years of filling empty pages; especially to my sister-in-law, Alma Nierenberg, and mother-in-law, Vogue Katz Berg, who both lived the story; and to my own mother, Jean Marino, who lived to "create" and make something beautiful out of scraps; and to my father, Anthony Marino, who lived to "invent." Thanks for passing down those genes, which my children, Janelle and Jeffrey, have inherited. And to Mike Gomez—my second son.

To my golden retrievers Jewel, Jude, and Joey, who sat by my side through it all, keeping me company in this isolated world of writing. And to my selfless sister, Judith Anne, who was my first reader; and to my blood sister from childhood, Kathy Ives Lamberta—a character in my book, who knows me like no one else. Thanks to my professors in the MFA Writing Program at Stony Brook University where I learned from the best, including the late, great Frank McCourt, the devoted Roger Rosenblatt, and my fellow students.

I am extremely appreciative to Professor Diana Cooper-Clark of York University, Toronto, Canada, who wrote the nonfiction book about the internment camp of Jewish refugees, titled *Dreams of Re-Creation in Jamaica.* I'd like to thank another relative who was at the Camp Gibraltar, David Cohen, who co-authored his nonfiction book with Robert Lemm (in Dutch and English), *One Rembrandt for 25 Jews,* and second cousin 100-year-old David Katz of Switzerland, who shared anecdotes of those days in Holland when he hid from the Nazis.

Here at the end, I have no words that can describe my gratitude for my husband, Bruce—my soul's mate . . . who wanted my dreams to come true as much as I did, and who believes we lived another life together before this one. I hope we share many more lifetimes where there will be more stories to create on blank sheets of paper.

CPSIA information can be obtained
at www.ICGtesting.com
Printed in the USA
LVHW022315150920
666084LV00005B/1103